Boys,
Book Clubs,
and Other Bad
Ideas

A Monday Night Anthology

Published by 84th Street Press in Seattle, WA, USA
Address: 84thstreetpress@gmail.com
Visit us on the Web! www.84thstreetpress.com

First paperback edition October 2021

Cover by Patrick Knowles
Editing by Morgan Wegner

ISBN 978-1-956273-01-4 (paperback)
ISBN 978-1-956273-02-1 (B&N paperback)
ISBN 978-1-956273-00-7 (e-book)
Library of Congress Control Number: 2021915899

Use of Nymphont font created by Lauren Thompson

To Marie Perella
whose dedication to and passion for nurturing artists
lives on in her grandchildren
and every life they touch

The Prompt

Write a story with the title "Boys, Book Clubs, and Other Bad Ideas."

The Anthology

You know those name generator memes that never stop circulating social media? The "find your high fantasy heroine name from the third letter of your last name, the color of your underwear, and the phase of the moon you were born under" — that sort of thing.

On October 14th 2019, our writing group came upon one such name generator entitled "Find Your YA Book Title." We had some laughs coming up with nonsensical titles — then hit on one that actually inspired us: "Boys, Book Clubs, and Other Bad Ideas."

I could write this story, each of us thought. *I have, like, six ideas already.*

So we did. Each one of us. No restrictions, just that title — that was our prompt.

We frantically penned our ideas, and after they were done, we swapped stories to see what each of us had come up with.

The results were surprising, not just because the stories were all so imaginative, but because each one was so beautifully and wildly different from the next. Individually these stories were good, but the true magic happened when they were read together.

We realized we were on to something special with this idea. For years, we'd written side by side but each on our own separate, disparate work. Now, for the first time, we'd collaborated on a single project. We got to see how our individually brainstormed ideas compared to those of the other members of our writing group and how our own unique styles shone. Even though we all began with the same seed of a story, we ended worlds apart—and that was truly delightful. The magic became most evident in the contrast each story had from the next and how that contrast highlighted each story in turn. Creating together in this way—and seeing these results—was a thrill unlike anything we'd previously shared as a writing group.

We wanted to do it again—but we needed another prompt.

After a brainstorm, we settled on "The Mistletoe Paradox" for our second collaboration. We wrote these in one sitting and enthusiastically critiqued each other's stories. Once again, the results thrilled us.

So…we kept writing. Our prompt list grew.

Eventually, we looked at each other and asked ourselves, "Should we do something with these?"

"Yeah, probably."

And so the Monday Night Anthology series began.

Table of Contents

Boys, Book Clubs, and Other Bad Ideas

by Kristina Horner

*❝*It's T-minus *four days* to prom, ladies."

Piper and her friends had spent every day this week trying desperately to ignore this countdown from Brynn's boyfriend Geoffrey, who was — as they generously put it — a bit eager.

"Just in case anyone had forgotten."

Piper rolled her eyes, trying to push down the dread creeping in her stomach. "We *know*, Geoffrey."

He gave her a pointed look. "Which is *well* past the cancellation window…"

"Finding a date will not be a problem," Veronica insisted, giving him a flippant wave of her hand. "For me, at least."

After a beat, all eyes turned to Piper, and she felt herself bristling. It wasn't *her* fault Geoffrey had gone and booked a limo on the assumption that all of Brynn's friends would find dates in time. It wasn't *her* fault Brynn just happened to be dating a party planning enthusiast with wildly high standards about creating "the best prom experience of all time."

She slammed her history book shut and pushed up from the table. She couldn't stand the humiliation of admitting she didn't have a date any more than she could bear the looks of pity if she admitted it was because no one had asked her yet.

And *besides* — she had bigger things to worry about.

"I'm heading home," she snapped, then turned to

3

the girls pointedly. "But I'll see you two tomorrow—at seven?"

Geoffrey looked confused, but Brynn and Veronica knew exactly what she was talking about—they saw each other at seven *every* month on the morning of the seventh day. *On the seventh day, at the seventh hour, re-seal the tomes of the seven demons...* yada yada yada. It had all seemed a lot cooler at thirteen—back when they were first initiated—but now it was usually a total snoozefest. Plus, Piper had a history test to contend with in the morning, Brynn had early morning swim practice, and Veronica was just a chronic oversleeper.

Not to mention all of this ungodly prom stress.

Why couldn't their ancestors have banished the seven ancient demons at a *regular* hour of the day? Clearly their former magical kindred never had to go to high school.

Geoffrey—who never had to think about things like clandestine magical mornings—wrinkled his nose. "What are you doing that early on a Wednesday?"

"Book club," Brynn said quickly and dismissively, always the best at coming up with covers for their strange morning trysts. "It's a bit of a family tradition, totally lame, can't get out of it." She and Geoffrey had been dating a few months now, but not quite so long that he wouldn't buy one of her signature stories.

Veronica cracked her gum loudly. "Been doing it since the dawn of time, you know," she added truthfully, despite the fact that it sounded very much like hyperbole.

"Your families have the strangest traditions," Geoffrey shook his head. "I always forget you three are distantly related."

They weren't, and Brynn didn't like lying to her boyfriend, but it was easier this way. They were like family — *closer* than family. And the old families were interconnected, so there was certainly crossover somewhere in their lines.

"*Seven at seven of seven,*" Piper murmured, still irritated about the whole prom date thing. But not so irritated that she didn't share in their intricate handshake first. They'd known it since they'd first developed their fine motor skills, and some things were bigger than prom drama.

"Seven what now?" Geoffrey scratched his head.

"I said I'll see the girls at seven," Piper coughed, turning on her heel. "Now I'm going home!"

"Tomorrow will be T-minus three days!" Geoffrey called after her, to which Piper gave him a middle finger on her way out the library.

The next morning, Piper rubbed her bleary eyes and raised her aching neck up from her desk — the very place she'd fallen asleep the night before. She'd slept in her clothes and was sure she had the circumstances of the French revolution permanently imprinted on her forehead. Whoever's idea it was to schedule any big tests this close to prom was a monster.

She checked her watch.

Shit. It was already a quarter to seven, and she'd planned on skimming the chapter again this morning, as well as running through her flash cards of important dates at least once more. But she *needed* to get to the school library by seven o'clock.

It was her duty, as a demon huntress. Well, demon huntress *in training*. Of course, it was her mother, aunts, and older sister who got to do the *fun* parts.

Piper and her friends were in charge of sealing the books, which was a *thrilling* task — one they were expected to carry out every month, no exceptions.

She looked at her notes again. She *really* needed the extra study time.

6:51am.

Shit.

It really didn't take all three girls to seal all the books. There were only seven in total, and in fact the ritual — while extremely important — was relatively simple. They met each month and rolled their eyes as they carried out the task while commiserating about how unfair it was that this was the only thing the elders would let them do. They didn't get to go to the interdimensional meetings or help seal up rogue tears in the world-fabric or anything. At least not yet.

What was the point of being the daughters of a centuries-old demon hunting force if all you got to do was hang out in a dusty library every now and then?

Piper *always* made it to the library on time, but she was *really* behind in history right now. She wasn't going to blame it *entirely* on Geoffrey and the fact that she'd been stressing about finding a prom date for weeks now, though that certainly didn't help.

Maybe Brynn and Veronica could handle sealing the books on their own *just* this once.

She bent her head low over her desk and continued cramming, immersing herself back into the political upheaval of late 1700s France.

It would be fine. It always was.

The morning was a blur until third period, where Piper did what she could only hope was at least an adequate job on her history test. The extra cram time had definitely helped. She hurried to the lunch room, excited both to catch up with her friends on the morning's ritual and to be done with France forever.

But they weren't there when she arrived. Only Geoffrey was seated at their usual table.

Great.

"Piper," he nodded at her as he folded his extra large, extra drippy slice of cheese pizza in half to make it better fit in his gaping mouth.

"Where's—" was all she had the chance to blurt out before Veronica slumped down beside her, the contents of her bag spilling out across the lunch table.

"What a *morning*," she said dramatically.

Piper stopped herself rolling her eyes just in time— Veronica was always like this on ritual days. "Early morning?" she asked, carefully unwrapping her turkey sandwich.

"The worst. Thanks again for covering for me this morning. I can't believe I need an entirely new engine. That's my entire prom budget, down the pipes. The *literal* pipes."

It took Piper a moment to register what her friend had said. "Cover for you?"

She dug a crumpled brown sack out of her school bag and unearthed a lumpy peanut butter sandwich. "At book club."

Piper's stomach lurched. "You... weren't there?"

Veronica stared at Piper. "What do you mean '*you weren't there*'? Of course I wasn't there. You would have seen me."

"V—I wasn't there. I thought you covered for *me*."

Veronica froze. "My car totally died this morning. I had to get towed and everything—it was a whole thing. Why weren't *you* there?"

"History test!" Now that she said it, it sounded like a pretty lousy excuse. "I needed some extra study time."

"Oh, well, that's just fine, Piper. Extra study time instead of *book club*. That'll go over well."

"Brynn," Piper said definitively. "Brynn was there. She'll have handled it."

"Well, not much of a book club by yourself," Geoffrey chimed in, licking pizza grease off his fingers, "but for the record, Brynn wasn't in homeroom this morning."

The color drained from both girls' faces. "What do you mean she wasn't in homeroom?!" Piper wailed, grabbing his shirt.

Geoffrey threw his hands up in defense. "I don't know where she was. She just wasn't there!"

Piper took a couple of calming breaths, then let him go. "Excuse us, Geoffrey."

She gripped Veronica's arm and dragged her friend out of the cafeteria. "What do we do?" she asked once they were alone in the hall.

"Find Brynn. Maybe she's still in the library," Veronica reasoned. "I'm sure it took a while without either of us to help. That's probably why she missed homeroom."

Piper nodded. That made sense. That had to be what happened. The girls turned on their heels and headed left toward the old library.

Piper's stomach rumbled, but she couldn't think about food at a time like this. If Brynn wasn't in the library this morning, they were going to be in *so much trouble*.

On their way, they passed a group of boys coming out of the locker room. Piper recognized them from the football team and tried not to make eye contact. One of the taller ones bumped into her as they darted past, knocking her into Veronica and sending all three sprawling to the ground.

"Watch where you're going," the football player said hotly, but one of his friends scoffed and pushed him out of the way, reaching down to help them. Veronica was hoisted up first, and then the guy — his name was Eric — extended his hand to Piper. His eyes pierced hers as he did this, and for a moment, she swore they flashed green.

She was so startled that she stumbled backward, almost tripping again until Veronica caught her.

"Easy there," she laughed, and Piper dropped Eric's hand, which she realized she was still holding.

"Sorry," she said stupidly, her face reddening. Then she grabbed Veronica and kept running toward the library.

"What was *that* about?" Veronica hissed, struggling to keep up with her. "Potential prom date material?"

"Oh my god, it was not like *that*," Piper moaned. "How can you think about prom at a time like — did you see his eyes?"

"What? Were they *gorgeous*? I'm always thinking about prom, Piper. And I didn't think you were into the jock type."

Piper rolled her eyes. "*No* — I mean — "

But she didn't get to say what she meant, because at that very moment Brynn walked through the front doors of their school, arm in a sling and bright blue slip in hand.

"Brynn!" they cried in unison. "Thank goodness."

"Hi… guys…" she said cautiously, eyeing the both of them. Then she held up the slip with her non-hurt arm, which both girls could now see was a doctor's note. "Listen, I am so sorry I bailed on you both this morning. I tore something in my shoulder at swim practice, and they whisked me off to the emergency room. I tried to stay, but they literally called an ambulance. It was so embarrassing."

It was like the floor had dropped out from beneath

Piper and Veronica.

"Oh. That's a *much* better excuse," Veronica finally said, defeated.

"A better excuse than what?" Brynn looked confused.

"We need to go to the library right now," said Piper, leading the trio the rest of the way down the hall, cold sweat prickling on her skin.

The library was nearly empty when they arrived, aside from one boy in the corner, aimlessly browsing the stacks. They always preferred when it was empty — fewer questions.

Piper led them back to the old books room, where the tapestry hung from the ceiling. The school always said it was just an old heirloom, but the three of them knew better — on it was emblazoned the crest of their families, the demon huntresses. And in a glass case at the back of the room sat seven old tomes: the demon tomes.

Of course, to the rest of Blackwood High, they were just "very old books," and the only people who had keys that unlocked the glass case were all standing in this room. The same three who very much weren't in the room at seven o'clock this morning, which explained why every single book was now flung open in disarray.

"I'm sorry, what!?" Brynn exploded once they explained what had happened. "You *weren't here*!?"

"I thought you'd be here!" Piper shouted back, but her voice wavered as she knew her excuse sucked hardest.

"I thought *you'd* be here," Veronica snipped back, and both turned to face Brynn.

She glared at them, pointing to her hurt shoulder. "Excuse me!"

"I know, I know, I'm so sorry." Piper slumped down on the ground in front of the glass case. "This is all my fault."

"No, it's on all of us," Veronica said charitably.

Brynn raised an eyebrow. "I'd argue it's definitely on you two," she said, but when she saw the looks on her friends' faces, she sunk down beside Piper as well.

"Thousands of years," said Piper miserably. "These books have been sealed for *thousands of goddamn years*, and now we've fucked it up over a history test."

Veronica, still standing, examined the books through the glass. "Are we definitely sure the demons got out? Maybe the whole '*seven at seven of seven*' thing was more of a precaution and not hard fact."

"The books are open," Brynn argued, her voice muffled as she rested her head on her knees.

"Let's get a little more positive energy in this room, okay, friends? Maybe the demons just wanted some fresh air."

Veronica dug around under her sweater until her fingers grasped the old skeleton key, identical to the one each girl wore on a chain around her own neck. She inserted it into the lock, twisted, and gently lifted the glass case. She then laid hands on the first of the seven tomes.

Piper felt herself holding her breath, waiting for Veronica's reaction. Maybe they hadn't just doomed the entire world. Maybe she wasn't about to get grounded for six lifetimes.

"Okay...yeah," Veronica said, closing her eyes as if waiting for an energy to flow through her.

"Yeah?" Brynn said hopefully.

"Yeah. That book is empty as shit."

Both Piper and Brynn let out cries of frustration. Veronica scooped up the rest of the books, dropping them in a stack on the floor near where the other two sat.

"Now what?" It was Piper who spoke, but they all stared at the useless books between them, feeling hopeless.

Veronica's eyes were wide. "Well, we obviously can't tell our parents."

"And we have to get them back," Piper said simply.

Both girls stared at her a moment. "Get them back?"

"Yes," Piper insisted. "We released the demons into the world; we have to get them back."

"Sure, okay, let's *not* tell our incredibly-skilled-at-demon-hunting families and instead entrust the task to the three of us, the glorified babysitters."

The three of them sat in silence for a moment, letting that thought sink in.

They complained constantly about how boring their job was and how badly they wished they could train to become actual demon huntresses already — get their magical staves, learn the ancient combat methods, don their amulets. But demon huntresses didn't get to begin training until they came of age at seventeen, at least not since the fourteenth century.

Hating this rule and their job was what brought the three of them together, so much so that they often forgot how critically important the job actually was.

"How would we even *find* the demons?" Brynn asked, reaching for one of the books. She could hardly lift it with her one good arm. Veronica reached out and heaved the top one over for her.

"They're just a bunch of crappy old books," said Piper, shuffling nearer so the book was draped across all three of their laps. "There's nothing here —"

But then she went silent. The book began to glow when all three of them touched it at once. Some of the pages floated upward, as if a ghost hand was flipping through, faster and faster, until the pages stopped entirely — laying flat on a certain page: 777.

Of course.

The letters began to float and rearrange themselves, moving magically around the page until the edges glowed green, as if to signal the tome was content with the new order.

"Read it," Veronica nudged Piper.

She gulped, then nodded.

"These monsters filled with ancient rage
Will wither here within the page.
Until powers of their own they wield,
Young huntresses must keep them sealed."

"Yes, yes, we know that part, thank you. Don't rub it in. What happens if we've fucked that up royally?"

The letters twitched again and began to swirl around the page once more. There was more about the ritual, the seventh hour of the seventh day — all things they'd heard before.

"But how do we *fix it*?" Piper yelled at the book. "Without telling our moms!?"

"To rid the world of demon kind,
It takes a demon huntress mind.
But if a novice let them play,
There is, perchance, another way."

"Okay," Brynn's eyes lit up. "We're listening."

"They latch-eth on to those you seek,
The ones you covet silently.
And to extract, inhale and draw
The demon from the vessel's maw."

With that, the glow faded and the book returned to its normal form — an ancient, dusty tome with lots of boring, nonrhyming text. The girls sat a moment, waiting for it to do anything else, but it appeared to be done.

"They latch-eth on to those you seek?" Piper repeated, confused.

Brynn continued, eyebrows knit together. "The ones you covet silently…"

Veronica rolled her eyes. "It's boys."

Piper and Brynn blinked at her. "What's boys?"

She smirked. "I think it's like... *all* boys. We seek and covet them, silently. Like... we have crushes on them."

"That's looney tunes, V." Piper tried to hide the fact that there was heat rising in her cheeks. "This has to have been written in, like, the Dark Ages."

"You don't think novice huntresses had crushes on boys in the Dark Ages?"

Brynn pinched the bridge of her nose, looking exhausted. "So you're telling me these demons are going to possess boys we have crushes on?"

"Do we even have crushes on seven boys?"

"V and I saw Geoffrey at lunch and he seemed fine. Not particularly possessed by demons."

Veronica chewed on her lip. "Maybe he doesn't count, since you're already dating him? Maybe it's new crushes."

"Poor Geoffrey," Brynn shook her head.

"Yes, poor Geoffrey, *not being possessed by a demon*." Veronica stuck her tongue out.

"Either way," Piper interrupted, "I don't understand what the second part means. How do we get the demons out?"

Brynn recited it from memory. "*And to extract, inhale and draw the demon from the vessel's maw.*"

As she spoke, her ears turned bright red, and Veronica burst out laughing.

"What?!" Piper asked, feeling left out of a joke. "I don't get it."

"Piper," Veronica said, putting a hand on her friend's shoulder, "we have to kiss them."

"Absolutely not," Piper said for what felt like the hundredth time as she and the others finally left the library. She held the entire stack of old tomes in her arms and could hardly see over them all. Lunch had to be almost over by then, and they didn't need to draw any more attention to themselves by missing class. "I'm not going to go around kissing strangers."

"Okay, great," Veronica said, pulling out her cell phone. "I'll just call up your mother then and let her know we need to summon a council of elders to—"

"Okay, okay, stop." Piper shot her a look around the old tomes. "That's not funny."

"Don't think of it as your first kiss," Brynn said, more gently. "Think of it as your first mission as a demon huntress."

That did help, a little bit. But Piper still had no idea how to do it. She still didn't even know how to get herself a prom date, let alone actually lock lips with a boy to expel an ancient demon from his being.

"And at least you don't have to cheat on your boyfriend to do it," Brynn grimaced.

"People break up and get back together all the time," Veronica offered. "Just tell him you need a break, hook up with a couple of hotties, and bam! Back together."

"Right before prom," she looked glum. "Poor guy.

This is going to break his heart. He *booked* the *limo*, guys."

"He'll get over it."

Brynn glowered at Veronica, but she didn't notice. Veronica had whipped a notebook out of her bag and was busy making a list.

"So, Piper, you said Eric had weird eyes, right?"

She nodded. "Yes. I saw them glowing green on the way to the library. That could be one of the indicators that there's a demon inside."

"Dibs," Veronica said, writing Eric's name in her column. "Now we just need to keep looking for weird eyes, get our smooch on, and get all these demons out before our parents can say 'no dating until you're of age.'"

"Seven demons means two each, and then a third for whoever finds their demons first."

"Three for me. Got it," Veronica said, reapplying her cola-flavored ChapStick.

"You're actually enjoying this," Brynn rolled her eyes at her.

"Listen. If I knew saving the world was going to be this easy, I would have let those demons out a long time ago."

"This isn't a joke," Piper snapped, unable to make light of the situation the way Veronica could. "You know what happens if we can't get them all back quickly."

Veronica sighed. "I know, I know. More tears in the world-fabric, raining fire, eternal despair."

"And toads."

The bell rang then, startling them all.

"Keep an eye out for more demons," Piper instructed, hoisting the stack of books into her locker, which Veronica opened for her. They all knew each other's combinations. "And meet back here after school."

"Roger that, boss." Brynn gave a little salute.

They went their separate ways: Veronica to math, Brynn to art class, and Piper to physical education.

As she laced up her sneakers in the locker room, Piper tried to give herself a pep talk.

The fate of the universe rests on your ability to do this.

Just find the boys with the green eyes and kiss them, and this nightmare will be over.

Just kiss them. It's no big deal. People kiss boys all the time.

She just wished she knew the first thing about kissing — or about demon behavior. Would they fight back? They just didn't teach these things in normal high school.

"Team one on this side of the gym; team two on the other," Coach Bickford called out once all the students piled into the gymnasium. They'd already numbered off, and Piper made her way to the far side with the other twos. It was dodgeball day, which made it a little tough to get close enough to anyone to inspect their eyes, but she was trying her hardest.

"You're out!"

It took Piper a moment to realize the coach was talking to her. She'd been hanging near the back, trying to sneak glances at her male teammates, and hadn't even noticed the ball that bounced off her leg. "Piper! Back behind the net."

"Sorry!" She ran behind the goal posts, stuffing her hands in the pockets of her gym shorts and hoping none of her teammates would score for a while. It was much less stressful waiting back here.

She couldn't see anyone's eyes from where she stood, but she did have an excellent view of... Simon Anderson's backside.

Piper sighed, feeling pathetic.

She knew she was supposed to be worrying about demons now, but she couldn't help but feel a twinge of panic about prom. It was only three days away, and she knew Geoffrey was going to be on her case again—and she hadn't even *remotely* implied to her long-term crush Simon that she was both available and interested.

It was just so... *hard.*

They had choir and P.E. together, and on top of that, they were even lab partners in biology. He frequently told terrible puns, but Piper loved the way he made himself laugh. She was fairly certain he didn't think of her like that, but it didn't stop her from pining anyway.

Focus, Piper, she berated herself. *Demons today; prom tomorrow.*

She watched as Simon attempted a trick shot just as someone else sent a curveball in his direction. He tried to jump over it, but the ball knocked into his ankle.

"Simon out!" the coach called, and he hung his head, jogging back to stand near Piper.

"Tough break," she said, shifting uncomfortably, suddenly all too aware of how dorky her shorts made her look.

"Thanks." Simon flashed her a smile, and Piper's heart stopped — not because of the way his lip tugged up higher on one side, creating the all-too-adorable crooked grin she loved, but because of the indisputable shock of green she saw when he caught her eye.

"Nothing," she said stupidly. "I mean, it's nothing!"

Her heart was jackhammering in her chest.

No.

Not Simon.

But of course Simon had the green eyes. He was her crush, after all.

I cannot be expected to KISS SIMON ANDERSON.

But at the same time, she didn't want Veronica or Brynn to kiss him, either.

Ugh, ugh, ugh.

She didn't have to worry about it right this second. It was the middle of class, after all. She could find her second boy first; get him out of the way. Then she'd at least have a little experience by the time she had to kiss Simon. Somewhere private, later. Not behind a dodgeball net in front of their entire class.

She couldn't believe she was contemplating casually kissing Simon while standing right next to him — in her horrid shorts. She hoped her face wasn't as red as she feared it was. She hoped there wasn't any reason Simon could read minds.

Can you read minds? she thought, as loud as she could.

"Hey," Simon nudged her arm, and it made her jump a foot in the air. "You're back in."

She nodded, heart in her throat. Dodgeball. She could play dodgeball. Focus on dodgeball.

After school, she met the girls outside Brynn's locker, just as they'd planned.

"How's it going?" Brynn asked, fiddling with the combination until the locker sprung open. "Wait — why are there only six tomes in here?"

Veronica unearthed the remaining book from her school bag, looking proud. The telltale glow emanated from the pages, cover shut tight.

"Ya girl's been working hard. One down, six demons to go."

Piper's eyes nearly popped out of her head. "You already kissed a boy?"

"Banished a demon, yes."

She was stunned. "How?"

Veronica shrugged. "It was easy. *Hey, Eric,*" she reenacted, putting on a sultry face. "*Meet me under the bleachers after fifth period.*"

"And he... did?"

"Of course he did."

"And then what?"

"I mean, I think you can use your imagination from here. I told him I'd been crushing on him for a while, acted irresistible, and then touched his hair."

Both Piper and Brynn waited for her to go on, but Veronica just grinned at them.

"You touched his hair?"

"It's a clutch move. Gets them every time."

"Geoffrey does like when I touch his hair," Brynn reasoned.

Veronica raised an eyebrow at Piper, as though to say, "*see*?"

"Well, I've got news," Brynn said. "You know Yuma? I've now got to figure out a reason to explain to my boyfriend why I need to make out with the foreign exchange student."

"Get it, girl." Veronica made a note on her spreadsheet.

Brynn sighed, and looked at Piper. "Any progress from you?"

For some reason, she didn't want to tell her friends that Simon was possessed. She didn't want the added pressure of seeing Veronica write his name under hers, making it all official.

"No," she said quickly. "Sorry. I guess I haven't had any classes with the demons yet."

"Fate of the world, ladies," Veronica reminded them, stuffing the sheet back in her pocket. "I'm assuming we're all staying after school?"

The other girls shrugged. Piper had wanted to spend the evening practicing doing her hair and

makeup for Saturday, but considering that she didn't
have a date yet—and that this whole mess was
basically her fault—she didn't much feel she could say
that.

"Okay. Piper: check the library, and maybe some of
the after-school clubs. Brynn: maybe head to the
mall?"

"And what will you do?"

Veronica flashed them her winning smile.
"Cheerleader practice, baby. I've got the whole field
on lock, and there are at least four sports that practice
today." Then she heaved three of the tomes out of the
locker, handing one to each girl and keeping one for
herself. "Just in case."

Piper stuffed the book in her backpack. She couldn't
very well just barge into classrooms looking for
demons in the after-school clubs, so she wandered her
way to the library. It was relatively crowded—much
more so than it had been that morning. Many of her
classmates were sitting at the rows of computers,
talking quietly amongst the stacks, or   doing
homework together at some of the open tables near
the windows.

It was hard to get a good look at anyone's eyes
while they stared at screens or down at their books,
but Piper got as close as she could to scope people out
without being awkward—well, more awkward than
usual.

First, she saw a group of boys looking up dirty topics on Wikipedia at the computers. But while their behavior was definitely demon-like, all their eyes were clear. A mixed group of boys and girls were poring over a periodic table around a circular workspace, but no one there looked out of the ordinary, either.

The old tome felt heavy in her bag, a constant reminder of what she was supposed to do.

She had almost given up, turning to leave the library, when a voice rang out, "Hey, Piper!"

She spun around, surprised to see that it was Simon.

"Hey," she said, giving a little wave.

He gestured for her to join him at his table, and she forced her legs to walk over to where he sat, heart thudding in her chest. Why was Simon calling her over? Was it actually the demon inside him? Did the demon know who — *what* — she was?

"What's... up?" she asked as he pushed a chair out across from him with his foot.

"I'm working on the biology homework," he said, pointing to his book. "Help?"

He looked up at her with pleading eyes, the unmistakable green reflecting there. For a moment she locked gaze with him, as though she could see straight through to the demon, but then Simon brushed his hair off his face, and Piper's insides melted, breaking her concentration.

"Sure," she said, plopping down in the chair and digging in her bag for her own biology book. But it wasn't there—just the old tome. She could feel an energy humming off of it, as if it was reaching out toward Simon, begging for her to do the deed.

She zipped her bag shut as quick as she could. *Not now,* she tried to will it with her mind. *I can't do it here. Too many people. Leave me alone.*

"I forgot my book," she apologized, hopping from her seat again. "I'll just run and—"

"You can share mine!" Simon said, gesturing to the seat right beside him.

Piper felt a whole flight of butterflies take up residence in her stomach. "Uh...okay."

She went to join Simon on the other side of the table, keeping her bag close. She dropped it on the floor between them and sat on the far edge of her seat to ensure there was no accidental arm touching.

You're his lab partner, she reminded herself. *You're the logical choice for homework help.*

"The human body is super weird, right?" Simon mused, leaning over to look at his anatomy worksheet. In doing so, his side pressed up against hers, his hair tickling the side of her cheek.

Oh god, oh god. Piper couldn't help herself. All she could picture was pressing her lips against his, sucking out an ancient demon while running her hands through his hair.

It's a clutch move, Veronica's voice rang in her head.

Piper spasmed away from him, nearly falling out of her chair.

"Are you okay?!" Simon caught her just as she was about to hit the ground. "What happened?"

Piper wanted to jump out of one of the library windows. "Sorry, just…jittery today."

She was such a moron. Piper felt any chance of kissing this beautiful boy evaporating into thin air. She was just going to have to break into his house and kiss him in his sleep when he wasn't expecting it. Then she'd probably get arrested and go to jail, but at least the world would be saved.

Or at least one-seventh of it.

Simon gave a little chuckle and brushed her chin with his thumb. "Well, it's very cute."

Cute.

What did that mean? Piper's face was on fire. Cute was condescending, right? Cute, like a small kitten, or someone's baby sister? Like a buffoon who didn't even know how to sit in a chair?

Or cute as in, I would purposefully touch your chin again?

Cute as in, I would totally let you kiss me and suck the demon out of my mortal soul?

"Piper?"

She snapped back to reality, where Simon was still staring at her. The green in his eyes was distracting, like she was looking at both him and the demon at the same time. He was acting relatively normal, but Piper couldn't shake the knowledge that an ancient monster was lurking inside him and it was all her fault. It was all her fault, and of course it was in *Simon* of all people, and the whole world was going to end because she couldn't pluck up the courage to just *kiss* him.

"What?" she shook her head, trying to clear it of all

her pesky, jumbled thoughts.

"I asked if you're excited for prom," Simon repeated, giving her an odd look.

Oh no. Piper had spent so long fantasizing about Simon asking her to prom that it hadn't occurred to her that he probably had plans already. It was three days away; *of course* he had a date already.

She couldn't bear to find out.

"I can't do this," she mumbled, gathering her things and jumping from the chair. "Here are my bio notes." She threw her worksheet at Simon, leaving him gaping at her, open-mouthed.

As she rushed away, Piper couldn't help but think how easy it would have been to expel the demon while he sat there like that, and the thought made her face burn so hot she didn't stop running until she made it all the way back to her house.

When her alarm went off the next morning, Piper groaned. She'd hardly slept all night for all the replaying of the library scene her mind subjected her to.

Simon obviously didn't *like* her. He thought she was *cute*. Boys didn't want cute girls; they wanted girls who were cool. Mysterious. Coy. *Sexy*.

She wished she could be all those things — she was a novice demon huntress, after all! But she wasn't like Veronica, or even Brynn. She was awkward. Timid. Who knows if she'd even be a good huntress someday? Maybe she'd be destined to seal the books forever with the next set of novices.

If there were any books to seal, a nagging voice reminded her.

Why couldn't she just *kiss a boy*? She could just spring an attack on Simon's face — dive bomb his lips, get the demon out, then immediately change her name and transfer schools.

The fate of the *entire world* rested on her shoulders. It was the least she could do.

Piper checked her phone again, wondering if she'd set her alarm wrong. It was shockingly dark out for seven thirty in the morning, but sure enough, it was correct.

Rubbing her eyes, she wandered into the kitchen, where her mother and aunt Cinda were waiting on high alert.

"What's going on?" Piper asked, still groggy.

"Sun isn't rising." Cinda's tone was much too brusque for this hour, and Piper's mother was gazing into a jeweled sphere. Her mother never gazed into her sphere when things were hunky-dory.

"We fear eternal night is upon us."

Piper almost choked on the glass of orange juice she'd just poured herself. "What?!"

"Don't be alarmed, my child," her mother broke her eye contact to give Piper a tight smile, misunderstanding her guilty look for more general fear. "We are investigating the matter thoroughly. We think there's perhaps a new tear in the world-fabric."

"That sounds like the most obvious answer,"

Piper's voice came out strangled and odd. "I'm sure it's that."

"Nothing off with the ritual this month, was there?" The question was casual, not probing—but Piper felt her blood run cold. She forced her face to stay neutral.

"Totally normal ritual, mother. But we can do another check today to be certain!"

Her mother's worried face softened. "No, no, don't let it get in the way of your studies. The demon huntresses will handle this. Just let me know if you see any other signs of the world's end."

Piper tried to give her mother an affirmative, but it only came out a squeak. She downed the rest of her orange juice in one gulp and slunk from the kitchen.

At school, Brynn and Veronica seemed equally alarmed.

"This is bad."

"Were your moms also in a state?"

"I don't think they have any idea what's really going on. They think it's the world-fabric again."

"For now. We have to do this *quick*."

Veronica pulled out another tightly bound book. "Emerson, track and field. I caught him on a run back through the woods. Very lucky timing, and he's an excellent kisser. Better than Eric."

"Because *that's* what's important," Brynn chided her, reaching into her own bag. She unearthed her own tome, sealed up and still lightly humming. "I caught Yuma this morning. We were texting late into the night and agreed to walk to school together. I managed to kiss him out by the bike racks, and now I have to burn my phone and wash my mouth out with soap because I feel so awful."

"Geoffrey not taking the break well?"

Brynn paused, looking guilty.

Veronica gasped, poking her between the ribs. "You haven't told him?!"

"It just seemed easier that way! I don't think anyone saw, and I told Yuma I needed to take things slow, like glacially slow. I'll tell him I had a change of heart before prom."

They both turned to Piper, waiting for her news.

Piper squirmed.

"Nothing?!" Veronica snapped. "Piper!"

"I tried!"

She was about to launch into the story about yesterday in the library, but Veronica didn't wait for her to explain. "*Try harder,*" she said, pulling open Brynn's locker, stuffing the sealed books inside, and swapping them with two more empties.

First period was choir.

Piper, an alto, was assigned to sit obnoxiously near Simon, one of two tenors in the class. She didn't want to think about Simon, so despite his best attempts to catch her attention, she spent most of the class ignoring him in favor of searching the eyes of other boys in the room.

Everyone looked normal.

When the bell rang, Piper hurried from the room, hauling her heavy bag over her shoulder.

There were no flashes of green in math class or English after that. Luckily Simon wasn't in either of those classes. However, Piper still wasn't able to relax. She dreaded seeing her friends at lunch and having to admit what a failure she was.

On top of that, everyone was talking about the darkness outside.

"What does it mean?" she overheard a girl asking on her way to the cafeteria.

"People online are saying it might be some kind of undocumented eclipse."

"Like a conspiracy?"

"Maybe it's the apocalypse?"

"I am *not* dressed for the apocalypse."

Geoffrey and Brynn were already at the lunch table when Piper arrived, deep in conversation about prom.

"So the limo will leave from my house at 5pm," Geoffrey explained, looking at a timetable he'd created on his phone. "We'll drive around downtown, stop for dinner, and arrive back here at the school fashionably late."

"Sounds perfect." Brynn sounded distracted, her eyes continually shifting from side to side as if looking for someone.

"Surely you've found a date by now, Piper?"

She was caught off guard by the question. "What?"

"Your date. To prom. Remember this exorbitant bill we're going to have if you and Veronica flake out on me? You promised."

This was not a stressor Piper could deal with right now, and Veronica chose just the right moment to waltz up and twist the knife. "How *is* everything going in your love life, Piper?" She gave a knowing look, and Piper did not misunderstand her meeting.

"It's... progressing," she said through gritted teeth.

Veronica sighed loudly, rolling her eyes. "Well, I found another one. I'll have it done by the end of the day."

"I'm not following you anymore." Geoffrey stared between them, but they were thankfully interrupted by Yuma, who sat down on the other side of Brynn without warning.

"Hey," he said to Brynn specifically, his voice full of meaning.

She went white as a ghost, but Geoffrey didn't notice her odd reaction.

"Hey, man," he said, extending his hand. Yuma took it, noticing how Geoffrey's other arm was wrapped loosely around Brynn's waist.

Yuma looked confused, but tried to shake it away. "Do you want to hang out after school?" he asked Brynn.

"Can't," she said, jumping to her feet. "I—have to

go."

Piper saw the telltale spine of one of their old tomes clutched in her arms as she darted away.

Yuma watched her go, then turned back to the group, who were all staring at him.

"Girls," he shrugged.

"Girls, indeed," added Geoffrey.

The rest of the day didn't go any better. Piper avoided Simon like the plague, even though she knew her time was running out to handle it. She spent all her free time looking for her second demon, but still came up empty-handed by the final bell. When she finally met the girls back at the locker, Piper was starting to wonder if it would be better to just let the demons win.

It would certainly be easier.

"I found another one," Brynn said miserably, "but I'm pretty sure Geoffrey is mad at me. I tried to talk to him after lunch, and he totally bailed on me. We always meet by the water fountains before fifth period, but he wasn't there."

"It *was* pretty awkward at lunch," Veronica said.

Brynn stuck out her tongue. "Thanks a lot."

"So where's the next demon?"

"Isaac."

"Isaac who?"

"You know, Isaac. Man-bun Isaac."

Veronica looked impressed. "Oh *yeah*! Nice."

"I managed to get detention with him, so I'm hoping that one's an open and shut case."

"And Geoffrey will never be the wiser," Veronica winked.

Brynn groaned, burying her head in her hands as Veronica dug another sealed book out of her bag.

"Well, I'm three for three."

"*How*," Piper gasped, jaw dropping.

"This one was in Mark, the cute guy who plays guitar in the commons during his free period."

"That guy *is* cute," Brynn piped up. Piper stared at her, and Brynn raised her hands in the air.

"What? I'm taken, but I still have eyes."

Veronica stuffed the book in the locker, pleased to see their stack of sealed books now outnumbered the ones remaining. "He was no problem. I sat and listened to him play after drama class, and after a particularly emo song... I just planted one on him."

"Were people... watching?" Brynn asked.

Veronica shrugged. "Yeah. So?"

"You're an icon."

"I think we need to move quickly, though. I noticed in this last one, the demon seemed to... put up a fight."

Brynn turned to look at Veronica. "How so?"

"Well, my first two boys were easy. Like the demon was inside, but the boys were still in control."

"Does it seem like the demons are getting stronger?" Brynn asked.

Veronica bit her lip. "Possibly. Mark tried to bite me. And not in a hot way."

Piper felt the blood drain from her face. Great. Just what she needed to add to her stress—demons that fought back.

"Noted," Brynn said. "I'll keep alert around man-bun Isaac."

Veronica nodded back, all business. "So that's four demons sealed, one more accounted for, and two at large. And prom is tomorrow."

There was a pause, and the girls turned to look at Piper. She thought maybe if she was quiet enough, they would forget she was there, but instead they looked deeply disappointed.

"It's Simon," she blurted out finally.

Both Veronica and Brynn looked surprised for a moment, and then rolled their eyes so hard Piper thought it actually looked painful.

"This is an *easy* one, Piper. Get it together," Veronica snapped.

"I'm going to do it," Piper pleaded with them. "I promise."

Veronica took the final book from the locker, looking murderous as she stuffed it in her own bag. "If we destroy the world and our parents don't let us go to prom, it's your fault."

Piper gulped and nodded. "I'll do it."

By the next morning—the morning of prom—Piper had definitely not done it.

Even as she washed and dried her hair and put it

in rollers for the dance, she had zero idea what to do.

The night before, she almost called Simon at least twelve different times.

She imagined meeting him at the movies, at the local diner, at the arcade.

She practiced kissing on her own hand.

She laid on the floor, staring at the ceiling.

No matter how she imagined it happening, it always ended in rejection. And Piper just couldn't handle it this close to prom—this close to the end of the world.

At least when she did nothing, there was still a chance that he'd want to go with her. Facing him, springing a surprise kiss on him—it was certain to end badly. And then she'd know, without a doubt, that he had no interest in her.

All the cats didn't even change her mind.

"We can't seem to find any new tears," Aunt Cinda reported over breakfast, "but cat swarms are a definite sign of the world's end."

The cats were everywhere. No one knew where they had come from. News stations were attributing it to global warming somehow, as well as making Harry Potter jokes, but Piper knew the truth.

It was her fault. It was all her fault.

"This is common demon behavior." Her mother sounded perplexed. "But there aren't any new demons in our dimension. Ours are all safely sealed away."

She smiled then at her daughter, and Piper wanted to climb under the table and die.

"Yep! Super safe! The safest."

She stuffed oatmeal into her mouth as fast as she could, desperate to leave the kitchen. But before she could do that, there was a knock on the door.

"I'll get it." Piper's mother swept toward the door.

It took a full minute of Piper continuing to stab at her oatmeal before she realized she recognized the voice wafting in from the front door. A panicked yelp escaped her, her dish clattering as she dashed to join her mother.

Simon stood in the doorway, shoulders hunched and hands stuffed in his pockets. The sky behind him was an inky black, and an orange tabby encircled his feet.

"Hi, Piper," he said, looking a bit uncomfortable as her mother stared him down. Luckily his eyes looked relatively normal at the moment, but her heart was beating in her throat all the same. She shoved her mom aside, joining him in the doorway.

Her mother would figure it out—if she hadn't already. Her mother was a Class A Demon Huntress, *and there was a demon literally standing right in front of her.*

"We need a minute, mom," she said, grabbing the backpack lying beside the front door before hurrying to pull the door shut behind her. Her mother put a hand in the doorway, blocking it from closing all the way.

"Aren't you even going to introduce me?" she asked, a curiosity in her voice that Piper thankfully recognized as the nosy mom type and not the suspicious huntress type.

"Later!" she squeaked, finally succeeding in pulling the door shut with a loud *click*.

Simon looked perplexed as Piper turned on him. "What are you doing here?!"

"I—I came to see you."

At first he looked bashful, but then his eyes flashed green, and Piper couldn't tell if she was looking at Simon or the demon. There was a funny look on his face, something hard and mean. But then Piper blinked, and it was gone, replaced with his usual crooked smile.

"Sorry if this is a bad time," he said.

"It's...fine." Piper was distracted, pulling him around the side of the house where her family couldn't see them talking. She caught her reflection in the window as they passed and only then remembered her hair was still in her pastel pink rollers. *Damnit.*

"A bad time for...what?" She dropped the backpack by her feet, just in case.

Simon shuffled his feet again, looking like he suddenly regretted coming over. Then something in his face changed again, and Simon was gone—the demon had taken over, his features sharp and unfamiliar, his lip curling as he snarled at her.

Piper was so startled by this shift that she let her guard down for just a moment too long, still in shock that Simon was at her house. Had he come on his own volition? Or had the demon brought him there?

In the time it took her to understand what was

happening, his hands had already raised to her throat, gripping with surprising force.

Piper tried to yell, but wasn't able to make a sound. He was strong—much stronger than a boy Simon's size should be. Finally her wits returned to her, and Piper sprang into action.

She may not have started her demon huntress training, but she did know self-defense. She managed to slip an arm beneath his, wrenching it upwards enough to ram her other elbow into his gut.

It's not Simon right now. It's a demon, she told herself.

The demon heaved backward, slackening his grip just enough for Piper to wriggle out, throwing her weight against him and knocking them both to the ground.

Piper was able to pin the demon down with her legs, the weight of her body enough to subdue him. She knew she only had a moment. She grabbed his wrists, pinning those down, too, on either side of his head.

You can do this, Piper told herself.

Her heart was pounding. Demon or not, it was Simon's face that stared back at her.

Just kiss him.

She only had a moment before the demon would find his strength again, throw her off, maybe get the better of her this time.

Fate of the world, Piper. It's all on you.

She hurled herself down at him, face-first, and her lips connected with his.

As Veronica warned, the demon fought back at

first—the kiss was wet and unpleasant, mostly teeth. But after a moment, they both relaxed, and Piper started to breathe in deep. The demon wasn't struggling anymore, so she reached over to unzip the backpack, sliding the book out one-handed, feeling it thrum in her hand.

She felt the energy of the demon start to pull from within Simon, a green light collecting and flowing through him, into Piper, and finally out into the book. It vibrated a moment, and with a final thrust, Piper was able to slam the old tome shut.

She'd done it.

The book was sealed.

The edges glowed, ebbing and flowing around the book's cover and down the spine, and then the whole thing fell still.

Piper let out a little whoop as she extracted herself from Simon's face, slipping the book back into her backpack.

"Wow," Simon said, as she returned her gaze to him. She was definitely still straddling him. He blinked, as if coming out of a daze. "So…is that a yes, then?"

Piper zoomed back into focus on what was happening, jumping off of him like she'd been burned.

"Oh my god," she said, mortified. "I'm so sorry." She gathered up her bag and hurled herself away from him, already imagining how many zip codes away she'd have to move.

She'd gotten the demon out. That was all that

mattered.

If Simon never spoke to her again, it would at least be worth it. Sort of.

Simon's face fell. "Oh. I figured you must have a date already. It's okay." This time it was Simon whose cheeks were tinged red.

Piper froze. "What?"

Simon gave her a sad smile. "I knew it was a long shot, asking on the day of prom. I won't make it weird in biology class. I promise."

"Asking...what?"

Her heart fluttered, but she couldn't believe it. Not after...after everything.

"Asking you to prom."

"*That's* what you came here to do?" Piper wished her voice didn't sound quite so incredulous.

Simon looked sheepish. "I've been trying to ask you for weeks, but you kept avoiding me. I was sure you didn't want to go. I shouldn't have come here. I'm sorry. Look at you — you're clearly already getting ready."

Piper self-consciously reached for her rollers again, but then decided it didn't matter.

None of it mattered.

She'd already banished a literal demon this morning. She felt invincible.

"Yes," she said, breathless. She closed the gap between her and Simon, helping him to his feet. Then she stood slightly on tiptoes, pausing only a moment before kissing him again, this time without a demon trying to murder her, without the fate of the world resting on her shoulders. Just a girl kissing a boy after finding out it *wasn't* just the demon that had brought him to her house—Simon really liked *her*. He liked Piper!

"Yes, Simon Anderson, I will go to prom with you."

On a whim, Piper reached for his hair as they continued to lock lips. The sensation was enough to sweep her away into a magical land where she could kiss Simon all day long—kissing was *wonderful*—but then she remembered Veronica. And Brynn. And the two remaining demons.

"There's something I have to do first, though." She pulled away from him.

Simon looked disappointed, but then he laughed. "I suppose I have to get dressed as well."

She wasn't talking about getting dressed, but she nodded all the same.

"We'll pick you up. Five o'clock. We've got a limo."

Geoffrey would be *so* pleased.

Two hours later, Piper stood in the small room at the back of the library beside her best friends, all three dressed in their fanciest dresses, hair curled and makeup applied.

Each of them held a final tome in their arms, and the four others were already safely back in the glass case.

"Piper, I have to say...I wasn't sure you had it in

you."

Piper tried to scoff, but she could tell Veronica was genuinely proud of her.

"To be completely honest... I wasn't sure I did, either. And while it's totally not fair my first kiss had to happen with a demon that wanted to kill me" — the other girls giggled — "my *second* kiss was awesome."

She stepped forward and placed her tome in one of the empty spaces in the case, feeling the last vestiges of the demon energy as it settled back into its eternal prison.

"*And* we have another seat filled in the limo, which will make Geoffrey *very* happy," Brynn added.

"How is ol' Geoffrey?" Veronica asked.

Brynn hung her head. "We had a fight this morning. He found out about Yuma, and Isaac."

"Detention went well, then?"

"As well as it could have," she said, holding up the book as proof before placing it in the case next to Piper's.

"So what happened?" Piper asked.

Brynn shrugged. "I told him the truth."

Both girls gave her the side-eye. "And what exactly was that?"

"I told him it's not cheating if it's a demon."

The others burst out laughing. "And that worked?" Veronica asked.

She shrugged again. "I told him very early on that there would be elements of our relationship that I couldn't explain. He trusts me. I told him this was one of those times."

"Fair enough."

Veronica stepped forward then. "And the final tome," she said, her voice dramatic. "Making me demon-kisser MVP at a whopping four successful captures."

She went to place the book in the case, and Brynn grabbed her arm. "Hang on!" she said. "You didn't tell us who it was."

Against all odds, it was Veronica's turn to get shy. She gripped both edges of the book, hiding behind it, only her eyes peeking out.

"It wasn't a big deal."

"Oh my god, V — you're *blushing*. Who *was* it?"

After a moment, she dropped the book below her face, letting a little half smile play at her lips. "It was Rien."

"Ryan Cooper?"

"Rien *Jennings*."

Piper's mouth dropped open. "*Girl* Rien?!" she exclaimed, to which Brynn gave a little hoot.

"No *wonder* I couldn't find the last demon," Piper said, shaking her head.

Veronica looked smug. "You were definitely not looking in the right places. Those you covet secretly…guess we needed my discerning eye to find the last one."

Brynn looked a bit emotional at this surprise coming-out moment, and for a second no one was sure what to say. This felt somehow even bigger than demon-banishing, than saving the world.

"So that's actually *two* additional seats in the limo

now," Veronica squealed, breaking the silence as a grin spread across her face. Piper let out a similar yelp of excitement, and Brynn started doing a little dance in place.

"Veronica!" they cried. "That's wonderful!"

This time when their friend moved to put the final tome in the case, the others let her, waiting only a moment before tackling her and engulfing each other in a messy group hug — the kind of hug you could only share with people who'd just successfully saved the world together.

Piper took her skeleton key out from beneath her prom dress and shut the case tight. The three of them stood there a moment, arms locked together while staring at the tomes that had caused them so much trouble this week.

"Let's never miss book club again, shall we?" Piper suggested.

"*Never*," they said in unison.

"Now what do you say" — Brynn pulled out her phone to call Geoffrey — "we go to prom?"

Boys' Book Clubs and Other Bad Ideas

by Stephen Folkins

The first hurdle was to get everyone to admit they'd read the book. The circle around Kyle was full of crossed arms and diligently nursed beverages.

"Well, I picked the book, so it would probably be better if someone else gave the summary," Kyle scanned the room. "Jace, you've got a lot of pages marked."

Jace was a large boy with a chin like a full rectangle protruding out of his jaw — a quintessential frat boy, equal parts protein shake and cheap beer at any given time. He was perched at the very edge of the love seat because the large wings on the ancient chair wouldn't admit his broad shoulders. He looked at the sticky notes extruding from the pages of his book as if they'd snuck up on him.

"Nah, man," Jace said, "I don't... nah." He shooed the request away.

"How about you? Isn't this kind of your thing?" Kyle asked Spencer.

Spencer started as if Kyle had shouted a challenge in a dark alley. He nearly spilled his drink but caught it in time and set it conscientiously on a coaster. Where Jace was large, Spencer was slight and slim, with a perennial baby face and lank blond hair that always made Kyle think he was going to suddenly start demanding chocolate in a German accent.

"Well, I don't know if it's really any of our *thing*,"

Spencer said, looking down at his copy as he idly thumbed through it. Kyle saw the margins were covered in notes.

"Are you sure?" Kyle asked, "I thought you were into fantasy."

"Okay, I like *high* fantasy," Spencer conceded, gesturing his hands left. "I like whole, awesome worlds where there's a whole universe and people go all over it and save it and stuff. This" — he shifted his demonstrating hands to the right — "was just a bunch of girls in pirate shirts sword fighting boys in tights with a bunch of talking in between."

"Well, that's the start of a summary, I guess," Kyle said. "Why don't you keep going?"

Spencer took a dainty sip of his Gland Blast, a banned energy drink from Thailand rumored to contain tiger adrenal gland and cobra venom. Kyle had found a dusty twelve-pack in his uncle's garage and used it to lure them to the book club. Jace had already been through two cans.

"I don't really remember the specifics," Spencer said, "except that she really wants to make out with this Ambrosius guy, but she also wants to make out with Sextimus, but she's supposed to kill one of them?"

He was interrupted by the basement door slamming closed and Denim's heavy footsteps pounding asynchronously down the stairs.

Denim plopped down in his armchair in a puff of weed smell. The year before, he'd been a standard frat guy, too, but he'd started experimenting sophomore year, and now he looked like if an Allman Brother needed an intervention: red-eyed, red hair in tangles to his shoulders, and his belly starting to strain the buttons of his ubiquitous jean jacket.

"We already get started?" Denim asked, cracking open a can of Gland Blast and scratching at his sideburns.

"We were just getting into it," Kyle sighed, relieved to see something like enthusiasm. "Spencer was giving us the summary."

"Hey, you know what, I'll bet Denim would do a much better job than me," Spencer said magnanimously.

"Yeah? I'll do it," Denim said, holding up his finger and stopping the conversation for a full ten seconds while he chugged his Gland Blast. He let out a soda-commercial "ah" and launched into it. "So, this girl Ophelia is like an orphan who's really good at sword fighting, but her friend Ambrose who does magic gets captured by this evil guy Septimus-"

"What?" Jace interrupted. "Septimus wasn't evil. He was just getting stuff done, you know?"

"I don't know," Kyle prompted eagerly. "Why don't you tell us?"

"I thought his name was Sextimus," Spencer said idly, still pretending he didn't know very well what the characters' names were.

"Nah, man," Jace said, fiddling with the stud in his left ear. "Sextimus was the older brother who was the Duke's evil advisor. Septimus was the one Ophelia fell in love with and tried to make switch sides."

Spencer switched gears and said, "Okay, I don't know that she was in love with him. It's more that she saw herself in his ambition and drive. She would have wanted him to switch sides anyway."

"Except when they were in the torture chamber, she held his hand to keep from going insane, and from then on, she can't choose between him and Ambrose," Jace pointed out.

Denim said, "Yeah, she keeps talking about how she loves Septimus now, but you're supposed to know that Ambrose is the right choice all along."

"Yeah, because he's nice, and they're on the same side and aren't constantly fighting with each other," Spencer said

Jace scoffed. "Fuck off. Ambrose is boring. Guys like that never pull. Septimus challenges her and makes her better."

Kyle leaned back with a happy sigh and took a sip of his Gland Blast. He had known that once they got over their initial reluctance, they'd all be really into it. Finally he'd have someone to talk with about *A Scrap of Liberty*.

It had been a lonely semester since he'd transferred in from community college. Kyle had always had trouble making friends. Descriptions of him usually included words like "nondescript," "basic," or "Wait, his name isn't Kevin?"

When he got assigned to a breakout group with

Jace, Spencer, and Denim in the geology class they were all taking to knock out their science prereq (except Denim, who was studying engineering), it was make-or-break time. They'd been leery of doing a book club, but the promise of some original Gland Blast had lured them in. This was the good stuff, where the inside of the can was coated in rubber to keep the drink from eating through the tin.

And now here they were, arguing about love triangles, just like the people he saw online. They were falling along the usual lines, split between supporting Ambrose and supporting Septimus based on who they thought was more like them. He'd stay out of it, for now. No point in spoiling the rest of the series for them.

"Ambrose does nothing!" Jace was shouting, bringing Kyle's attention back to the debate. "He just shuffles his feet and asks Ophelia if she's making the right decision. He doesn't even help."

"And he ends up being right!" Spencer's energy drink almost sloshed out of his can with the force of his argument. "If they hadn't tried to board Sextimus' ship, Old Carmello wouldn't have died."

"He had to die, dude," Denim said. "He'd taught her everything he knew, and it was time to pass the torch."

"But they don't know that." Spencer slammed his paperback copy with the movie poster as cover art down on the table. "In the story, they're real people, and Old Carmello dies because Ophelia goes along with Septimus' plan even though Ambrose warns her..."

Of course, Kyle had seen all these arguments before, but that was online and mostly punctuated with gifs. He'd always been uncomfortable when the fights became threatening or harassing, but he'd figured removing the anonymity would prevent that.

"You're full of shit." Spencer was standing up now and pointing at Jace.

"Am I, dude? Am I full of shit? Dude? Am I?" Jace pushed his chest out but kept his arms on either side as he rose to meet Spencer. "Or do you just like Ambrose because he sits there simping for a girl but doesn't have the balls to do anything about it?"

Spencer tried to square up, but both of them were extending their necks as far up or down, respectively, as they could in order to make eye contact, and it was just uncomfortable.

Spencer thought better of that quickly and turned on his heel to huffily stomp back to his seat.

"Yeah, that's right," Jace said, swaggering back to his own place.

"Okay," Kyle said in a calm voice, trying to power through the unpleasantness. "What do we think the themes were? Denim, you were saying—"

"You son of a bitch!" Spencer lunged at Jace with what appeared to be a hand grenade. He shook the hand grenade violently, popped its tab, and sprayed its unnaturally yellow contents into Jace's face.

Jace lashed out, pushing Spencer over, causing the fizzing can of Gland Blast to spray wildly over Kyle, Denim, and the basement in general.

By the time Spencer picked himself up, Jace had seized a new can of his own and was shaking it vigorously.

"Come on, guys," Kyle moaned. "I had to pay my uncle like forty dollars for that twelve-pack."

But Jace and Spencer were in no mood to see reason. Spencer dove for a fresh can right as Jace popped the top of his own, but askew, sending a concentrated spray sideways onto Kyle and Denim again.

Spencer grabbed a can and tried to do a roll to escape Jace's redirected stream, but he just ended up flipping onto his back, so Jace knelt over him, pouring the energy drink directly into his face.

Kyle tried to pull Jace off of Spencer, but there was no way that was happening, and Spencer just had to splutter until the can was empty. Jace then snatched the can Spencer had been holding and shook it vigorously.

"Denim, give me a hand here," Kyle waved him over. Denim rose and laid one hand over Jace's other shoulder and just kind of let it rest there. "Ugh, whatever. Jace, man, come on. If we don't get some baking soda on this right away, we'll never get it out of the carpet."

But Jace let out a guttural Schwarzenegger howl, raised the can above his head, and popped the top. A torrent of the sickly yellow soda spiraled out like a lawn sprinkler, soaking the whole boys' book club, and the geyser was still rising as Kyle jumped up, ineffectually trying to grab the can out of Jace's hand.

The fountain of Gland Blast rose and rose until it hit the bare fluorescent lights suspended from the ceiling. Sparks flew, and the lights blinked.

"Oh shit!" Denim yelled. "Stop, drop, and roll!"

"That's for fire—" Spencer started, still spluttering from the seemingly never-ending spring of fizz raining down upon them, but he stopped short.

"Huh," Spencer said.

"What?" Kyle asked, wringing out his shirt, as if it would make a difference.

"There," Spencer said weakly, pointing to the ceiling.

They all turned their heads, Jace included, to see a mini galaxy of Gland Blast orbiting above them, arcs of electricity shooting through it every few seconds. Drops ran in grand spirals around a central halo of foam, spitting out far more volume than could possibly have been in the whole twelve-pack. It cast a sickly brown-yellow glow over the basement. And it hummed. Maliciously.

"Oh," Kyle said. "Huh."

Jace seemed to come to himself and pushed his hair back, sending a wave of soda behind him, onto Denim.

"Dude, I'm sorry about that, Spencer. That was out of line."

And then the room exploded.

And there was everything and nothing.

When Jace came to, his arms were asleep, so he tried to roll over to a more comfortable position.

Then tried again.

He would have gone a third and maybe a fourth time, but a cold, throaty voice interrupted him.

"I wouldn't bother, Priest. Those chains were forged specifically to hold your kind."

Jace finally opened his eyes, hocked up some phlegm, and spat. Instead of passed out on Kyle's faux leather couch, as he had been expecting, he was leaning against a stone wall with his arms suspended from chains above his head.

"Like I said, Priest, there's no point in — hey — hey! Stop it!"

Jace continued to ignore the voice rising from its moody depths to nasally highs as he jiggled his hands back and forth, pretty sure he could pull the chain off the wall if he could get the right torque or something.

"Quit it!" The voice echoed into endless halls behind the barred door of Jace's cell.

Jace looked up and noticed, for the first time, a figure skulking in the shadows on the other side of his cell. He stopped playing with the chain.

"Oh, hey. Bro, where are we? Where's Kyle and the guys?"

The figure stepped out of the darkness, resolving into a young man, maybe a junior in high school, dressed all in black. Black overcoat, black jacket, black cravat, everything black down to his boots. His hair, though, was a golden blond, glowing like a halo as it fell in curls to his shoulders. He had a kind of rodenty face, Jace thought, and his scowl wasn't doing him any favors.

"I don't know where your friends are, Priest, but by the time I am done with you, you will—"

"Jace," Jace said.

"What?" The kid fully flinched at being interrupted.

"Name's Jace, and I for sure could never be a priest. Couldn't do the sibilancy, if you know what I mean." Jace raised his right hand as much as the chain would allow for a high five, but none was forthcoming.

"If you are not a priest, as you claim, then how did you materialize midair in my quarters, pray tell?" The kid kept putting on that weird sneer, but it just kind of looked like he had to sneeze.

"I don't know, man, we were talking about this book, and I totally owned Spencer with some Gland Blast, and—oh, shit dude, I think we got sucked into the book."

"You what?"

"Yeah, we got Freaky Friday'd into the book."

"I told you, Priest, these chains suppress your magic. Spare me your incantations!"

"Yeah, yeah, I get it. Okay, you think I'm one of the magic priests like in the book. Holy shit, if I got sucked into the book, maybe I am a magic priest. Yo, unchain me so I can see if I have magic."

"No."

"Did any of the other guys appear with me?"

"As I was saying, I do not know what rat holes your little friends are hiding in, but by the time I'm done with you, you will give me the name of every traitor you have ever met." Jace's interrogator clenched his fist in front of his face.

"Shit, bro, you're going to torture me?"

"I am not my brother!" The boy screamed, bolts of red magic arcing between his hands.

"Oh. Ha!" Jace bonked his head on the stone wall from laughing. "Shit. Ow. You... you're Septimus, right? I totally should have guessed from all the black. I thought you'd be, like, hot though, from the way Ophelia's all obsessed with you."

"Looks don't matter! Only power matters! I mean... so you *do* know the Revolutionaries! I mean... she is?"

"Yeah, dude, she's totally up for it, but she's holding off because you're all evil and shit."

"Is it evil, what I do?" He totally dropped his menacing air and started pacing with his hands behind his back. "Is protecting my family evil? Protecting the realm?"

"Hey, man, I'm not the one you need to convince."

"But every time I see her," he suddenly clenched his hands in front of his chest, "she says these *things*! And I know they're true, and I just get so mad."

"Tell me about it, bro. Hey, you got anything to

drink?" Jace raised his head up so that one of his bound hands could scratch it.

"Huh?" Septimus seemed to remember he was in the room, "What? Oh, yeah. Hold on. Let me get those chains."

Denim awoke, as usual, to the scents of incense and body odor.

"Oh, man, cottonmouth," he said as he sat up.

"Drink this. It will help," said a soft, kind voice. Denim looked to see a teenager holding out a wooden cup full of sparkling liquid. Denim took it without question and downed it all.

They were in a large room, a stone dome supported by six stone arches. Dust flowed nearly opaque through the pink tinged sunbeams that peeked through holes in the masonry. The floor was covered in worn rugs, and the sounds of a rowdy crowd rang up from the street below.

"Pretty good," Denim wiped his mouth. "Is this Gland Blast?"

"It's a restorative potion. It was supposed to last the Sanctuary for the rest of the week." His benefactor was in some kind of monk's robes, his head shaved on the crown, but he was built like a star quarterback, with broad shoulders, a broad chin, and a beatific, idiot grin.

"Oh, my bad. I got the next round, then."

"You didn't know. What is your name, stranger? I

am Brother Ambrose, of the Brothers of the Cloth."

"I'm Denim." They shook hands, and the Brother placidly kept still while Denim did his extended sequence of grabbing the hand, pulling it in, slapping it five, and doing wiggle fingers. "Super cool to meet you. So, we got sucked into the book, didn't we?"

"I have no idea what you're talking about, Denim."

"Yeah, probably not. We're in Pardio, right?"

"Yes, it's good that you remember."

"How did you find me?"

"You were passed out in the gutter."

"Okay, sounds right. Was there anyone with me?"

"No one."

"Bummer. Anyway, you're one of those magic priests, right?"

"I am of the Arcane Brotherhood, yes."

"Sweet. Okay. We can work with this. Have you ever had someone travel here from the real world?"

"I understand we do not have the wealth of Windblow, nor the great empire of Herrenverr," Ambrose smiled indulgently, "but we still do consider this the real world."

"Yeah, of course you do. The opposite, then," Denim said. "Have you ever heard of anyone coming here out of a book?"

"Of course. It is a staple of the serials that are written for children, published in weekly pamphlets on the cheapest paper. It often seems like pure fantasy, but I find they actually have a great deal to say about our own society. For example, The Island Boys seems like a simple adventure beyond the bounds of laws and norms, but—"

"Yeah, cool, really deep. I need to go to a library."

"Now is perhaps not the best time. You may not have noticed, but there is a war on."

"Oh, um, yeah," Demin improvised. "I need to research the... ancient texts... for Ophelia?" Ambrose's demeanor changed instantly.

"You know my Lia?" He grabbed Denim's hands and pulled him uncomfortably close.

"Oh, yeah, we're super tight." Denim racked his brain. "Like, I know her favorite color's lilac-"

"Lilac!" Ambrose shouted, nearly before Denim could get the word out, "You truly do know my beloved. What work has she for you at the library?"

Denim didn't see any way this could backfire. "She wants me to comb the records for a world beyond this one."

"A world beyond this? I do not understand, but if it's Lia asking, she's definitely got a plan. I've seen no mention of it from the Mages or historians, though. Where would we find these writings?"

"Um... young adult literature?"

Spencer woke from one dream into another.

A beautiful woman was leaning over him, wiping his brow with a warm cloth.

"Good. You're awake." She smiled. Her black hair fell in tight ringlets over her face, and she brushed it back with her fingers, her dark skin liberally spotted with freckles.

"Where am I?" Spencer said, reaching out subconsciously. She gently placed his hand back on his chest.

"You're in Revolutionary Headquarters, deep in the slums of Pardio."

Spencer sat straight up, nearly headbutting the woman. "No fucking way."

He was in a smoky room with light poking through the gaps in the boarded walls. His caretaker stepped back in alarm. She was wearing breeches and tights, a jacket and cravat… and a sword.

"Revolutionary Headquarters. We got… I'm actually here." He gave a shrieky laugh. "I'm in Pardio. I'm with the Revolution."

"Old Carmello thought you were a spy, suddenly being discovered in the pantry. He was ready to slit your throat and have done with it. But we're trying to make a different world, a better world. We won't resort to their methods."

"Old Carmello? Then it's the same. That means —"

"You know Carmello?" the woman asked.

"By reputation," Spencer said hurriedly. "So if Carmello's here, then that must mean that Ophelia's here, too."

The woman blushed.

"Wait," he said. "You're Ophelia? But you're…"

"I know," she said sadly. "I'm not like all the propaganda, all beautiful. I'm skinny and lack a woman's curves."

"Oh, no, that's not what I —" Spencer stopped that

thought. "I just always pictured you as... that is, the book always said dark, but I assumed... Anyway, I think you're a really beautiful girl."

"Thanks?" she looked like she was giving the throat slitting a second thinking over.

"Sorry, I mean—" he stumbled to his feet, then dropped immediately into a deep bow. "My name is Spencer, and I'm super honored to meet you, Lady Ophelia."

"Thank you, Spencer," Ophelia smiled indulgently, "but I am no Lady. I am a simple, filthy peasant, like you, raised above my station by War."

"I look like a peasant?" Spencer crossed his arms over his Big Dog graphic tee in embarrassment.

"I'm sorry. I didn't mean to assume. It's just that you wear cloth all down your leg, but it is torn and tattered."

"It's distressed."

"Do not be distressed; all are welcome here. Now, Spencer, what brings you to our cause?"

Spencer sputtered. "Oh, I've, uh, I've heard of your speeches of liberty and of your battles against the evil Septimus of the Guard."

"Is he evil, though?" she said, suddenly clasping her hands and turning to look into the distance, which was a wall a couple of feet away.

"I mean, yeah, he tortures and kills people. If that doesn't qualify, I don't know what does."

"But what's in his heart?" she asked decidedly not-him.

"Probably also torture and murder? Hey, what

about that Ambrose guy?" he said, a little desperately. "I heard he's pretty nice."

"What? Of course he's not evil."

"No, I mean for, like, being in love with…" Spencer mumbled the end.

"What?!" Ophelia gave a choking laugh of disbelief. "I'm not in love with Septimus."

"I know. I was talking about Ambrose."

"Oh, Ambrose," she said sadly and, frankly, a little patronizingly. "We've known each other since we were children. Everyone's been saying for years that we would end up getting married, but I just don't… want to?"

"But he's objectively better, right? Like, he's always there for you and helps you with your problems. Septimus just sword fights with you and screams insults about your low birth."

Ophelia blushed again, turning away to hide an indulgent smile.

"No! No, that's bad. You see how that's bad, right?" Spencer was running out of patience. "He's not your friend. He's dangerous."

"That's it!" Ophelia nearly jumped in the air. "That's what it is!"

"Thank God… the gods? The gods. Thank the gods. You understand."

"Yes, I feel this way when I think about him because he's dangerous. If I defeat him, I'll stop having these feelings."

"I mean, yeah, sure, that will work. Just kill him, and—"

"No! I can't kill him," she clutched her hands together. "But would he kill me? Is it sexy that he'd kill me?"

"Of course not! I mean, I guess I can see it if I think about you killing me."

"Don't worry, little one. I will not harm you."

"I could have done without the 'little one' part, but thank you."

"There's something about you I just can't put my finger on." Ophelia leaned close and looked into his eyes.

"Oh?"

"Something… nonthreatening."

"Oh."

A door slammed open. A hunched man with a drooping white mustache sidled in, out of breath.

"What is it, Carmello?" Ophelia asked.

"They've found us, 'Phelia. I told you this one was a spy!"

"How would he have told them where we are? He's been here the whole time."

Carmello looked to the same wall Ophelia had used to stare into the distance and said, "Magic."

"Well, I trust him. Spencer, now is your chance to prove yourself to the Revolution. Do you know how to handle a sword?"

"Yes? I mean, in theory… Okay, I don't have time to explain what LARPing is right now, but—"

Kyle was woken rudely by a kick to his ribs. He rolled over onto his hands and knees, wheezing.

"Up, boy!" A furious voice shouted. "The City Guard is charging the barricade!"

Kyle looked up to see a bearded man in stained leathers holding a hand out to him. The other hand held a smoking musket.

"Where am I? Who called the cops?"

"You hit your head, boy? You're at the barricade! The Blind Quarter!" the man snatched Kyle's hand and pulled him up. "You're in Pardio, but you'll be beyond the Seal if we don't get out of here."

Kyle staggered, "Okay, okay, I'm up. Is there any coffee? Wait, did you say Pardio? Jesus Christ, I'm in the book. I'm in Pardio! It's actually happening! I've fantasized about this so much; this is amazing."

"Aye, lad, welcome to the Revolution!" the man smiled kindly and clasped his forearm in the style Kyle had read so much about. "Now get running or the best you can expect is a bullet to –" the man's head exploded into a mist of blood and bone shrapnel, and Kyle finally took his sage advice and ran.

Sadly, he wasn't sure what direction to go in and ran directly into a large wall of broken wagons and furniture stacked up in the middle of the street. He figured he had gone the wrong way, and this was confirmed when the first shot rang out from above. Atop the barricade, a line of muskets poked over and shot a volley over his head into a screaming crowd running the other direction. A stream of men in black, hooded coats began descending toward him.

"There's one!" one of the hooded men shouted, pointing directly at Kyle.

"Shit, shit, shit, shit." Kyle pushed off the wall and ran as fast as he could away, the only person upright and moving in a street full of dead and dying men.

"Get him!" someone shouted, and dozens of men cheered and took off after him.

Kyle sprinted down an alley, clutching a stitch in his side and actually crying a little. Old women in headscarves looked down on him from second story windows but offered no help. The guardsmen behind him were jeering and throwing their musket balls with their hands, laughing at the yelp he gave each time one found home.

He finally hit a dead end and collapsed against a stinking heap of what was hopefully mostly food waste. The guards quickly spread out in a bully's lineup, just to make sure he knew there was no escape.

Kyle held up one finger to indicate he needed a second and tried to catch his breath. Strangely, this seemed to work. After a minute, he picked himself up and wiped off the worst of the filth he'd been sitting in.

"Okay, now what?" he said.

"What is that glowing amulet?" one of his pursuers asked, pointing at him.

Kyle patted himself down for a second before realizing they were looking at his left hand. "Oh, you mean my Smart Watch? Yeah, it's just lit up because my heart rate's going crazy."

"Is it magic?" one of the guards far in the back

yelled.

"Huh?" Kyle was leaning over with his hands on his knees, still breathing raggedly. "Oh, yeah! Yes! Actually — " Kyle found himself uniquely prepared for this moment. "Have you ever been to the Holdings across the sea to the south?" he asked as mysteriously as he could. The guards looked at each other and shook their heads, but they were definitely intrigued.

"There are great spirits in Jiris that are full of ancient magicks, as I'm sure you've heard," Kyle gestured grandly, placing his watch more prominently. "I came across one in a cave full of treasure while I was there. As he gloated over me, threatening me with a death that lasted centuries, I acted aloof and pretended to be unimpressed. He boasted of ever greater feats, but I turned my head at each. 'Spirit,' I said to him, 'it is easy for anyone with magicks to be great and grand, but it takes true mastery to be small and subtle. For all your power, I'll bet you can't even shrink yourself down small enough to fit in this — "

"Hey, Sarge," one of the guards tugged at another's sleeve. "I think that's just a glowing wrist watch. It's showing the time and everything."

Kyle and the Sergeant had a brief staring contest, and then Kyle jumped into the pile of ordure.

Luckily, all of the guards had discharged their shots earlier at the barricade, so they could only plunge their bayonets through the muck, cheering whenever they hit something that felt thicker than the general slurry.

By the time they discovered the open sewer grate beneath the pile, Kyle was long gone.

Jace tried to put some swagger into his walk as he followed Septimus down the narrow lanes surrounding the palace, but it just didn't feel right.

"You're sure dudes wear this stuff?" Jace asked, pulling at the black tights and hooded coat he'd been given.

"Of course," Septimus scowled back at him. "I'm wearing them, aren't I?"

"That's what I'm talking about. You've got long, flowing hair, and you swish your cloak around a lot."

"I am the height of masculine fashion."

"I'm just saying these tights are kind of girly."

"And I suppose where you come from, men walk around with their privates dangling freely, girding their loins only for battle? Here it is women who go about with only drapes between the gods and their shame."

"Yeah, totally. Nah though, where I'm from, dudes wear full-on pants. Like, straight-up cloth, all the way down the leg."

"Your people must be quite wealthy."

"Yeah, my dad pulls down a good six figs. Anyway, my point is, if you want to pull that Ophelia girl, you're going to have to butch up, you know?"

"I do not know." Septimus stopped in front of a heavy oak door and banged on it. "City Guard. Open the door!"

"Yeah, you wouldn't," Jace continued, leaning against a wall. "I mean, a nice haircut, maybe some product in there, you'd look pretty hot. To a girl, I mean. I bet."

"Ha, you would have me let a barber-surgeon hack at my hair with a blade and bowl, like the anemics in Windblow?" Septimus pounded on the door again. "Last warning!"

"No, man, my cousin's girlfriend works in a salon. She could hook you up. You've got to put gel—er, animal fat in it, so it stands up. Drives girls crazy. They think you're a soccer player or something."

"I leave the athletics to my brothers," Septimus said through gritted teeth. With the last warning already given, he removed his sword—the whole thing a shimmering green steel, just like Jace had read about in the book—and slammed the hilt against the door, which promptly exploded into splinters, prompting a chorus of screams from inside. Septimus swept in, sword extended, and Jace followed him casually.

"And don't those big floppy sleeves get in the way?" he asked. They didn't seem to, since Septimus was cutting down rebels one at a time as they rushed him. It was kind of cheating that he had a magic sword, though.

"The sumptuary laws allow only the son of a Duke to wear cuffs longer than eight inches," Septimus answered without pausing his slaughter. "It is a mark of my status and wealth."

"Yeah, man, but you've got to show off those guns." Jace used the standard steel sword he'd been given to lazily knock the house's few possessions off a shelf while Septimus did the killing. "Or grow out a chin strap, you know? Anything so you look less like the ghost of a ballerina."

"Ophelia grew up among the large, muscled, hairy gutter scum that you describe, and yet she finds herself drawn to me. You would have me mimic the brutes she is running away from?"

"You got me there. But look, I know chicks, man. They may put posters of pretty boys up on their walls and talk about how hot they are all the time, but when it comes time to bone down, they pick guys like me."

"And the times they've picked you, have there been any of these pretty boys around?"

That shut Jace up for maybe the first time since they'd met, and Septimus was able to continue his massacre in peace.

Jace turned to a scratched, foggy silver mirror hung on the wall and tried brooding. It wasn't half bad. He tried to enhance the effect by pulling his hood over his eyes, but then he couldn't see himself in the mirror.

"Hey, Sep-dog, how do you get your face so pale?"

"Lead powder," he said, pinning the last rebel to the wall through his stomach, the sword sliding through like a hot knife through butter. "You are going to die," Septimus said to the rebel. "It can be over now, or it can take a week as your intestines fester in the dungeon. Where is the girl: Ophelia?" He twisted the sword, causing the man to gasp.

"Up..." the old man leaned in close to Septimus, breathing into his face, "your butt."

The old man let himself drop, and the enchanted sword split him like paper as he fell.

Spencer swirled the sweet liquid around his mouth to wash out the taste of bile. His clothes from home were ruined, covered in blood and other, even less savory fluids.

Old Carmello plopped down on the bench next to Spencer and patted him roughly on the back. "It happens to all of us the first time," he said kindly, his moustache blowing out when he spoke.

"It does?" Spencer asked.

"No! Only to you!" Carmello let out a great laugh. "Because you are weak and unmasculine."

While fleeing the hideout, Spencer had mostly managed to stay clear of any combat. Staying a few feet back from the real warriors, he'd swung his sword at empty air to look busy. At some point, though, his shoelaces came untied, and he'd tripped sword-first into one of the Guardsmen Ophelia was fighting.

Everyone had hailed him as a hero once they'd got to the safe-house, but then he'd just thrown up a bunch.

"Ignore him," Ophelia said, seating herself gracefully across the table. "He couldn't keep food down for a week after his first kill."

"That was your cooking," the old man said crossly.

"Young Spencer, if you think this one mangles the bodies of her enemies, you should see what she does to a chicken! Ha!" His point scored, Carmello gave Spencer another needlessly heavy blow to the back and sauntered off, looking for more arguments.

"It's true," Ophelia said ashamedly. "I have no skill in the domestic arts, like most women who men want to marry. I am more comfortable on the battlefield or around the fire with other soldiers."

"You were amazing," Spencer said, taking a sip of what they called Surgeon's Muck, overly sweet and tart, reminding him strangely of home. "I was scared out of my mind, but you were literally slicing musketballs out of the air."

She unsheathed her sparkling, golden sword and put it on the table. "It is my greatest gift..." she paused dramatically, "and my deepest curse. Can a man love a woman who kills? Who wants to come home to a bloody warrior?"

"You don't exactly seem short on options," Spencer said a little sullenly. Ophelia didn't notice.

"Ambrose is so dependable, but he is a healer. He could never accept that I find my true self in fighting and killing."

"I think you might be surprised what guys can get over."

"And Septimus is like me. He knows the rush of battle, the sound of your own heart in your ear. But he is a tyrant, cruel and unyielding. Could I change him? But if I did, would it be the same between us?"

"Yes? Probably?" This conversation had become

familiar over the past few hours. "Look, just from what I've heard, both of these guys are absolutely obsessed with you, so you really just have to choose one and you're golden."

"But it's impossible to choose! One is a good person, but the other I'm actually attracted to." She tucked her hair behind her ears absent-mindedly, as the book had described so many times to show she was thinking hard.

"I feel like it's not, though. Let's say you hookup with Septimus? What happens next?"

"He is my sworn enemy. We'd have to carry out our forbidden love in secret, meeting for hidden trysts, agonizing in our sweet guilt. Stolen kisses and caresses in the shadows. The crushing fear of being exposed. Every embrace an opportunity for a stab in the back." She was getting really worked up, breathing heavily.

"Wow, okay. I didn't realize you'd put this much thought into it. And what if you started dating Ambrose?"

"I don't know. We'd move in together or something?"

"I was going to ask which one of those sounds better, but I'm rethinking it."

"I am so glad you came here, Spencer." She took his hand, and he pretended not to panic. "I feel as though I can truly talk to you about these things because you are so sexually nonthreatening."

"Thank you? I mean, isn't that a good thing, not being sexually threatening? Don't you think Septimus is sexually threatening?"

"No, not at all. He is threatening and sexual. It is entirely different."

"I could be sexual and threatening."

"No," she smiled sweetly. "No, you could not. Don't worry, Spencer. I'm sure there is at least one woman out there who could be attracted to you. I'd even introduce you, but I don't have any female friends. I've always been more comfortable in the company of men."

"Cool. Look, Ophelia, please just promise me one thing: before you kiss Septimus, make him promise he doesn't actively want to kill you."

"Ooh," Ophelia let out a breath. "That's a pretty big ask."

"If he truly loves you, he should be able to say it, no problem."

"What? No, I meant for me."

"This one appears as you describe, Master Denim."

"Huh?" Denim looked up from the poorly bound stack of waxy papers he had been reading. "Oh, thanks, 'Brose. It's got cars and stuff?"

"Yes, and people speaking to each other over many miles with the use of wires. It even mentions this America you are so fond of."

"Really? Give it here."

"Yes, though it refers to it in the past tense. It is now called the Greater Western Reich."

Denim threw the book over his shoulder. "We can probably skip that one."

Ambrose dutifully picked it up and brushed off the dust. "You are certain that one of these carries the secret to victory, and to Ophelia's heart?"

"Hundred percent. All great truths can be found in Young Adult Literature."

"Who said that?"

"I dunno. Some teen wizard? Yep, here's a good one. It's got cell phones and everything. Oh, there are vampires though. Put this one in the 'maybe' pile."

"I've been meaning to ask you, Master Denim—" Ambrose was wringing his hands in a way oddly reminiscent of Kyle or maybe Spencer.

"You want to talk about Ophelia, right?" Denim had this kind of conversation on autopilot and so kept skimming. "How to make her like you?"

"I'd do anything for her." Ambrose folded his hands within his long priest's sleeves. "In fact, I *do* do anything for her. I treat her many injuries. I lend her my sleeping pallet when she must hide from the Guard. I listen to her troubles and offer what advice I have. I have been by her side since childhood and offer her unconditional acceptance. Why then does she not love me?"

"Those are all nice things you do for her, but what do you do that's not about her? You know, what cool things are just you?"

"I am among the most powerful of the Mage Priests and can destroy and repair entire buildings with a gesture."

"Hmm, that's pretty good. I'd be into that. I don't know, man. She's probably just not attracted to you."

"So what do I have to do differently?"

"Do you play any musical instruments?"

"Yes, the pan flute."

"Nope. How's your bod?"

Ambrose pulled up his sleeves to show well-muscled arms. "I have the stocky build of a laborer, like my father. Not at all the lithe grace of *Septimus*." He hissed the name.

"Dude, you're jacked. Okay, this is going to sound harsh, but I don't mean it that way: it's probably because you're bald."

"Bald?" Ambrose brought his hand to his scalp. "This is a monk's tonsure. I shave it to show I am a member of the holy order of Mage Priests."

"If you grew it out, would you lose your powers?"

"Of course not. Magic doesn't work that way."

"If you say so, man. Anyway, it looks terrible. Also your clothes. What you need is a makeover."

"You know this spell, this... makeover?" Ambrose asked, looking at his sacred robes with a new, critical eye.

"Of course, dude. You think I always looked this good?"

"You are dressed like an inebriated peasant musician."

"Exactly."

"And women are attracted to men who look like filthy Norther boat raiders?"

"Yeah. I don't know why either, man, so don't ask

me."

"Let us do it, then, this makeover."

"Sweet. Let's get to it."

"Don't we first have to find the book containing the Secrets of War and Love?"

"If I'm being honest, I'm pretty bored of that. Let's just bring the 'maybe' pile. It's probably in one of those."

Kyle woke up in a panic, jumped out of the straw bed he was laying in, and sprinted into a wall.

"Oh, sounds like someone's awake," came a ringing voice from below.

As Kyle massaged his throbbing nose, he took stock of his situation. He was in some kind of attic and dressed in a long, white nightgown. The sound of footsteps creaked up a wooden staircase, and a powdered wig bobbed into view. It was followed by a woman with a white-painted face wearing a dark green evening gown and velvet cape.

"So you have returned to the waking world, young Master Keela?"

"Uhh, you mean Kyle?" Kyle said, "Wait, how do you know my name?"

"It is printed here on your Student Id." The woman pulled Kyle's wallet miraculously out of her décolleté and flipped it open to show his ID.

"You... you're Madame Bickford, aren't you," Kyle said, pointing subconsciously.

She smirked, and the signature beauty mark penciled in over her lip rose. Madame Bickford—the spymaster of the slums, beautiful and seemingly omniscient—drove a great deal of the sequel's plot from behind the scenes. She was a personal favorite of Kyle's.

"You are well informed, Master Kyle, for being fished unconscious out of the sewers. You're lucky the Reclaimers who found you thought your watch was magic. They knew to bring you to me." She pulled a pile of clothes from her bag and threw them to him. "Make yourself decent. We have much to discuss."

Kyle waited a moment.

"Aren't you going to…?"

"No," Madame Bickford said. Kyle grinned like an idiot. This was definitely her. This was real. He began to get changed, and then paused.

"But you don't show up until the second book," he said. "How are you here, if I got sucked into volume one?"

"You say you arrived here by book? Tell me exactly what happened."

"Well, Spencer was on Team Ambrose, so when he said that Septimus was evil—"

"Tell me about getting sucked into the book."

"Oh, yeah, well, we and the book got covered in Gland Blast, and then we got shocked by the lights, and then we exploded."

"So you applied a potion, exposed it to magic, and were thrown into Pardio?"

"Yeah, that actually sounds cooler."

"Okay. I think I have a solution for us." Madame Bickford cast her hand once more down her neckline and withdrew in one smooth motion an entire glittering sword. She brandished it expertly before flipping it and catching its flat side against her arm, the hilt extended to Kyle.

"F-for me?" he asked.

"For you. To have been brought to this world under such incredible circumstances is surely a sign. This sword was meant for you."

Kyle took the sword gingerly and held it up. A white light began at the hilt and climbed in a spiral up the blade until the entire thing was illuminated.

"This is a magic sword," Kyle whispered.

"Go forth, Kyle, and seek your destiny." She put a hand to his back and guided him down the stairs.

As soon as he was out of earshot, she crossed her arms and smiled.

"See you on the other side."

Ophelia gave a great cry of triumph every time she dismembered another black-clad figure, laughing as she kicked them off the rampart of the Smaragdinewood Prison. A riot had broken out at its gates around dawn, and the Revolutionaries had hurried to seize the advantage. Ophelia's sword sang through the air, painting great arcs of blood across the dusty stone of the prison walls. Old Carmello was there, mowing down faceless guardsmen with a giant club studded with nails.

And Spencer was trying his best.

He ran in circles, trying to look busy but not actually engage in any of the fights. It was as if the Guard could smell his fear, and they kept approaching him shouting challenges and curses. He would wave his sword once or twice in their direction and then run back to Ophelia, who would absently cut down his pursuer as he ran past. It was undignified but certainly effective.

He was getting pretty tired, though, so he resolved to ask Ophelia if he could take a break when he next passed her.

A black-hooded figure appeared before him and thrust at him with a sword, and Spencer was astounded and delighted to find that he blocked it easily. He tried poking his own sword back at the assailant, but it was blocked in turn. Adrenaline filled him as he entered into a rhythm of thrust and parry with the Guard. Perhaps he was becoming part of this world. Was he destined to be a great Sword Master like Ophelia? It all hinged on defeating this random Guardsman, who had evidently ripped the sleeves off his black overcoat to show his tattoos.

"Goddamn it. Jace, is that you?" Spencer yelled and backed away from the duel.

"Hey, Spencer. Why'd you stop?" Jace asked, pulling the hood back and wiping the sweat off his forehead. "We were doing really good."

"What are you doing, Jace? I could have killed you."

"I wasn't really that worried, man."

"Yeah, thanks for that. Why are you in a Guard uniform?"

"Dude, you won't believe it. I met up with Septimus! From the book! We're in the book, dude."

"No shit, Jace. I'm here with Ophelia."

"Is that who that is over there killing everybody? She's pretty hot. You two do anything?" He raised his hand for a high five.

"No." Spencer walked over next to Jace, now that they were done fighting, but he did not give him five. "She just wants to talk about Septimus."

"Yeah, I got some of that on my end. Where are the other guys?"

"I haven't seen them. You haven't seen them?"

"Haven't seen them. Oh, here's my boy."

There was a flash of light followed by an explosion as the front gate of the prison erupted into fiery debris. Ophelia was at their side in a flash, magic crackling in her sword.

"He's here," she said, staring with such intensity that she didn't notice Jace beside Spencer.

The cloud of dust parted, and Septimus stepped into the courtyard.

"Oh," Ophelia said, and she might have even gulped.

"Yeah," Jace said, apparently unconcerned that she had just killed a couple dozen people dressed just like him. "I gave my boy some pointers."

Septimus brushed some rubble off his black coat, the sleeves now ending at the shoulder, revealing long, thin, pale arms. His hair had been sheared close on the sides, and the great blond arc of his fringe fell down over one eye.

"Oh," Ophelia said. She took a step in his direction and reached out a hand.

Septimus saw her and smirked. He tossed his hair back exactly the way Jace had told him not to.

"Prepare to die, you gutter dog!" He extended his sword and charged at Ophelia, who sighed contentedly and rushed to join him in battle.

"Those two are fucking weird, right?" Jace said.

"Yeah, super weird. So how are we going to get home?"

"It's actually pretty chill here." Jace gestured around. "Why do we need to go home?"

There was a gurgling sound nearby followed by a thump, and a severed head rolled between the two.

"We should find the guys and go home," Jace said.

"How do we get back, though?"

"With this," Denim said, handing him a book.

"What the hell? Denim?" Spencer pushed the book over to Jace and embraced his friend. "How did you get here?"

"I got in over there." Denim pointed to a giant arch that had opened in the previously solid stone wall. A man in all white was floating in the air, launching the freed stones at fleeing guardsmen, his eyes glowing electric blue, hair shaved to stubble.

"He looks like a metal album cover," Spencer said.

"Is he wearing all white...?" Jace started.

"Denim," Denim finished with a smile.

Ophelia and Septimus broke off their duel upon seeing the spectacle.

"Who is *that*?" Ophelia said, appreciatively.

The man noticed her attention and raised a hand in a wave.

"Ophelia! I came to help!"

"Oh, it's Ambrose," Ophelia said, and lunged back into battle with Septimus.

"Eh, it was worth a try," Denim said, "Anyway, we've got to get sucked into this book to get home."

"And you know how to do it?" Spencer asked.

"Yep. We've just got to spill some Gland Blast on this book and electrocute it, and it'll suck us back home."

"They have Gland Blast here?" Jace asked.

"They call it different stuff. I scored this healing potion from Ambrose. Here, take a pull."

Jace grabbed the flask and took a sip. He swallowed quickly several times in succession in order to keep it down. "Oh, that's Gland Blast, alright."

"Cool," Spencer said. "Now we just need to find Kyle and get out of here."

"Oh, yeah, Kyle," Jace said.

There was a great clanging of metal, and Ophelia went flying back into a wall. Septimus approached her with his sword raised, ready to land the killing blow.

"This is how it ends, girl. This is how it was always going to end. You are a mere mortal, playing with the tools of gods. I will take your sword for my own and plunge it into the heart of your little revolution. All these scum you have riled up will fall back in line under the lash, knowing that they will never prevail against their betters. Know that you have failed, girl, and in this moment of failure," he lowered his sword, "know what it is to truly love."

With that, the two fell on each other in a tangle of passionate kisses and groping.

"Halt, villain!" a voice rang out behind the observers.

All turned to see the new arrival. Even the two lovers pulled apart to get a look at the interloper.

Kyle stood on the rampart, in doublet and breeches, holding aloft a glowing sword. He swung it impressively a couple of times and then slid one-handed down the steel ladder bolted to the wall. He rolled at the bottom and came up in a flourish, the air crackling around his glowing blade.

"Holy shit, Kyle," Spencer said. "Where did you get that?"

Kyle smiled mysteriously and said, "Spoilers."

With that, he charged Septimus, swinging the sword so that arcs of light followed him.

Septimus moved into a dueling stance, getting a safe distance from Ophelia, who was refastening the many straps on her outfit.

Kyle jumped into the air, swinging his blade to meet Septimus', which sliced easily through both Kyle's sword and his chest.

"Huh?" Kyle said. He fell to the ground with a plop. There was an enormous gash running diagonally from his ribs to his shoulder. He looked at his severed sword, the end of which revealed two copper wires flopping around. A few sparks arced between the exposed wires, and the sword flashed once or twice.

"That bitch," Kyle said.

Spencer went to Kyle's side and held his head up. "Kyle. Kyle! Stay with me buddy. You're going to be alright."

"What are you talking about, Spencer?" Jace shouted. "He just got can opener-ed! He's not going to be alright."

"Well, don't tell him that, asshole!"

Ophelia knelt by Spencer and put a hand on his shoulder. "This man is a friend of yours, Spencer?"

"Okay, well, I don't know about friend —"

But the emotional reality had fully caught up to Jace. He threw himself, crying, onto Kyle, who was well into shock now and barely seemed to register his presence.

"I'm so sorry, Kyle," Jace sobbed. "I don't want to see you go out like this, man. This is all my fault."

"Jace." Spencer put a hand on his shoulder, expanding the web of shoulder grabs.

"I really liked the book, man. I didn't want to admit it, but I really liked the book."

"Yeah, me too, man." Spencer said, smiling sadly.

Septimus approached warily. "So, are we stopping the battle?"

"Yes, man!" Jace shouted. "Who cares about the Revolution, or Universal Rights, or the food shortage! I'm losing my little buddy."

"Hey guys!" Denim called, running over with his arms full of metal flasks. "Don't worry. I've got this."

Before they could ask him what he meant, he shook one of the flasks, popped open the lid, and sprayed a viscous green liquid into Kyle's face.

"Ah, shit, what the hell man?" Kyle sputtered.

"That's right!" Spencer said. "You've got healing potion."

"Even better," Denim grinned at him, shaking another flask.

"What do you—" but Spencer was cut off by Denim spraying him in the face. As he coughed out the potion, Denim turned to Jace.

"Woah, man," Jace said. "This is a new jacket."

Denim ignored him and sprayed him in the face, then took his last flask and poured it over himself and then a bound leather book.

"What the hell are you doing?" Jace demanded, grabbing him by the collar.

"He's bringing us home," Kyle said, breathing more steadily but still bleeding. "He's recreating the way we got here. But we still need the electricity part."

"Like in this?" Ambrose said, handing Denim the remains of Kyle's sword, still sparking.

"Hey, good job, Ambrose," Denim said. "You helped."

Ambrose smiled and walked over to join his own cast.

"She didn't screw me over after all," Kyle said, breathily, staring at the sword. "She gave me exactly what I needed."

"Who?" Spencer asked.

"Spoilers."

"I suppose this is goodbye," Septimus said, clasping Jace's forearm. "You are a strange and insulting man, but I will miss your counsel."

"Yeah, dude. You should totally come to our place next time."

"I would like that."

Ophelia gave Spencer a deep bow. "You are truly a great warrior and great friend, Spencer. Surely there will be a woman somewhere who can love you."

"Yes," Spencer sighed. "Thanks, Ophelia, for always saying that specifically."

Ambrose waved, and Denim waved back.

"Okay guys," Denim said, holding the soaked book out between them. "Let's do this."

They each put their hands on the book, and Denim held the blinking sword above it.

The silence stretched on, as something clearly needed to be said.

"I didn't actually like the book all that much," Denim said and plunged the sword into the book, sparks flying everywhere.

Then, they exploded again.

They awoke together with a gasp in Kyle's basement, piled on top of each other on the floor. There was much elbowing and cursing as they pushed off each other.

"We made it!" Jace shouted, disentangling himself and falling back into the chair he had left just hours ago.

Kyle inspected his un-bisected torso under his original, modern clothes and sighed in relief.

Spencer picked up his copy of the book they had just been inside. It was clean and dry.

"That was messed up," Denim said, picking up and looking inside his still-full can of Gland Blast.

"What book should we go into next?" Jace asked excitedly. "We should get one of those Star Wars novelizations."

"I'm not going anywhere," Kyle said, picking up a bag of chips and collapsing onto the couch. "I'm never going to read anything more dangerous than Reader's Digest again." He crunched into a chip and then sat up with a yelp. "Ow, I bit my tongue."

The others laughed.

"No, I'm serious," Kyle said. "I think I'm bleeding."

He pulled his lips back to reveal his incisors were now long, pointed fangs.

Jace and Spencer looked at each other and then tested their own teeth with their fingers.

They had fangs.

"Denim," Spencer said, "where did you get that book?"

Boys, Book Clubs, and Other Bad Ideas

by Jennifer Lee Swagert

Something was different about the new Darkness Dawns event, and no one knew exactly what. The promise of change enthralled the playerbase. Player message boards were ablaze with speculation, vidstreams dedicated hours to theory breakdowns, newsfeeds spun irrelevant details into dramatic reports, influencers milked content out of fake leaks—and Bickford Studios, powerful and commanding as always, remained close-lipped.

Like nearly every player of her caliber, Jimmy had spent the last several months devouring every crumb of information, desperate for any clue that might give her an edge. The initial announcement from Bickford Studios had been deliberately vague: just the title "Fire & Stone Arena" with a release date overlaid on a single flame. No new promotional material came for months, which was unexpected and confusing from the most popular fantasy VR game—so unexpected that the lack of concrete information was news enough, and critics unwittingly promoted it for lacking promotion.

Finally, an update came through: "Light the way," read the promotional banners, horns and fire filling the dark images. The press release promised a shake-up to the game's special event meta. In interviews, studio reps repeated the same thing: "New mechanics, new meta, new play."

Several theories on what that meant dominated player discussions, but Jimmy was firmly in the "Hellfire Battle Arena" camp. Battle arenas were standard fare, and the fire and brimstone imagery wasn't exactly subtle. Darkness Dawns was a hodgepodge of archaic Greek, Roman, and Biblical imagery, the lowest hanging fruit glued together by sheer force of will no matter how mismatched. It had been a while since an update from the underworld had come through, anyway. A bit of hellfire was overdue.

An underworld battle royale suited Jimmy just fine. She had spent years playing Darkness Dawns, spending entire paychecks updating her VR console and neural link. At 24 years old, it looked like the investment was finally going to pay off. She was approaching the Top 1000 on the leaderboard. Once a player was in the Top 1000, they were looking at sponsorship money, vidstream contracts, and, best of all, prestige. Jimmy had earned her 1084th place in the ranks through dedication, hard work, and a single-minded intensity that perhaps wasn't entirely healthy. Plus, she was absolutely phenomenal at battle arena events. Her steady victories meant steady rank-climbing. This new arena could be the arena that broke her past the Thousand Line.

And it was minutes away from going live.

Jimmy idled in game alongside thousands of players stretched across a dry, dusty field, waiting beneath a gray sky for the event lobby to allow entry.

The bright colors of the players stood out oddly against the grim backdrop.

Jimmy wore her best. Her black robes reached her knees and wrapped around her like a toga, held in place by a bronze pin — a limited edition Bronze Snake Pin to be exact — on her shoulder. Her limbs were covered in armored plates, dyed black and bronze to help her hide in the shadows. The black helmet and boots she wore were top-tier Event Exclusives few players owned. Every item optimized her Snaker class skills, granting stealth and boosting the range of her attacks.

She might have looked frightening, she thought, if she weren't a cherub. Her bouncy hair and four small wings were dyed black, but there wasn't much anyone could do to make a four-foot-tall angel look threatening. She carried no weapon, but none of them did; this event only allowed players to enter with clothing items equipped. Everything else they needed was inside.

Most players around her were, like her, decked out in hard-won storyline or Event Exclusive gear, every piece complementing another to optimize skills and boosts. Not everyone was, though. Some new or casual players mingled among the rest, their weak gear and default brown cosmetics marking them as out of place. She didn't really understand why players like that bothered to show up for event releases when entry into an arena could take hours, but she was glad to see them. Arena events turned many a new player's budding interest into a giddy, spiraling obsession. It had happened to Jimmy. Plus, she liked to imagine they looked upon her rare armor and expensive cosmetics with respect — even envy.

New players didn't bother her, no. But swanks did. At least half among the crowd were swanky players covered from head to toe in gear from the Gold Shop, which charged real-world money. The gear was as good as any Event Exclusive, but no one had to lift a finger to earn it. She bitterly watched as swank after swank walked by her, each one bright from Gold Shop cosmetic dyes. They formed a bumbling rainbow, every color of moron represented. Cherubs, seriphs, pucks, you name it — it didn't matter. Swanks were all guilty of the same sin: buying their way to the top.

Jimmy frowned at the crowd. Even if any of these morons could stomach damaging their swanky, market-exclusive gear, they wouldn't know how to play without the gear buffs. They were useless, and Jimmy wasn't the only one who thought so. The swanks in the Top 1000 might be wealthy and prestigious, but at least half of the playerbase hated them. Jimmy might not be the kind of player who wrapped herself in Gold Shop exclusives, but she didn't need to be. She had something these idiots didn't: skill.

God, Lucky better get here quick. He was the only player on Jimmy's level in her alliance, and he had promised to be here. Fire & Stone was a pair arena, so Jimmy was depending on Lucky to keep his word.

"Only five minutes to go," said a cheery voice.

Jimmy looked to her left. Not Lucky. A pink cherub was speaking to a tall, armor-clad neph warrior, who nodded silently. They were using the public voice channel rather than a private one, which was a bit of a faux pas, but Jimmy said nothing.

Like Jimmy, the cherub—BEETSOUP46, according to the public channel record—had two massive, ale-brown eyes and four small wings folded against her back. Outstretched, they'd be no longer than her torso. In contrast to Jimmy's black wings, this player's were still the default white. This made for a shocking contrast with her expensive gear—expensive *market-exclusive* gear. Rather than wearing the spoils of hard-won battles, this player was yet another swank drowning in market-exclusive armor and robes, all dyed a hideous pastel pink. None of the items added any meaningful skill boosts. That wasn't the only difference between Jimmy and BEETSOUP46, though. The pink cherub stood no more than three feet tall.

BEETSOUP46's neph companion towered over both of them, but then, all nephilim seemed to tower over other players. Their ashen, wraith-like bodies hovered at least a foot above the ground, flickering in and out of view and waning into shadows that seemed only to exist in their proximity. That design had made nephs the most popular choice for Snaker stealth builds, but Jimmy had taken one look at their pupil-less eyes and decided she'd rather be an adorable, child-like angel.

The nephilim's billowing robes were market-exclusives just like his companion's, although their usefulness was much more apparent. The public channel record showed his player name was Arsenick1.

Before Jimmy could make a smart remark, a flash of golden light alerted Jimmy to a new message. She opened her player dash screen.

Alliance member [LuckyLLucre] is nearby.

Thank God! Jimmy stepped around the two swanks and scanned the crowd. The golden glow of an Ally Halo marked Lucky's tall, broad form, and she sprinted up to him. His Divine Knight armor had the intimidating thickness and sharp edges typical of his class, but the dagger-like spines along his shoulders and back marked his armor as a cut above the rest. The limited edition gear had been acquired through one of the many special events Lucky and Jimmy had completed as a pair. The default skin was silver with sapphire spines, but Lucky had dyed his solid crayon yellow.

"You look like a satanic Peep," said Jimmy.

"Nice to see you, too, you ugly rat baby." He grinned.

"Seriously, what's up with the yellow?"

"Aren't I supposed to draw attention away from you?"

"True, but you look toxic. Everyone's gonna go straight for you."

"That's the point!"

"Whatever. Just don't die. You're no good to me dead."

"You think I could die in *this*?" he asked, placing a hand on his hip and jutting out his rear in a mock supermodel pose.

Jimmy laughed and pulled up her player dash. "Come on. There's only, like, two minutes left."

They made a good team—the perfect pair. Lucky was a beacon of noise and color, distracting players with a barrage of attacks as Jimmy slunk through the shadows and struck the enemy from behind. Their system hadn't failed them yet.

The crowd waited in a clamor of activity and chatter for the lobby queue to open. Time dragged, and after two hours, two minutes had passed. Jimmy and Lucky stood with their player dashes open, hands outstretched and ready to open the event once the announcement came through. With any luck, they'd make it into the early rounds rather than having to wait hours for a lobby.

A gold flash of light across her dash announced it had refreshed, and **Fire & Stone Escape Arena Live!** appeared on the screen.

"It's here!" shouted Lucky, not that Jimmy needed telling. She had already joined the queue.

The players around them blinked out of view and the landscape effects froze in place, the dry landscape turning unnaturally still as a sheer golden dome descended around Lucky and Jimmy.

Entered lobby. Players: 8/10

Lucky and Jimmy gave loud shouts of triumph.

"Can't believe that was so fast!" Jimmy shouted. Having Lucky around really had brought her luck.

Six other players stood in pairs a few feet apart from each other, their faces bright with the same joy. Each player wore competitive builds, the kind that would make them hard to kill—for most players, anyway. The challenge excited Jimmy. She sent a few flares of glittering purple dust and stars into the sky, and the others did the same—bright oranges and pinks and blues spiraling upward in streams. Flares were for aesthetic purposes only and despised by most players, now that using them to bait other players into fights and traps had become common practice, but it was tradition to pop them off in lobbies. She loved the comradery of these rooms. Once everyone crossed the threshold into the arena, they would be enemies, but right now their shared excitement in the unmoving dome brought them together.

Occupancy: 10/10 players.
Entering Escape Arena in 10 seconds, 9 seconds...

Jimmy turned to identify the new arrivals. A sick thrill ran through her at the sight of the garish pink swank and her neph companion from before. She hoped no one else killed them. She wanted to do the honors herself.

2 seconds...

The swank caught Jimmy's eyes on her and waved, smirking. Who the fuck actually smirked?

1 second...

Golden light wrapped around each person in the lobby. A message sprawled across the loading screen:
Escape the Minotaur. Light the way.

Jimmy had just long enough to wonder what the hell that meant before an unseen force lurched her upward, wrung her through a darkened sky, and dumped her onto the map. Her fall was cushioned by a cluster of dry, jagged shrubbery.

"Where'd we land?" Lucky asked.

Jimmy assessed the prickly, dead bushes freckling the landscape around them.

"Not far from the Mouth, I think."

"We're on Devil's Mouth? I love this map!"

"Me too. It's been too long since we've had an event here."

"Too true. Alright, let's get farming." He reached both arms into the bramble in search of crafting materials.

Jimmy appreciated his hustle. Post-drop, it was a mad dash to collect resources. They'd need to work fast to brew enough potions and find the best weapon chests before the others. Luckily, the bony shrubs held the key ingredient in health potions, so at least they'd have a head start on those.

After collecting what they needed and brewing a heap of health potions, they started toward the only worthwhile landmark in this dead place: Devil's Mouth, a dark hole leading to an endless system of caves and chambers below. The darkest chambers promised the best loot, so into the dark they'd go.

A massive cracking reverberated through the clouds, stopping Jimmy and Lucky in their tracks. Red tore through the sky until it reached the edge of the distant mountains and shot downward in a streak of lightning that lasted far too long. At the same time, both Lucky and Jimmy received an event message. Once the red lightning had faded, they opened their player dashes in unison.

Torch lit.

That was all. She checked the player counter at the corner of her dash on reflex and saw that all 10 players were currently alive and uninjured. Beside the player counter, however, was something new: a small torch icon with a count of 1/7.

The message had said, "Light the way." Apparently, that had meant literally. But how the hell were they supposed to do that? She didn't know what the torches were or where to find them—never mind actually lighting one or dealing with what happens once they're lit.

"Christ, you think that lightning was whatever these torches are supposed to be?" Lucky asked.

Jimmy looked over to answer and froze. An inky black fog several paces behind Lucky was rapidly approaching. Light seemed to disappear in its depths, erasing any sense of depth or form. The fog billowed upward, and Jimmy realized it wasn't fog—it was some sort of creature. Its shadowy form had no texture, almost as though it was the absence rather than the presence of something.

Jimmy could just make out two red eyes and the outline of horns when she shouted, "Run!"

Lucky did, only looking behind himself once he'd caught up with Jimmy.

"That's the Minotaur, isn't it?" he shouted. "Christ, it looks like a black hole!"

It was gaining on them, and they still had no weapons. They'd run out of stamina points before finding a good place to hide in this barren field.

In the distance, Jimmy saw a faint red glow. As they neared, the glow began to shimmer and oscillate. Fire.

"Shit, Jimmy!"

"I know."

"We're at the skid mark? We're screwed!"

The wall of fire they were approaching was the fiery wreckage marking the set path phoenixes flew through the map. Globular chunks of fire fell from their tails in a fashion players had taken to calling "phoenix shit." The shit set the ground on fire in a clear strip across the landscape, which players naturally called "the skid mark."

"We must have dropped on the wrong side of it. Shit." Jimmy continued sprinting forward, scanning the length of fire for any opening.

They stopped at the edge, the flames rising above their heads. The long trail of fire stretched before them was solid — an impenetrable wall between them and the weapons they needed to win.

"We're gonna have to go through," Lucky said.

"Walk through fire? Are you insane?"

"We have like 300 health potions!"

"So? I don't want my armor to take that kind of damage!"

"What good is armor if you're dead?!" he shouted, giving her an imploring look with his obnoxious yellow eyes.

There wasn't any time left to argue. The air around them darkened and the huffing of the Minotaur grew louder and louder as it reached them.

Lucky barreled into the fire. Jimmy followed.

Fire filled her vision. The Minotaur's loud, omnipresent huffing penetrated through the blaze, and her game nav blared glowing red damage alerts in rapid succession.

Armor 190/200
Health 170/200
Armor 120/200
Health 90/200
Armor 60/200
Health 8/200

Jimmy reached the other side and scrambled for her waterskin, drinking the contents to douse the flames that still clung to her. The absurd mechanics of that usually irritated her, but she was grateful just then. She twisted her head to see if the Minotaur had followed through the fire—it *was* an infernal creature, after all—when an iron spike thrust in her path halted her. She turned toward the source.

The pink swank, BEETSOUP46, smiled at her from the other end of an oxgoad.

At least the Minotaur hadn't followed.

Behind the swank, Lucky stood with his arms outstretched, his yellow gear singed and dirty. His gold ally halo had faded almost to white, indicating he was severely injured. And the swank's tanky neph companion held a low-grade pickaxe to Lucky's throat.

Their attackers' gear had clearly been put together with no thought for skill optimization at all, but it was pristine and undamaged, and they held weapons in their hands. Just a commonplace oxgoad and pickaxe, neither intended to withstand much use, but that was more than Jimmy and Lucky had.

"Hand over your items, and we'll let you live," said the swank. "Or maybe we won't," she added in a light tone, shoving the iron spike of her oxgoad at Jimmy again. Goading her.

Of course they wouldn't. This was a *battle arena*. They had already lost.

Jimmy's face flushed red, and not for the first time, she resented her neural link for making her emotions so plain on her face. Being at the mercy of such unskilled players was utterly humiliating. She hoped they weren't fame-seeking hopefuls vidstreaming their gameplay. She considered warning them about the Minotaur and banished the thought.

The swank poked her stick again. "Come on."

This time, Jimmy glared at Lucky, furious at him for getting them into this situation. She shouldn't have listened to him. She was going to lose to these garbage players and miss out on this arena's exclusive loot, all because she was killed by a swank and the fucking *skid mark*.

"Fine," said Lucky.

"Drop your items here," the neph ordered, his gravelly voice strangely two-toned.

Lucky obeyed, and Jimmy moved closer to do the same, swiping her potions from her dash screen into the dusty field. She stared at the neat pile of blue potion bottles, briars, and grass tufts they'd collected. What a waste. Health 8/200 and she was being robbed for grass tufts. Christ.

"That's it?" The neph's eerie eyes narrowed.

"Yeah," Jimmy said.

"It's junk," the neph said.

"They're lying," the swank said.

"This was a total waste!" The neph let out a whine.

"Yeah, it was." Humiliation still coursed through Jimmy, burning her cheeks. "All these potions given to players who won't even survive their next battle. Total waste."

The neph's face squashed in on itself, and he drove the point of his pickaxe into Lucky.

Player [LuckyLLucre] killed by player [Arsenick1].

A great black hole yawned open beneath Lucky and pulled him into the screeching, howling abyss. The screams of the netherworld grew louder as the hole stretched wider, reaching Aresenick1. The abyss swallowed him whole and closed in the space of a blink.

Player [Arsenick1] sacrificed to the nether domain.

What the hell? Jimmy had never seen the abyss consume a living player.

"Nick! Nick!"

The pink cherub spun around the empty area, no longer focused on Jimmy. Red tinted and blurred Jimmy's vision, courtesy of her untreated injuries. She needed to heal. She also needed to run, preferably without getting an oxgoad to the gut. She took a few slow steps away before her game nav burst to life.

New cooperative party member auto-assigned: [BEETSOUP46].

What—

"We're allies!" BEETSOUP46 dashed over with a wide smile, swinging her oxgoad onto her back. Apparently, Nick's death was forgotten. Well, Jimmy couldn't judge. The same was true of Lucky's for her. The boys didn't matter now.

"We aren't," Jimmy protested, but the gold ally halo above BEETSOUP46's head said otherwise.

"We are!" She beamed as she pulled healing potions and bandages out from her player dash.

Jimmy scanned the area. Fire to her left. Open field in every other direction. There was nowhere to hide.

"I've never played with someone so high rank before," BEETSOUP46 said. "It's exciting!"

BEETSOUP46 began healing Jimmy, so she stayed put. The red injury haze faded from her vision, but she was still decidedly off-kilter. The swank's suddenly pleasant demeanor had Jimmy's head reeling.

"Listen... Thanks for healing me, Player *BEETSOUP46*"—she applied herself to sneering the name—"but—"

"Call me Soup!"

"What?"

"That's what everyone calls me! Soup. What do I call you, Player *Cherubjim*?" She said the name with significantly more cheer than Jimmy had said hers.

"Jimmy." This wasn't the conversation she wanted to be having. "Ugh, thank you, but I don't play pairs with strangers."

Back to full health, she strode off without ceremony. That oxgoad wouldn't be able to kill her now.

Soup followed.

"Go away," Jimmy said over her shoulder.

"We can't split up! The point is to play together!"

"Where'd you get that idea?"

"It's obvious. Why else are we in pairs?"

Jimmy turned around in disbelief. "That's completely ordinary."

"Well, yeah. At the start. But auto-assigning a new co-op partner mid-game is completely new."

As true as that was, Jimmy didn't have the energy to discuss and dissect new game mechanics with someone like this. "Listen, I don't want to carry you."

"*Carry* me? I know how to play!"

Jimmy doubted that, but she didn't bother arguing. "Doesn't matter. I still don't play pairs with strangers."

"How else do you make friends?" Soup asked, voice hard. She jerked her hand in midair, opening her player dash.

An alert chimed on Jimmy's player dash.

New friend request from player [BEETSOUP46].
Message: [*Buddies?*]

Decline or Accept?

Jimmy pinched her lips.

Decline.

Soup's face crumpled like a child's, tugging at Jimmy's chest a bit more than she would have liked. It didn't help that Soup was wrapped in soft pinks and a *literal cherub*.

"Listen, I'm close to breaking past the Thousand Line, and I can't have hangers-on holding me back."

"I won't hold you back, then. But I have to stick with you. That's the game's doing, and I'm not going to ignore it. I don't want to throw my first match any more than you do. I have to see what's out there."

Her voice rose with each word, desperate and determined. Jimmy knew that feeling, that almost aggressive need to explore and learn the game. Against her better judgment, her resolve bowed.

"Alright, okay. You can follow me."

"Accompany you," Soup corrected.

Jimmy walked on, and Soup followed.

Soup was still trailing behind her, pink cloak flapping in the wind, somehow unhindered by her tiny cherub wings—the game's chaotic design apparently hated physics—when she heard huffing. Faint, omnipresent huffing. Jimmy looked around but saw nothing. The sound grew louder, and she knew it had to be nearby.

"Do you hear that breathing sound?" Soup asked. "What is it?"

"Minotaur. We need to hide."

She instinctively reached for her Bronze Snake Pin and swore when she found it unusable. The skid mark had too badly damaged most of her gear, pin included, leaving her vulnerable until it was repaired. Only her boots retained enough HP for use, and she engaged their stealth boost.

Her efforts were rendered futile as Soup's Swank Shop sandals crunched and crackled through the dead grass. There was nowhere effective to hide in this barren, wide open space, least of all when attached to a bright pink signpost of a person. She rushed them toward the nearest patch of spindly, waist-high brambles. It wasn't enough to cover them, but maybe the Minotaur would be too busy killing Soup to notice her. Hopefully her bronze attire was enough to blend her into the landscape.

Soup crashed against the shrubbery as she crouched, apparently never having heard of stealth in her life. Jimmy shot her a glare.

"What?" Soup asked in a hushed voice.

Jimmy could barely hear her. The Minotaur's heavy puffing overwhelmed and flattened all other sounds.

The air darkened around them just as it had before, and the Minotaur was before them, rising through the ground in a squall of shadow. Christ, it had been *beneath* them. Its body had thickened, the tendrils of darkness seeming to hold shape just a little better.

It moved at a steady pace around the field, head oscillating as if searching for something. For the first time, Jimmy was able to target lock on the creature and register its life bar.

Name: Minotaur
Domain: Nether
Life: ∞

"Infinity?" Soup must have clocked the life bar at the same time as Jimmy. "Does that mean it can't die?"

Jimmy shushed her as the Minotaur drew closer. Darkness pressed in on Jimmy, blurring her vision. She pressed against the ground as best she could and waited. Wisps of shadow threaded through the bramble, nearly touching Jimmy. The huffing grew manic. She inched backward on hands and knees, praying her stealth boost was enough to keep her hidden.

Soup made to shift back as well, but Jimmy held a hand up to stop her. Her loud movements would only draw more attention. A dark tendril undulated through the air near Soup's shoulder, dangerously close, but she held position.

After a moment, the tendrils slowly drew back. When the huffing ebbed, Jimmy and Soup peered through a hole in the dead bush to see the Minotaur with its back to them several paces away, head still swaying rhythmically to scan for prey.

Soup leaned toward Jimmy's ear. "It's leaving. We should attack now while we have the element of surprise."

Jimmy's face must have conveyed her shock, because Soup pointed to her oxgoad and continued, "It's fine! I have this!"

Jimmy sucked in a breath. "You idiot! That's a terrible idea. You can't kill something like that with farming equipment!"

"I'm pretty sure it's not for farming!" Soup whisper-shouted. "I got it in one of those fancy Amberwood Chests!"

Jimmy very much doubted that, but she focused on what mattered. "I don't think stabbing it in the back will do much damage to its infinite health."

"Aren't you a Snaker? This is what you do! Hide, then stab people in the back!"

Without waiting for Jimmy's input—of which she had plenty regarding that colorful characterization of Snakers—Soup rose and jumped out into the open. Jimmy tucked her head low, cursing the game for tying her to such a foolish partner.

The uptick in deranged huffing signaled Soup had reached her target.

Jimmy peered over the pathetic shrubs to see Soup in a fighting stance, oxgoad drawn.

The Minotaur was a gaping, horned abyss towering several feet over the cherub. Soup's tiny wings fluttered uselessly—it's not as if they could actually take flight. A single swipe from the Minotaur's arm would knock that pink idiot to Hell and back, probably literally. Jimmy wondered why it hadn't yet. The Minotaur stood frozen.

Soup jabbed the oxgoad toward it. It took a step back. She jabbed at it again. It took a few more steps back, red eyes trained on the oxgoad.

My god. She was shepherding the fucking Minotaur.

The absurdity of the sight sent a thrill through Jimmy, and she leaped out from her hiding spot to join in. She wanted to be able to take credit for this.

"Back!" shouted Soup. "Back! Back!"

"Back!" added Jimmy helpfully.

Soup continued to herd it back several paces before Jimmy realized the problem. There was nowhere near to herd it *toward.* Soup glanced over at her, apparently having had the same realization.

"What now?" Soup asked.

Jimmy had no idea. Devil's Mouth was still too far. Were there animal pens on this map? No, they'd need to herd it back to Hell.

"Herd it downward," Jimmy commanded. "Toward Hell."

"How do you propose I do that, exactly? I'm three feet tall!"

"Just try pointing down!"

She did. The Minotaur's eyes snapped away from the oxgoad. A roar scraped through the air.

"That didn't work!" Soup said.

"Point it back up! Point it back up!"

Soup lifted the oxgoad, but whatever spell the Minotaur had been under had broken, and it took a massive step forward.

A violent rumble wracked the sky, obscuring the Minotaur's huffing. The Minotaur looked skyward just as Soup and Jimmy did. Red swept across the clouds.

Torch lit.
Torch lit.

Two bolts of lightning struck, one at the west edge of the map and the other at the east. The Minotaur rocked its gaze between the two unbroken streaks of light, ignoring Soup and Jimmy now, and vanished.

Jimmy stood staring at the empty field for a moment, stunned and confused. Beside her, Soup took a few tentative steps into the area where the Minotaur had been, jabbing her oxgoad in the air as if to confirm it hadn't simply turned invisible. Nothing was there.

"Did we do that?" Soup asked.

"No," Jimmy said. "The red lightning scared it, I think."

"What do you think the lightning is? Something to do with the torches?"

"Obviously. It appeared immediately after the torch alert."

Soup twirled to face her, beaming and apparently unfazed by Jimmy's cold tone. "What if the red lightning is an alert for the Minotaur, just like we get alerts?!"

"I suppose—"

"—and maybe the lightning strikes where the torches were lit, or near it or something, and the Minotaur runs toward the strike points—"

"—to hunt the players!" Jimmy finished with her, excitement welling up inside her too.

The idea had merit. Perhaps they'd finally discovered the new event mechanics the game had promised.

Jimmy stayed close to Soup after that — she wanted to be near that oxgoad — and the pair set about gathering resources. They found a few crafting tools and the necessary metal ore to repair Jimmy's armor and Bronze Snake Pin, but none of the chests they had found had yielded any weapons. Jimmy would have settled for an oxgoad of her own, but they hadn't even found that. Jimmy was beginning to suspect Soup had been telling the truth about having found it in an Amberwood Chest, despite the ultra-rarity of those chests.

Two more torches had been lit in that time (which were not simple hand torches, they discovered, as crafting those had not brought the sky down upon them), bringing the count up to five out of seven. What exactly happened at seven was still unknown.

Soup and Jimmy made their way toward the Devil's Mouth mostly in silence. The swank had attempted some lighthearted chatter, but Jimmy had kept the conversation one-sided enough that Soup got the hint and stayed quiet. She did have some questions that needed answering, though.

"Why do you think that Arse Nick guy died?" Jimmy finally asked.

Soup let out a bark of laughter. "Arse Nick? No, it's *Arsenick*, like *arsenic*."

Jimmy turned her dark eyes on Soup. "It's literally spelled Arse Nick. Someone should tell him."

"A lot of people have," Soup said through her bubbling laughter. "He still won't change it. I think he likes it."

"So he's an arse man?" Jimmy gave a cheeky grin.

"Oh, don't say that!" Soup said, covering her ears with her hands. "He's my son!"

That stopped Jimmy in her tracks. "I—what?"

"He's my son!"

"Your actual son? In real life?"

"Yes. He usually plays those gun games, but I can get him to play DD with me sometimes. Took ages to convince him to queue up for an arena release, though."

"Oh. Cool." That made Jimmy uncomfortable, and she wasn't sure why. At least part of it was shame for having taken delight in the idea of slaughtering a ten-year-old playing a game with his mom.

Soup looked ready to say more, so Jimmy quickly changed the subject. "The torches—any new ideas about them?"

"Well, I was thinking..." Soup kept her eyes downcast and her cheeks flushed, looking surprisingly shy.

"Yes...?"

"Well, I know you're a pro and all, so you've probably already thought of this, but you know the Bickford Books?"

Jimmy did indeed. She was obsessed with them, as were many players. They were a collection of player guides, handbooks, and general notes on the world and lore from Billy Bickford himself, the creator of

Darkness Dawns. Jimmy couldn't imagine a player like Soup knew much more than what a few oversimplified fan videos described.

"I do. Go on," she said anyway. She began to walk toward their destination again, and Soup stayed in step beside her.

"Well, there was that scrapped idea for the Throne."

"Right. They replaced it with the mountains." Jimmy pointed toward the distant mountains. This was beginner stuff.

"Yeah, well, the Throne had seven lamps."

Jimmy turned toward Soup. That tiny detail had been turned over and over by many fans in the past, but it hadn't occurred to Jimmy yet. It certainly wasn't in basic introduction videos to the Books.

"Yes," Jimmy said. "Yes, seven lamps, like in the Bible. And that can also be translated to *torches*. God, you're right!"

"Oh, you can just call me Soup."

Jimmy ignored that. Her excitement was building far too much. "Do you think this has something to do with the Throne, then?"

"I'm not sure. I don't really know how the Minotaur plays into that. Then again, I don't know if it needs to. Bickford Studios is never consistent with symbolism."

"Too true," Jimmy said. "Have you actually read the books?" She hadn't meant for it to sound quite as rude as it did coming out, but Soup didn't seem to mind.

"Oh, definitely," she answered. "They're the whole reason I started to play. The worldbuilding and legends and all that."

"I love them, too. I used to be in a book club for them." She wasn't sure why she was telling Soup this, but she could read the excitement in the cherub's face, and it reminded her of her own. She wanted to see more of it.

"Really? I've heard of those."

"Yeah. My club sort of petered out, but there's a lot of good ones."

"I've always wanted to join one! What was it like?"

Jimmy shared some of the highlights from her old club, spurred on by Soup's rapt attention. By the time she ran out of interesting anecdotes, she had the strangest impulse to offer to create a new club with Soup but pushed it down.

Soup's delight seemed to lead her to the same idea. "Could we make one?"

An alien shyness clenched Jimmy's gut. "I don't think so."

"Oh. Why not?"

"I think we're a little too different. That's all."

"How so?"

"Well, your clothes make no sense, for example. None of their skill boosts work together." Jimmy sounded like a petulant child even to herself.

"That's not why I wear them."

"Oh? What are you—the toxic type who lights off flares and dresses in pink to irritate everyone else?"

"It's not that I want to antagonize other players. I just like looking cute," Soup said, calm rather than defensive.

"Well, it looks bad."

"Rich coming from you. Your entire ensemble is so drab!"

Jimmy bristled. "This is tailored to be fashionable *and* practical for stealth maneuvers! It looks good!"

"Oh, come on! You have a poop pin!"

"I—what?" Jimmy looked down at her clothes, where Soup was pointing at her Bronze Snake Pin.

"This is the snake pin from the Celestial Serpent Arena!" Jimmy protested. "It's extremely rare! And imbued with divine transformation powers! And—and—"

"It's a swirl of poo."

"It's a coiled snake!"

"It's a swirl of poo. It's brown!"

"It's bronze!"

"Well, it wouldn't look like poo if you dyed it pink," Soup said, crossing her arms.

"Oh, sure! Let me just intimidate all my enemies while wearing a pin of a cuddly, coiled *earthworm!*"

Soup let out a bark of laughter. "*Cuddly*? What exactly do you do with earthworms?"

Jimmy was laughing too, then. Because it did look like a swirl of poo, and she had never noticed, and it was absurd and ridiculous and funny. Soup's laughter grew, face open and bright. The sight filled Jimmy with inexplicable affection.

Devil's Mouth was near now, and Jimmy instinctively shrunk down to minimize the risk of being seen in the wide-open field that stretched before it. If other players hovered inside the edge of the Mouth, though, there wasn't much she could do to avoid detection, especially with a ball of bubblegum walking beside her.

No one accosted them as they breached the entrance. They began a cautious expedition into the caves. Both held hand torches out ahead of them, watching for threats. The player counter still showed six of the original ten players in the match. Jimmy and Soup didn't know for sure what had happened to the two who weren't Lucky and Nick, but they had a fair idea.

"Where are all the netherbats and sagspiders?" Jimmy asked. "Keep an eye out."

The space was eerily quiet. The usual globs of viscous monster goo trailed down the cave walls, but the monsters themselves were absent. They were getting deeper into the caves now, where the higher-powered vermin sprung out from dark corners, but none appeared. Jimmy didn't like that, but she trudged on. Deep enough into the cave were several promising treasure chambers. She'd find a weapon there, and if she was lucky, it would be this arena's Event Exclusive.

They found a few decent chests and breakable vases throughout the channels, but none yielded any weapons.

"Kind of strange these haven't been looted yet," Soup said. "Isn't Devil's Mouth a go-to?"

"I think it's stranger none of the loot vases have any weapons. They really messed up the drop rate for this arena."

"I don't think there are any weapons for this one. I think that's the big twist they were hyping up." Soup smashed an intricately painted Greek vase against a slimy cave rock. Mediocre bandages and salted meat spilled around their feet.

"You're carrying one on your back," Jimmy reminded her, gathering the salted meat.

"Oh, that's just a tool. There aren't any *real* weapons."

They resumed their trek through the dark halls, salted meat and bandages in their stash.

"Of course there are." Jimmy felt strangely irritated by Soup's foolishness. "How do you expect people to *battle* in a battle arena otherwise?"

"But this isn't a battle arena."

Jimmy gawked at her. She knew swanks were prone to ignorance, but this was on another level. "What do you think this is, exactly, Soup?"

"An *escape* arena."

That gave her pause. The event screen *had* said escape arena, and there was a very clear monster to escape. Still, it didn't make sense to pair up players and send groups out just to play hide-and-seek with a beast from the underworld.

"I think that's just about the Minotaur," Jimmy finally said. "Not the players."

"You can't be serious. My son was sent to Hell for killing your friend." Soup's tone was a lot lighter than her words.

And damn, that made sense. "He killed another player, and he was banished for it."

"Exactly!"

"Well, then what are we all here for? To light some torches?" Jimmy still hadn't even seen one of these torches, and she very much doubted one would be buried underneath ground if they were meant to light the Throne.

"Well, and to *cooperate*. Work together to light the torches."

"Maybe," Jimmy conceded. The idea rubbed her wrong.

"Don't you think it's innovative? Encouraging collaboration instead of competition and all that."

Jimmy gave that some thought before responding. "It's boring is what it is." The more she thought about it, the more irate she became. "If people wanna play collaborative games, they can buy a cooking game for toddlers or some shit. No one's forced to join in on the arena events, anyway. They can just build farms or whatever. Christ. The rest of us live for the battle arenas."

"That's a fair point. Innovation is always nice, but you have to think about what loyal customers want, too." Soup sounded like a corporate training video.

"Loyal customers?" Jimmy made sure Soup saw her disgusted look. "We're not 'loyal customers.' We're loyal players. You're the only customer here."

Soup drew her tiny pink brows so close together they nearly met. "What do you mean?"

Jimmy stopped walking and dragged her eyes up Soup's pastel ensemble. "All that," she spat, waving her hand in a circle that encompassed Soup's entire being.

"That's not very kind..."

"Not kind? What are you, 80?"

"No. I'm 46."

Jimmy's eyes went round.

"Anyway, being kind has nothing to do with age," Soup said quickly, turning her back to Jimmy. An awkward tension grew in the silence.

"Sorry." Jimmy was unsure why she was apologizing. She felt awkward. She'd never knowingly played with someone so much older than her before. It shouldn't matter, and she chastised herself for getting flustered.

"I know you think I'm a swank," Soup bit out, a challenge in her voice.

"Well... You are."

"And why exactly is that a bad thing? Like I said— I'm 46. Can't I spend my money how I want by now?" Every word from Soup's mouth was soaked to the bone in defensiveness.

"Of course you can!" Jimmy snapped. She didn't like the steadily growing guilt weighing her down. "I just don't like when people buy their victories!"

"I don't buy my victories, Jimmy," Soup said calmly. "I just buy cute togas and sandals."

"I know! It's just... The Swank Shop makes everything unfair. There are people working really hard to do well, but someone who works a fraction of that can just buy the rank someone else worked for. It's wrong!" Jimmy's voice had risen alongside her anger, and it echoed off the walls.

Soup was silent for a moment as they walked. When she finally spoke, her voice was very soft. "I agree, you know. About the pay-to-win stuff being wrong."

Jimmy's anger deflated. "Okay. Good."

"It would be a lot better if the shop was just for cosmetic stuff."

"Yeah... Yeah, that would be fine. It's the rank cheating that gets to me."

"Yeah, I see. I don't really play for ranks, and I forget how important it can be for others."

"It can be, yeah. Did you see how much Robo-Scope got from his Gland Blast sponsorship? It was outrageous."

"No, I didn't. I don't really pay attention to the Thousand, though."

That surprised Jimmy. Even non-players followed news on a handful of the more scandalous players at the top. "How can you not?"

"I just play for fun," she explained. "I like the lore and the world. I'm more interested in finding easter eggs from the Bickford Books and that sort of thing. Top players aren't really on my radar."

Jimmy took a moment to digest that. "I haven't played like that in a long time... But I like those things, too."

Soup smiled at her.

"And, well..." Jimmy tried to think of what to say. "Well, I'm sorry. For being unkind or whatever. It's okay if you want to buy excessively pink clothes."

Soup's smile grew. "Thanks, Jimmy. It's okay if you want to wear limited edition poo pins, too."

They reached the chamber they'd been searching for soon after. At the center of the dank and slimy hollow stood a pristine, white pedestal, glowing gently against the filthy backdrop of the cave. Atop the massive pedestal sat a wide, metal basin containing kindling.

"That's got to be a torch!" Soup squealed and surged forward. The wet rock beneath her feet shifted under her weight with each step, jostling her and the torch.

"Careful!" Jimmy shouted.

Soup stepped back on solid ground.

"Ground's a bit uneven," Soup said.

"Christ, I wish we could fly," Jimmy said, not for the first time.

She took a tentative step forward and watched the ground lurch sideways, toward her foot. She moved to step on the other side and watched the ground tilt again, still toward where she applied her weight.

"It's a scale," Jimmy said.

"Okay. We go in together," Soup said. "You on the right, me on the left, to balance it out."

"Right. Okay. Slowly."

They stepped onto the shaky platform, arms and hand torches outstretched. A thin layer of filthy water sloshed at their feet as they walked. Every few steps, they turned to check on the other to monitor each other's balance. They managed to reach the center pedestal having only made a few shaky missteps.

Up close, the soft glow emanating from it somehow seemed brighter. The metal bowl reflected back their images, the same round faces and big eyes facing each other, pastel opposite earth tones.

Jimmy held her hand torch to the tinder in the bowl. Nothing happened.

"Why isn't it lighting?" She pulled her torch away and searched around the pedestal for some kind of latch or puzzle.

Soup placed her hand torch inside the bowl with the same non-results.

"Add yours now." Soup held her flame steady against the bowl as she spoke. "At the same time."

Jimmy obliged.

A progress bar appeared above the fire, marking the time necessary to light the torch.

10/100, 15/100...

Soup and Jimmy stood perfectly still.

20/100, Skill Test—

The ground pitched to the side sharply, knocking Jimmy off-balance and Soup against the pedestal. A spark of red light clipped the bowl the instant their torches slipped away. Both cherubs regained their footing quickly and shoved their torches back into the basin. Jimmy cursed. The progress bar was back to zero.

"Let's keep our balance next time," Jimmy said.

15/100...

Soup rolled her eyes and nodded.

20/100, Skill Test—

They each braced an arm against the pedestal and swayed in rhythm with the floor, keeping their torches tightly tucked in the basin.

Soup let out a breath as the floor righted itself again. The progress bar continued ticking away.

"No lightning this time," Soup said. "But I think it might strike at the end."

"We're underground, though."

"We just saw some!"

"True..."

"So if it strikes, the Minotaur might follow."

"It might," Jimmy agreed. "We'll have to go hide in another chamber."

They swayed through another skill test at the 50 mark, bracing against the pedestal again. Jimmy imagined they'd look like very confused surfers to any onlookers and felt ridiculous.

60/100...

"We might not get the chance to hide. It'll throw us off-balance when it arrives," Soup said.

"That's true. Good thinking, Soup," Jimmy praised. "Okay, I think I have an idea."

70/100...

"Alright..." Soup's voice encouraged Jimmy to continue.

"You pull the oxgoad on it and trap it in here while I run."

Soup let out a bark of laughter.

Another skill test struck and Soup gripped the pedestal. "That's a terrible plan! You couldn't make it anyway!" She had to shout over the rumble of the shifting floor.

90/100...

"No, it'll work. See? I have this!" Jimmy unfastened her Bronze Snake Pin from her robe and held it up for Soup to admire before she let it plonk into the water on the floor. The pin transformed into a shimmering bronze serpent and began slithering in the direction Jimmy had aimed it.

95/100...

"I'm not sure that makes sense," Soup said frantically. "I'm not big enough to balance out the Minotaur's weight alone."

"It barely has a body," Jimmy countered, not entirely as confident as she made herself sound.

The progress bar reached its end, and fire burst to life inside the basin, bathing the chamber in a warm glow.

Torch lit.

They yelped in victory, but constrained their movements to avoid destabilizing the floor.

The moment they drew their hand torches from the basin, a thick band of red lightning struck the pedestal.

In an instant, the Minotaur sunk through the ceiling, loud huffing echoing against the chamber walls. Its massive form appeared more solid, more threatening, the faint ridges and curves of a powerful beast visible in the torch light. Shadows billowed at its hooves, elevating the creature a few feet off the ground.

"Soup! Your oxgoad!" shouted Jimmy, like an idiot.

Soup had already drawn her oxgoad and was pointing it directly at their target. But the Minotaur wasn't looking at her. Its red eyes were focused on Jimmy and her loud mouth.

It lunged.

The Bronze Snake Pin serpent reached its destination and snapped Jimmy to its location just as Soup sent out swirling pink and lavender flares into the chamber.

Pink and purple ricocheted off the ceiling and walls, showering Soup and the Minotaur in shimmering streams of pastel.

The Minotaur turned its red eyes to Soup, pink sparkles rippling down its almost-form.

The Bronze Snake Pin had transformed back and was now pinned neatly in its place on Jimmy's robe, recharging. She stood at the entrance to the chamber and watched as the ground she had just been standing on lurched sideways, hurling Soup and the torch against the greasy cave walls. The oxgoad flew from Soup's hand and clattered several paces away. The floor and wall now joined at a near forty-five-degree angle, Soup trapped in the crevice.

To Jimmy's dismay, the Minotaur stood perfectly stable, hovering above the swaying floor. Faint remnants of the pink and purple flares dusted its shoulders. Her plan had failed. She'd completely failed her co-op partner.

She could run now — hide on her own. She'd get to see what this Throne was all about before thousands of other players. She wouldn't have to wait or queue up again. This was her chance, with the Minotaur's focus entirely on Soup, but the idea of failing Soup again didn't sit right in her belly.

Laughter rose through the chamber. Jimmy turned to see that the source was Soup. The Minotaur's dark tendrils were spreading around her, and she was *laughing*.

"Well, that failed!" Soup said through giggles. "We're dead now!"

That wouldn't do. At least one of them could make it out. "MINOTAUR!" Jimmy bellowed.

It turned its gaze on her.

"What are you doing?" Soup shouted.

"This is my fault! You run and hide!"

"No, it's fine!" Soup said, scrambling for her oxgoad. "I don't care like you do! Minotaur! Minotaur! Look here!"

It didn't. Darkness crawled around Jimmy. She turned to run, to pull the Minotaur away from Soup, giving her time, but there was no time.

The last thing she saw before she was consumed by the screaming pit of Hell was Soup's surprised face framed by a useless, pretty pink cloak.

Jimmy felt oddly empty once she exited the match. It was as if a vacuum had sucked up all the air around her. The post-game metrics had cheered her up some, but not enough. She hadn't broken past the Thousand Line, but she had scored surprisingly well in some of the event's unique new point systems, Covenant and Fortitude. Playing with Soup had worked in her favor more than she had anticipated. Soup's play style had resulted in Jimmy gaining way more points than she would have if she'd abandoned Soup by the skid mark. If Jimmy played through a ton more matches in the arena, she'd still have a shot at the Thousand. She wondered what Soup would think of that.

Player message boards and vidstreams confirmed Soup's theories. She'd been right about the emphasis on co-op, the Throne, all of it. Jimmy had been amused to learn that the oxgoad had been the Rod of Revelation, the arena's limited edition Event Exclusive item. It could be used to temporarily stun and control certain diabolical beings. She wondered if Soup had been able to grab it before going to Hell.

She wondered a lot about Soup, frankly.

She had worried surprisingly little about her rank while playing with Soup, and it had felt good. It had been *fun*. She wanted that again.

As she prepared to queue up for another match, she opened her player dash to draft up a message.

Recipient: [BEETSOUP46]

Message: [*Wanna lobby up?*]
Send message?

Jimmy pressed yes before she lost her nerve.

An alert seconds later sent her rushing to her notifications.

New friend request from player [BEETSOUP46].
Message: [*Yes! Wanna be book buddies?*]
Decline or Accept?

Jimmy smiled. Why the hell not?

Accept.

Boys, Book Clubs, and Other Bad Ideas

by Katrina Hamilton

ACT ONE

❖ You stare down a giant pile of school books that need to fit into your backpack. You struggle to get them in, pulling at the zipper. It's the first week of freshman year of high school, and you can't be late.

❖ You're at school an hour early because there's a special college prep seminar happening today in the gym. Jayden, a cute boy with short, messy hair and a nervous demeanor, approaches you.

   "Is this seat taken?"

❖ The seminar is led by a guest consultant, along with the regular school counselors.

   "Hundreds of thousands of students from all over the country are vying for just a handful of spots in the nation's elite colleges. If you want to be one of them, you can't just be *among* the best in your school. You have to be better than everyone else."

❖ The counselors push everyone to get involved in as many activities as possible as a way to build up their college resumes. They explain how a recent grant will allow them to run outdoor sports in both the spring and fall, and winter sports year-round, to encourage greater participation. At the end of the seminar, they give out a lengthy checklist of all the activities, clubs, and sports available at your school.

❖ Jayden attempts to make small talk with you.

"Wow. No pressure, right?"

"Yeah, none." You shove the checklist into your overstuffed bag before leaving Jayden alone on the bleachers.

❖ In English class, Ms. Bartleby explains that part of your homework will be to read a new book every month for the rest of the school year and turn in a 5-page book report for each one.

"You can choose any book in the school library that's over 200 pages. I don't care about subject matter; I just want you to follow your interests. Read something you actually *want* to read."

❖ You're overwhelmed at the thought of having to read even more than you're already expected to read. After class, you explain to Ms. Bartleby that you can't imagine choosing to read additional books "just for fun" when you already have so much school work. Ms. Bartleby says that it's important for everyone to read, and that the assignment is mostly about finding out what kind of literature you enjoy. She suggests that if the reports themselves are a problem, you could always propose an alternative way of completing the assignment.

> "Like writing a poem or a song about it," she suggests. "Shooting a short film — that sort of thing."

> "That sounds like even more work."

> "Alternative assignments usually are."

❖ After school, you head straight to The Mountaineers Club with your friend Eva. Jayden is also there. You're already one of the most skilled climbers in the club, so you're surprised when Jayden is able to keep up — though just barely. You aren't racing him on purpose, but it still feels good to beat him every time. Coach Gregor tells you to take it easy.

> "Remember the Mountaineers' Motto! It's not the top; it's how you get there."

❖ You complain to your friend Eva about all the pressure the school is putting on students. Eva suggests that maybe you don't have to do *everything* on your list.

> "There's more to life than getting into a good school, ya know."

❖ You're in a group text with Eva and three other girl friends at school: Charlotte, Hazel, and Mae. They agree that the expectations for college applications are completely impossible.

> YOU
>> it's ridiculous. they want us to be in both honor society and model congress even though they both meet at the same time on tuesdays

> HAZEL
>> and how am I supposed to do softball AND volleyball AND track?!?!?!?!

> HAZEL
>> i'll need a knee replacement by the time I'm 25

> CHARLOTTE
>> the deck is rigged. totally stacked against us. my mom expects to see acceptance letters from at least three ivy league schools

> CHARLOTTE
>> there's just no way

> MAE
>> i'll be lucky to keep up my gpa at this point

> EVA
>> hey what are you guys gonna read for bartleby's book report thing?

> EVA
>> she said 200 pages but I don't know how to search for the shortest books in the library lol

YOU

> we should just figure out the 9 shortest
> books and all read those

CHARLOTTE

> better yet

CHARLOTTE

> each of us read 1-2 books, then share
> the reports with each other so we don't
> have to write all 9

HAZEL

> that's cheating

HAZEL

> besides if the reports look too similar
> bartleby will figure it out

YOU

> i have an idea

❖ You propose that you all take Ms. Bartleby up on her offer to do an "alternative" to the book reports. You'll start a book club, where you all read the same book each month and meet to talk about it.

> "One book club meeting will take way less time than writing a full report. We can rotate who takes notes and turn those in as proof that we met. Best of all, we can all count it as an extracurricular on our college applications."

❖ The girls all love this idea, and Eva suggests one super short book you can start with.

❖ The first month of school goes by. You and the others sign up for as many clubs and sports as you can fit into your schedules. It's exhausting, but you're making it work. Sort of.

❖ Jayden keeps trying to talk to you during The Mountaineers Club. You're starting to suspect he might have a crush on you. You're not sure if you like him back, but you know it doesn't matter either way. You don't have time for boys right now.

❖ You have your first Book Club meeting in the school library. All five of you read the same short book last month (except Mae, who *almost* finished it). You have your quick chat about the book, Hazel types up some notes to turn in to Ms. Bartleby, and Mae, Hazel, and Eva go ask the librarian for a list of the shortest books in the library.

❖ Charlotte tells you this was a great idea and that it's too bad it can't be this easy with everything.

> "I wish there was some way to have just one of us go to band practice for the whole group, you know?" she says.

> "Seriously," you reply. "Nothing happens in most club meetings anyway. You could summarize for me in five minutes what happens in Chemistry Club every week, and I bet we could guess what goes on in Key Club, because Mae says every meeting is the same anyway."

"I'm sure there are people who just lie and throw everything on their resume even though they never go."

"I'm sure. But I bet the colleges can tell. I mean, you wouldn't be able to talk about any of the stuff you did in your application or essay, and your transcript addendum wouldn't show a club if you weren't listed as an official member. Plus, your recommendation letters wouldn't mention anything about seeing you in the different clubs."

"Please. You really think Mr. Sanders is paying attention to how often we actually show up to Film Club? He's not even there himself half the time."

"Too bad we can't show up half the time and get full credit."

"Too bad we can't just go one at a time and do a fifth of the work, like with Book Club."

❖ You both realize the solution at the same moment. The other three girls return, and you start scheming on how it could work. You figure out all the clubs, sports, and activities everyone is supposed to be doing, when the various organizations meet, and how much work each person has to personally do in order to seem like they're really a member.

❖ Eva and Mae both express concerns. But you and

Charlotte have an answer for everything, and Hazel is quick to agree.

"Isn't this cheating?" Mae asks.

"No way," says Charlotte. "I mean, Book Club isn't cheating, right? We're just doing the same thing: taking advantage of our group resources."

"What if we get caught?" asks Eva.

"Get caught doing what?" you reply. "Participating?"

"You know what I mean," says Eva.

"Until we put it on our college applications, we aren't doing anything wrong," you say. "Except being lackluster Chess Club members."

"You're right," says Hazel. "I mean, it's a little unfair, but so is the system, right?"

"Exactly," says Charlotte. "And it's not like we're hurting anyone else. Just making the impossible a little more possible for ourselves."

❖ You decide Book Club is the perfect time to coordinate your activities, which means moving it out of the library so no one can hear what you're planning. Eva volunteers her old childhood treehouse as a meeting location. You see Jayden walk into the library and start eying you like he's going to come over.

"Dammit, it's Jayden," you sigh.

"Who?" asks Charlotte.

"Jayden," you say. "He's in The Mountaineers Club with me."

"Oh right," says Mae. They all look over toward Jayden, who waves and shoots you a dumb smile. "Him."

"Alright," you whisper to the group. "First *real* meeting of the Greenwood High Book Club is tonight at Eva's treehouse. I'll get rid of the boy."

❖ The other girls leave, and Jayden takes the opportunity to come talk to you. He is shy but sweet, and you can't remember if his shoulders always looked this good or if it's the extra time in Mountaineers. But it doesn't matter, because you're not interested. You don't need a boy; you've got a plan. You wiggle your way out of the conversation and head to class, excited about school for the first time in a month. You finally know how you can beat this.

❖ That night the Book Club meets to form a plan of attack. You list out who is already in charge of which clubs, who can join what, etc. As you figure out where everyone will be sent, it becomes clear that some members are going to have to spend less time at the clubs they enjoy in order to keep up with the new schedules.

"But I actually like Film Club," says Mae.

"You can still go," you tell her. "You just won't be able to stay until the end."

"So I have to miss the ending of every movie?"

"You can finish watching them in college," says Charlotte. "What's next?"

❖ Some girls are going to have to attend clubs they have no interest in or actively hate.

"Why do I have to be the one stuck with Spanish Club?" asks Eva.

"I thought you liked Spanish," says Charlotte.

"I like Spanish *class*," says Eva. "Because I like Andrew Evans. He's not in Spanish Club. It's just Bradley and those other losers."

"Andrew is in Robotics Club with me," says Hazel. "I'll give you the first Thursday of the month if you take on one of my Speech and Debate meetings in exchange."

"Deal."

❖ Before adjourning, you give each other official titles so everyone can all be listed as members of the leadership team. You do this based on who needs what to pad their resumes: Charlotte isn't Vice

President of anything, Mae wants Treasurer because she thinks it sounds smart, etc. You all agree that these titles are meaningless, because there are no actual roles in Book Club. The Book Club, after all, isn't real.

ACT TWO

❖ For the next month, you stick to easy subterfuges. There are several clubs that don't take attendance, so you just rotate through the meetings, having a different girl go each time and report back what happened. You take notes and offer suggestions of what to say at the next meeting to make it seem like all of you were there.

> "Asmita suggested we should ask the teachers to make donations to the bake sale as well, but Dylan totally wasn't listening to her. So I bet you anything next week he's going to suggest the same thing, and you should point out that Asmita suggested it last week. If we can get her and Yusef believing we're active members and on their side, no one will question it."

❖ For Anime Club, Charlotte and Eva show up for the first 15 minutes, just until the show starts. They then excuse themselves to go to the bathroom so they can attend the Astronomy Club meeting upstairs. Whenever the Astronomy Club turns off the lights to show slides and images, they sneak back down in time to make comments on the Anime. They always read the show synopsis ahead of time so they can ask good questions that make it seem like they're paying attention.

❖ You end up attending most clubs alone, but whenever there're two of you at the same activity together, it makes it easy to cover for the others. Like when you and Hazel are at golf practice.

> "Where are Mae and Eva?" asks Coach Marks.

> "Oh, Eva was having...feminine issues," you say.

> "Mae was waiting for her to make sure everything was okay," adds Hazel. "I'm sure they'll be out any moment."

> Coach Marks swallows uncomfortably and averts his eyes, still unsure how to handle the anatomical issues of teenage girls even after 12 years of teaching.

> "Don't worry, Coach Marks," you say. "You go ahead to the next hole, and we'll wait for them here."

> "I'd love to give this first hole another go anyway," says Hazel.

> "What a great idea," you add. "I'll watch your form." You and Hazel grab your clubs and head back to the first hole, leaving an

uncomfortable and dumbfounded Coach Marks in your wake.

❖ By the time of your next Book Club meeting, there's a new development to discuss. One of the teachers has noticed the extra enthusiasm you all seem to have for extracurricular activities.

> "Mrs. Travers wants Hazel to serve as the Scorekeeper for Quiz Bowl," Charlotte explains, "and thinks I would be the perfect Secretary for the Chemistry Club."

> "We can't take on more leadership roles," says Eva. "It's too much work. And besides, if you're the Secretary, it means you have to take attendance, which means being there the whole time."

> "Yeah," says Mae. "Same with Scorekeeper."

> "Exactly," Charlotte replies.

> You smile. "Don't you get it?" you say. "They'll control the attendance sheets for both clubs. The rest of us won't have to go at all."

❖ You and Eva start playing chess with the Chess Club members at lunch, because everyone assumes that if you're playing with the Chess Club at all, you must be in it. This convinces the advisor that you're both members, since he just sits in the corner grading papers during Chess Club and never pays attention to who is there or for how long.

❖ At Track practice, you and Hazel are present at the start, so the coaches can send you off on a long run. You've purposely signed up to do Cross Country, because the Cross Country team is always getting sent off on long runs through the surrounding neighborhood. Hazel lives nearby, so you just run straight to her house and work on your homework together. When you're getting near the end of practice, you run back.

> "Wait, Hazel! Over here!" you yell.

> "Why?" she asks.

> "The sprinkler," you say, the effort of actually running again interrupting your words. "Run through it!"

> "Are you kidding?" she says. "It's not even that hot out today."

> "Yeah," you say, "and you're not that sweaty, either. Not sweaty enough to have been running for 90 minutes, that's for sure." Hazel smiles as she finally understands your plan. You both run through the sprinklers and arrive back at school just in time for the end of practice and in obvious need of a shower after all your hard work.

❖ Everyone in Book Club is thriving on the success. You're halfway through the school year and as far as anyone is concerned, you are each participating in two sports, five activities, and nine clubs.

❖ You enjoy this work more than you ever enjoyed school work before. There were only a few extracurricular activities that interested you, and everything else always felt like a slog. It's not that way now, because every moment you are sitting in some boring activity you don't want to be doing, you start thinking up ways to get out of it or somehow double up your time.

❖ Jayden catches you in the hall between classes one day.

> "I haven't seen you around as much," he says. "You seem so busy."

> "Yeah, well, you know," you say. "Gotta keep active. Gotta make sure you look attractive to all those top-tier schools." You spot Mr. Sanders at the end of the hall. You need to catch him before third period starts.

> "Oh, I'm sure you'll look attractive to them," Jayden says, though you're only half paying attention. "'Cause you are. I mean, the schools...like...I'm sure you look good to them, too."

> "I'm sorry, what?" you ask.

> "Nothing," says Jayden. "Hey, are you still in The Mountaineers Club? I haven't seen you in a while."

> "Yeah, I am," you say. "Sometimes I'm just a little late is all. I'm sure you're just not

noticing when I arrive."

"I doubt that," Jayden says, laughing to himself. "I always notice when you arrive."

"You do?" you ask.

"Of course I do," says Jayden.

"Dammit," you say, under your breath.

"What's wrong?" Jayden asks.

"Uh, nothing," you say. You glance past Jayden's shoulder in time to see Mr. Sanders disappearing into his classroom. "I gotta go," you tell Jayden, before running down the hall and yelling back, "but I will definitely see you at Mountaineers later, okay?"

"Okay!" he yells back, a hopeful smile on his face.

❖ You catch Mr. Sanders right before he has a chance to sit down at his desk, and you ask for a specific movie to be played next month at Film Club.

"I just feel like we've been watching a lot of post-classical Hollywood lately," you say, repeating the exact words Eva told you to say, "and I really think the group would benefit from a few examples of the Golden Age of Asian Cinema."

"Uh, sure," says Mr. Sanders, still a bit confused and flustered.

"Great," you say. "Hazel was right; you are a great advisor." Mr. Sanders would have never seen either you or Hazel in Film Club, but a little fact like that isn't enough to stop the Greenwood High Book Club.

❖ You start going to Mountaineers Club again, knowing that Jayden would notice your absence. He volunteers to be your spotter every chance he gets, and the two of you start talking more and more. You find yourself name-dropping clubs left and right, because it feels like it's all you have to talk about anymore.

> "I can't believe you can keep up with all that stuff," he tells you. "I feel like I'm barely scraping by just keeping my grades up and doing a few sports."

❖ Mae is struggling to finish her history paper and asks you to cover for her in Key Club the following week. When you arrive, you're surprised to see Jayden sitting in the front row. You know that if you grab the seat next to him, it will cement in his mind that you're a member, but it might also make it obvious when you never show up again. You decide to risk it.

> "I thought you said you didn't have time for extra activities," you whisper when there's a lull in the agenda.

> "I probably don't," he said. "But the Key Club runs the blood drive every year, and I

think that's really cool."

"You became a member just to do that one thing?"

"I mean, I help with some of the other projects occasionally, but yeah. School is full of stuff I have to do. But the blood drive is something I actually want to do, you know? So it's worth sitting through the meetings."

❖ You ask Mae if you can switch with her more often. You start going to Key Club every other week.

❖ You're spending more time with Jayden than you spend with any of the girls in Book Club.

❖ You've got a lot of plates spinning right now. Getting involved with someone would just be a time suck.

❖ You can't put "had a boyfriend" on your college application.

❖ This is a bad idea.

❖ You're in the library one day, fixing the books on the Poetry Club attendance rosters. Jayden comes in. You try to hide what you're doing, but he tells you not to bother.

"I know you're up to something," Jayden says. "You and the other girls. I know you are doing something to trick the teachers."

"How'd you figure it out?" you ask.

"Come on," he says. "All the stuff you talk about—all the clubs you're in—it's impossible. You were telling me how much you loved Gymnastics while we were in Mountaineers Club."

"So?"

"So they practice at the same time," says Jayden. "No one can be in both."

"But they expect you to be in both," you say. "They expect all of us to be in everything."

"So you're lying about it?" he asks.

"Not lying, exactly," you say. "I really have gone to meetings and practices for all the stuff I talk about. Well, almost all of it. None of us are actually in the 4H Club."

❖ To your surprise, Jayden has no interest in turning you or the other girls in. He doesn't seem very pleased with the whole situation, but he won't stop you.

"If this is what you want to do, I won't get in the way," he says.

"And you really don't think anyone else has noticed?" you ask.

"A few people are suspicious," he says. "Principal Bickford is smarter than you give him credit for, and Chelsea Chang definitely knows something's up. But no, I don't think

153

anyone else knows."

"How'd you figure it out?" you ask.

"I'm not that stupid, you know."

"And you notice me."

"Yeah."

"Thanks for not telling anyone." You hesitate. "You're a...really...good friend."

"Yeah."

"Yeah."

There's silence.

"What if I were able to help?" he asks.

"How could you possibly help?"

"Well, you need a better way to be in Mountaineers and Gymnastics at the same time, right?"

"Yeah..."

Jayden leans in close and whispers, "You ever been on the roof?"

❖ The next day at Mountaineers Club, Jayden shows you how to get from the catwalk at the top of the climbing wall to a roof access door. You both cross to the other side of the building, where a separate roof hatch opens down onto the extra mat storage area in the Gymnastics gym.

"Just hop down from here," Jayden says.

"Spend an hour or so working on your balance beam, then come back over and rappel down the wall. No one has to know…except for your climbing partner." He smiles a big, satisfied smile.

"Thank you, Jayden," you say. "And you promise you won't tell?"

"Of course not," he says. "What are…friends…for." There is disappointment in his voice.

"Maybe…not friends, so much…" You avert your eyes, staring at every spot on the roof and every distant building. You aren't sure how to do this.

"Not friends?" he asks.

"Not if you don't want to be," you say. "I mean, if you want to be not friends. I mean, other than friends, like, more…"

"Yeah," Jayden says. "I mean, I do, like…"

❖ You kiss. It is more dramatic than any kiss you've had before because you're sneaking around breaking rules together and it's happening on the roof and the wind is whipping through your hair and as soon as Jayden breaks away from the kiss you jump down the hatch and land on the crash pads.

❖ At the next Book Club meeting, you let the others know that Jayden figured out what you're doing and is now working to help. Hazel, Eva, and Mae are worried about letting someone else in on the plan, but Charlotte is fine with it.

❖ In fact, Charlotte has already enlisted her own set of helpers. She's recruited a couple members of the various clubs to be a part of the scheme. The others are worried they'll be found out if they let more people in on it, but Charlotte assures them that everyone is on a need-to-know basis.

> "No one but us knows the extent of what we can do," says Charlotte. "They all think we're cheating on one, maybe two clubs at most."

> "And none of them have gotten suspicious?" Eva asks.

> Charlotte hesitates. "I've got it under control," she says. "Trust me."

❖ Things continue as they have, but the addition of Jayden and the other helpers means all of you are running around even more than usual. You're exhausted and sensing that some of the others are, too. You're rappelling in and out of the sports you're involved in; you're memorizing meaningless meeting action items alongside memorizing for your tests. It's draining.

❖ Jayden says he's been hearing whispers from around the school of other people being involved in the Book Club's scheme.

❖ You and the others are getting sloppy. Your grades

are slipping, and subjects you used to ace easily are now difficult. You don't have time to think or breathe, let alone process any of the stuff you're learning in class.

❖ The other students Charlotte recruited are starting to notice there's more going on than what she told them, and Charlotte's solution is to cut them out completely. Anyone who questions the system gets kicked out of it.

> "Once they know enough to ask questions, they know too much," says Charlotte. "Better to cut them off now than to wait for them to get greedy."

> "What do you mean, 'greedy?'" asks Mae. "What would they want?"

> "To be at our level," says Charlotte. "And we all know how difficult it is. They wouldn't survive. They'd blow it and accidentally reveal the plan to everyone. We can't have that."

❖ You go to turn in this month's Book Club meeting notes for English. Ms. Bartleby asks how you liked the book, as it's one of her favorites. You are tired and zoned out, and it wasn't actually your turn to read the book this month. You stumble over the phrases Hazel used to describe it during the meeting.

> "Are you okay?" Ms. Bartleby asks.

"I'm fine," you say. "Just a little tired is all."

"You've been really running yourself ragged," she says. "Don't forget to take a break now and then."

"Yeah," you say. "Sure."

"Maybe you can relax this weekend?" Ms. Bartleby asks.

"I've got a Speech and Debate tournament this weekend," you say as you pick up your bag. "And a Gymnastics competition." You begin to head for the door. "And movie night...I think."

❖ At the next Book Club meeting, Eva confronts Charlotte. Apparently, cutting people off wasn't enough to keep them quiet. Eva found out that Charlotte has been threatening people.

"You told Sarah Kim you'd take her off the attendance rolls for Anime Club!" yells Eva.

"She was going to tell Principal Bickford that Hazel was skipping out on Basketball. What was I supposed to do?" Charlotte says.

❖ Hazel and Mae both agree with Charlotte and her actions. Hazel admits she's had to threaten one or two people herself in order to keep them quiet.

"I don't like it either," Mae tells Eva. "But we have to keep the secret. It's in the best interests of everyone."

❖ Eva looks to you for support, but you're torn. You're worried about everyone you've gotten involved. Not just Jayden, but the other students you've pulled in over time. For now, you agree that this is for the best.

❖ At school, Principal Bickford approaches you in the hallway and asks you to come into his office.

> "Ms. Bartleby says you've been tired lately," he says.

> "Oh, you know, just busy with lots of school work," you say.

> "And that you're doing both Speech and Debate and Gymnastics?"

> "Yes, well, they are my passions."

> "Both of them?"

> "Yes."

> "That's interesting, because I thought you were more interested in climbing, and Mountaineers meets at the same time as Gymnastics."

> "Well, I was," you say, having grown accustomed to this particular lie. "But you know how your interests change quickly when you're a teenager. I'm just much more focused on Gymnastics now."

> "Must be hard competing on the same level as the others, having gotten such a late start."

"I don't have any aspirations to place at the meets or go to districts or anything," you say, perking up now that you're solidly back in your comfort zone. "I'm more of a Renaissance Woman. I like to be a little good at everything."

"I see."

"Is that all?"

❖ Principal Bickford decides that since you're so invested in both academic and athletic pursuits, you'd be the perfect candidate for the upcoming article the local newspaper is doing on "Healthy Scholars." You agree because you can't figure out an excuse to say no, but you know that you don't have the time for it. You're already stretched to the breaking point.

❖ Charlotte announces via group text that the next Book Club meeting will be held in the library rather than Eva's treehouse, since Eva is no longer a part of the group. She refuses to explain further.

"Eva made her choices. This is how she wants it."

❖ Jayden is getting frustrated, because helping you sneak into other clubs has meant he sees less and less of you. You've gotten to kiss occasionally, but never actually gone out on any dates. No one even knows you are dating, and he's starting to wonder if you are.

"Why are you even doing it?" he asks. "Why are you spending every minute running around school pretending to be interested in everything?"

"It's just temporary," you say. "Just for the next couple years, until we can write our college applications and get into good schools."

"And what will you do then? Pretend to be on the college football team?"

"No. Then we'll have made it. We can do whatever we want to do."

"And what about doing what you want right now?"

"This is what I want."

"Is it?" he asks. "Because you seem miserable. And you're not getting to work on your climbing, you're not even talking to Eva anymore, and you hardly spend any time with me. Unless...maybe that's exactly what you want."

❖ Jayden gets mad and walks away. You aren't sure if he's just mad or if the two of you are finished. You may have messed this one up big time.

❖ At the next Book Club meeting, you suggest that maybe it's gone too far — that you need to pull back. Charlotte thinks you're just being emotional over a boy. Hazel tries to play peacemaker and even makes a joke about being the president of Book Club.

> "You're not actually the president, Hazel," snaps Charlotte. "We just let you say that because you're the only one who couldn't get herself elected president of any other club."

❖ Charlotte suggests that if you aren't happy with how Book Club is run, perhaps it's time for you to leave, just like Eva.

❖ You are kicked out of Book Club.

❖ You're scrambling to pick up the pieces. You're halfway involved in every sport, activity, and club in school. People are stopping you in the halls asking for updates. Coaches are asking why you haven't been practicing the things they've told you to work on. You can't remember where you're actually supposed to be and where you were merely pretending to be.

❖ Jayden approaches you, saying you need to talk. But you can't stop to talk; you've got math homework to finish and an Honor Society contact roster to fill out. On top of that, you actually need to read this month's book for Ms. Bartleby on your own, since there's no way Charlotte will be giving you a synopsis now.

❖ The guys in Chess Club ask you to join them at lunch, but you can't because you're still trying to figure out where you're even supposed to be.

Principal Bickford stops you and asks if you've filled out the initial questionnaire for the newspaper article.

"I'm sorry. I haven't gotten around to it yet," you admit. "But don't worry. I'll finish it right after Chemistry Club today."

"Oh," he says. "I thought you dropped out of Chemistry Club."

"What makes you think that? I'm there all the time." Chemistry Club was one of your staples for the Book Club. You took on the majority attendance share for the whole group.

"Oh, it was just something your friend Charlotte mentioned this morning. I was wondering when I might catch you and asked if Chemistry Club would be a good time. She said she hadn't seen you there in weeks."

"I gotta go," you say, backing into a near run down the hall. "But don't worry," you yell back. "I'll get you that questionnaire by the end of the day!"

❖ You start running through the school, darting into classrooms and stopping friends in the hall. You're looking for staff advisors and fellow students who are on sports teams with you or engaging in the clubs with you. With each person, you stop in a panic to ask about whatever activity you share, and each one gives some version of the same answer.

"I thought you weren't doing that anymore."

"Oh, Hazel said you quit."

"I heard you gave that job to Mae."

"Wasn't Charlotte going to take over for you?"

❖ Each stop, each person, gets progressively worse, until finally:

"Oh hey! You're still here! When are you transferring?"

"Transferring where?"

"To boarding school, of course. Aren't you leaving us?"

❖ You turn the corner and see the back of three familiar silhouettes by the lockers: Charlotte, Hazel, and Mae. You reverse around the corner to stay out of sight. You need to get to the main office. You want to believe Charlotte wouldn't have gone so far as to unenroll you from school, but at this point, anything is possible.

❖ You head over to the climbing gym, knowing that with the rest of the Book Club by their lockers, you should have a straight path to the office if you can get to the Gymnastics gym. You've taken the shortcut over the roof dozens of times by now, though usually you had a spotter. Usually, you had

Jayden.

❖ You get to the climbing wall and put your ropes together in a panic. You start to climb, but you've tied the ropes wrong. They give out halfway up the wall and you fall flat on your back. You feel all the air get punched out of your stomach in an instant before you pass out.

ACT THREE

❖ The faces of Jayden and your climbing coach are hovering above you. Coach Gregor asks you what you were thinking by climbing without a spotter.

> "My usual spotter wasn't around," you say, your eyes on Jayden.
>
> "Well, then you wait," she says. "Hey, hey," Coach Gregor grabs you gently by the chin to get your attention. "What's our motto? It's not the top…"
>
> "It's how you get there," you say, still groggy from the fall.
>
> Coach Gregor goes to get the nurse, insisting that she take a closer look at you before you can be released. "Jayden, you stay here and keep an eye on her," Coach Gregor says.
>
> "I'll try," Jayden says, mostly to you. "If she doesn't try to run away again."

❖ You and Jayden have a heart-to-heart. You apologize for pushing him away; he apologizes for not realizing how bad the situation had gotten. He's heard the rumors, too, and knows that the Book Club is now determined not just to remove people like you who don't go along with their plans, but to destroy them.

❖ You think you know how to fix this, or at least how to make it better. You ask Jayden to find Eva and then come meet you in the nurse's office.

> "Oh, and stop by the counselor's office on your way," you say. "Pick up that checklist they have of all the school's extracurricular activities. We're going to want a clean copy."

❖ After you get cleared for serious head injuries, you, Eva, and Jayden start going around the school, talking to the students and faculty, setting up the plan. Sometimes you are together; sometimes you split up. All the time, you are avoiding any direct contact with the Book Club or the students known to be direct Book Club cronies.

❖ It takes a couple days, but eventually you talk to every person you need, make every convincing argument required.

❖ The announcement comes over the intercom three days later. In order to make it easier for the advising staff and to encourage interclub projects and collaborations, the Astronomy, Chemistry, and Robotics Clubs will all start meeting at the same time after school in the cafeteria, rather than in separate classrooms on different days.

❖ You're not there when the Book Club hears this and realizes they're going to have to regroup.

> "What are we going to do?" asks Mae. "People will notice someone sneaking between clubs if they're all in the same place."

> "We'll have to pick one and give up on the others," says Charlotte. "But it's fine. It's only two clubs."

❖ You're not there when a member of the Speech and Debate team approaches Hazel, telling her they're adding an extra meetup this Friday.

> "The Model Congress asked for our help with identifying arguments," he says. "So we need to come up with a lesson plan."

> "Wait," says Hazel. "Since when does the Speech and Debate Team work with the Model Congress?"

> "It's a new thing Mrs. Thomas wants us to try," he says. "Next month, they're going to go over Robert's Rules of Order with us."

❖ You're not there when Charlotte sees a member of the Film Club putting up a poster for an upcoming Miyazaki Film Festival, jointly hosted by the Film Club and the Anime Club. You don't see the look on her face when she realizes they're screwed.

❖ You are back in Mountaineers Club, along with Eva and Jayden. Coach Gregor approaches to say that she talked to the two Gymnastics coaches, and they're really excited about the cross-training idea. They're going to alternate Fridays, with the climbers going over to the gymnasts one week and the gymnasts coming to them the next. They really think it will improve the overall strength and mobility of both teams.

> "Honestly, we all felt a little dumb for not thinking of it ourselves," Coach Gregor says.

❖ The days of conning your way into every club are over. There is too much collaboration in the school now, too many different groups working together for any individual to sneak by unnoticed. People actually notice who they are working with and who they haven't seen before.

❖ Charlotte avoids you for two weeks. You finally manage to find her in the hall between classes.

> "You know we still have two more book reports due for Ms. Bartleby," you say. "And as far as she knows, we still have a Book Club."

> Charlotte pauses, waiting to make sure the offer is genuine. "Talking about the books was a lot more fun than writing about them," Charlotte finally says.

> "Did you have one in mind for this month?"

"I hadn't even thought about it."

"Well, you pick something out and let me know what we're reading."

"Something short?" asks Charlotte.

"Something good," you reply.

❖ You meet Jayden in the library, where he sits behind a mountain of thick books.

"Hey," you say, sitting down at the table across from him.

"Hey," he says.

"You going for extra credit or something?" you ask, pointing at the giant books.

"I asked Bartleby if I could read one really big book over three months instead of three short ones."

"Why?"

"I don't know, exactly. I just realized I'd never read a super long book before, and I thought it'd be fun."

"It should give you some interesting things to talk about with your girlfriend at least," you say, catching his eye and smiling.

"Girlfriend?"

"Yeah."

Jayden leans back in his chair. "I don't know

about that," he says with a smile. "Do you really have time for boys right now?"

You lean forward. "You can always make time for the things you really want."

❖ And from then on, you do.

Boys, Book Clubs, and Other Bad Ideas

by Shay Lynam

There's something about Yellow Wood Academy after hours that Violet loves. Maybe it's the fact that just a little while earlier it was filled with hundreds of students, and now it's empty and silent as a tomb. Maybe it's just how big and old the place is; the school was built two hundred years ago, and it shows in the brick facade, the dark wood casings around the doors and windows of every classroom, and the marble statue of the founder in the front hall. Or maybe it's the fact that a certain upperclassman volunteers every Thursday after school in the library, when the Night Owl Book Club congregates around one of the long oak tables, and so she gets to spend the evening nervously twirling the end of her braid around her fingers and exchanging shy glances with him from where he stands behind the desk organizing books.

Being the type of girl who's always focused more on her academics and who happens to like getting dressed in her uniform every morning, it stumps even Violet why she would be drawn to the rowdy boy whose blue hair is as brash as his personality. One thing Yellow Wood Academy is known for is its strictly enforced rules and guidelines, yet somehow Peter Yeong found a loophole that allows him to maintain his sapphire locks. Then again, the boy tends to get in trouble a lot, so maybe they allow the bright hair so he's easier to keep an eye on.

"Well, I'd say this was a productive night," Savannah says from across the table, getting up and pulling her bag off the back of the chair. "Don't forget we're reading *The Light Between Oceans* next month."

Garrett scoots his own chair back. "How could we forget with you reminding us every week?" he mutters.

Violet and Leslie share a glance, both knowing this isn't going to end well. In hopes of avoiding the inevitable argument, Violet stands and grabs her backpack off the chair. "I'll just let Mrs. Bickford know we're leaving," she says as she makes her way toward the office, leaving Leslie to listen to Savannah scold Garrett while she collects her things. Violet can feel Peter's eyes following her as she crosses the big room.

"You guys heading out?"

Violet looks in his direction. "Yeah, I was just going to tell Mrs. Bickford."

Peter peers over at the others, then back at her, and smiles. "Or..."

"Or?"

He leans in, resting his elbows on the desk and lowering his head as if he's about to share a secret. "Or you could stay." A corner of his mouth quirks up and Violet can feel it reverberate down to her knees. "Ever been in the school at night before?"

She furrows her brow. "Have you?"

"I might have a few times," he says, then straightens up again. "It's pretty cool. We could go exploring."

"And get in trouble."

"Only if we get caught," Peter says nonchalantly. "Don't you think it would be fun?"

Violet can feel the heat blooming in her cheeks, and she looks back at the others waiting for her by the table. Savannah watches them, a curious expression on her face.

Violet turns again to Peter. "Just you and me?"

"Just you and me."

"Alone in the school?"

"Alone in the school."

Violet chews the inside of her cheek, fingers coming up to fiddle with her braid. She's always been one to follow the rules. Not just follow them, but enthusiastically so. To do something so rebellious that could reflect on her permanent record is so completely out of character. Then again, does she enjoy following the rules because she likes to or because doing the opposite would disappoint her parents? Peter said he's done this before. He knows how to not get caught.

"Okay," Violet says at last, and she can see Peter perk up at the word.

"Okay," he repeats with a nod. "Well then, I'll let Mrs. Bickford know we're *leaving*."

"You ready, Vi?"

Violet jumps, not expecting Savannah to come up behind her.

"Um, no, I think I'll stick around for a little bit," Violet says, hoping that'll be hint enough for her best friend to leave her alone.

Instead, Savannah cocks an eyebrow. "But the library closes in five minutes," she says slowly. "Is Peter walking you home?"

"Um," Violet looks to the office where Peter stands in the doorway, his back to them as he talks to the librarian. "Not exactly."

"Vi."

"Peter asked me if I want to stay."

Savannah blinks. "He what?"

Violet already regrets telling her. "I think it sounds fun."

"Fun?" Savannah asks. "To be alone in the school? With Peter Yeong? Who are you and what have you done with my best friend?"

"I like Peter."

"So do a lot of other girls, Vi," Savannah says. "And do you know why?"

"Because he's cute and sweet?"

"Because he's a charmer," she corrects. "I know his type, and it's not one you should be alone with."

"Oh, hey, Savannah."

Violet startles as Peter's voice comes from directly behind. How long has he been there? How much did he hear? Hopefully not a lot.

"Hey Peter," Savannah says suspiciously. "We were just leaving."

"Actually, I'm staying," Violet blurts out, and her friend rips her eyes away from Peter to look at her. "I'll see you tomorrow, Sav."

Savannah breathes a sigh and then stands up tall. "Okay," she finally says. "See you tomorrow then. Night, Peter."

"Night, Savannah," Peter says almost smugly, then makes his way back around the desk, grabbing his backpack off the floor and slinging it over his shoulders—his shoulders that look so broad in his school-sanctioned navy sweater vest. "Shall we?" he asks.

Violet nods, watching as Savannah trudges back over to Garrett and Leslie. The two best friends exchange one more glance before the three head for the exit. She wonders if maybe she should go after them.

But then she feels Peter's hand slide into hers, his fingers encasing her own, and then he's pulling her along behind him, a dimple appearing as he smiles, and leading her toward the mystery section, furthest from the entrance.

As they sit on the floor across from each other waiting for Mrs. Bickford to leave, Violet is positive her heartbeat can be heard throughout the whole library and that it's surely going to give them away at any second. It doesn't help that Peter is just staring at her, mouth curled upward in a slight, mischievous grin, so she tries her hardest not to look at him, but at the titles of the books surrounding him—because she knows that if she does look at him, the librarian will be left wondering why the mystery section suddenly has a pulse.

Footsteps echo off the hardwood floor, and they both hold their breath as they listen to each step. Violet imagines Mrs. Bickford's shiny, black heels strolling across the room, her skirt brushing the middle of her calves, swishing as she walks.

The footsteps pause, and Violet straightens up. Why'd she stop?

Just then, a sneeze rips through the silence, and Peter mouths the words *"bless you,"* causing a rush of air to escape Violet's lungs in a very unattractive wheeze. She slaps her hand over mouth and nose, eyes growing wide in horror. Peter covers his own mouth with both hands as he doubles over, shoulders shaking with silent laughter.

The footsteps start up again, much to Violet's relief, continuing to grow fainter as the librarian nears the entrance. Then with a click, the lights turn off and she hears the door open and close with a firm thud. They are finally alone.

They wait only a few more seconds before allowing their laughter to burst forth, and then Violet really is on the floor, full-fledged spine to the hardwood, arms wrapped around her already aching middle.

"We almost got caught thanks to you!" she exclaims, reaching up to playfully swat at Peter. Her fingertips brush his hair, causing an electric pulse to climb her arm, and she jolts up again, eyes wide, mouth twisted in horror. "What am I doing?" she whispers.

Peter is up a beat after her, the smile on his face faltering when he notices her distress. "Hey, it's okay," he says. "It'll be fun. You'll see." Then he gets up and holds a hand out. "Come here," he says, and she takes his hand — once again feeling a spark ignite when her skin touches his — and lets him pull her to her feet.

He leads her to the big arched window that looks out over the faculty parking lot, and the two watch in silence as the figure of Mrs. Bickford walks across the asphalt three stories below, then gets into her silver Cadillac. Neither say anything until the car has disappeared from the parking lot, leaving the expanse of black unmarred by any vehicles. "See?" Peter asks, nudging Violet's shoulder. "Nothing to worry about."

She lets out a breath, then looks at Peter and smiles shyly. "Okay, so now what?"

Peter steps closer to her until his face fills her vision completely, and once again her heart stirs, knees going weak at the proximity — a sensation she hasn't experienced before, but one she's already becoming addicted to. She never noticed the small freckle adorning the right bottom edge of his lower lip, but now she can't stop staring at it. And maybe that's the reason he leans in further, one hand squeezing hers just a bit tighter, the other coming up to touch her cheek. His fingers tremble a little, perhaps from his own nerves. Hers are on fire.

Just as his bottom lip grazes hers, a crash erupts from another corner of the room, causing the two to blast apart like pieces of shrapnel.

"I thought we were the only ones here," Violet says exasperatedly, an icy spike shooting down her spine.

Peter's eyes are wide, head moving frantically as he searches for the source of the noise. "We're supposed to be."

"Geez, Garrett, do you even know how to walk?"

Violet squints into the shadows. "Savannah?"

"Leslie was the one who crashed into me. Educate *her* on the mechanics of walking."

"Guys?" Violet calls.

Peter groans as the other three members of the Night Owl Book Club emerge from one of the darkened aisles.

"What are you doing here?" Violet asks, mortified. "I thought you went home."

"And leave you alone with him?" Savannah asks skeptically. "No way."

"Hey," Peter says. "It's not like I forced her to stay."

"Oh geez." Violet covers her face with her hands.

"Well, what's wrong with us being here, too, then?" Savannah asks.

"I only invited Violet."

"Well, it's not like you own the school," she says. "And the more the merrier! Right, Garrett?"

"Right!" he says enthusiastically. "Right, Leslie?"

"That's right, Garrett," Leslie replies, also with exaggerated gusto.

Peter turns around now, pleading eyes falling on Violet, but all she can do is stare back at them. She's never been someone who others would look to for help, and now that she is, she doesn't know what to say to make everyone happy.

"Um, I mean, it could be fun with more of us, maybe," she says quietly and can instantly see that this isn't the answer Peter was hoping for. But from one moment to the next, his expression softens.

"Well then," he sighs. "Shall we unleash chaos upon the halls of Yellow Wood Academy?"

"Lead the way," Savannah says with a triumphant sweep of her arm toward the entrance.

Peter saunters towards the door, but when he goes to turn the knob, it doesn't budge. He swears under his breath.

"What's wrong?" Violet asks.

"The door's locked," Peter says, then grunts as he pushes against it, trying to no avail to get it to open.

"Locked?" Leslie asks.

"I didn't think Mrs. Bickford locked the library door," Peter says, more to himself. "The school is already locked. Why would the library be, too?"

"Maybe so idiots who like to try and sneak around after hours can't get in," Savannah says.

"Or out," Garrett adds quietly.

"Hey, don't forget that you're here, too," Peter growls, and Violet feels like she's watching a tennis match.

"We're only here to keep you from making a move on Violet," Savannah says.

Peter scoffs. "She can make her own decisions, you know."

"As her best friend, it's my responsibility to protect her from creeps like you!"

"I'm not a creep!"

"Guys!"

The two stop arguing to look at Violet where she stands between them, hands on her face while she watches the two bicker about her as if she's not right there. "Instead of arguing, could we actually try to come up with a solution?"

"Is there a spare key or anything hidden somewhere?" Leslie asks.

The others turn to Peter again. "Don't look at me," he says.

"You're the one who got us into this mess," Savannah barks. "And besides, you volunteer here every Thursday."

"Doesn't mean I'd know where a spare key is."

"I'm surprised you haven't gone snooping through all the drawers in the office," she utters.

Peter steps forward now. "I told you I'm not a creep," he says.

"No, just someone who's trying to take advantage of my best friend by convincing her to risk expulsion."

"I'm not trying to take advantage of her!"

"You were just—"

"GUYS!" Again, they all turn to Violet, who is now so anxious she can feel the anger burning in the pit of her stomach. She takes a deep breath. "How about we just try to get the door open?"

"I think Mrs. Bickford has a letter opener somewhere," Peter says and starts toward the office.

"Ah, so you *have* been through her desk," Savannah says, and Violet notices the material of Peter's sweater vest grow taut as his spine stiffens.

Leslie pulls out her phone. "I'll try to get help."

"Don't you dare call one of our parents," Savannah cuts in.

"Or any of the faculty," Garrett adds. "Unless you wanna get us all expelled."

Leslie rolls her eyes. "I'm not an idiot," she says. "I was going to call Justine. I'm sure her dad keeps a set of keys somewhere." She goes to one of the tables, phone already out and dialing the headmaster's daughter.

Violet follows after Peter, finding him sitting at Mrs. Bickford's desk, looking through the drawers in a huff. Without a word, she turns to a tall cabinet on the opposite wall and opens the doors. The top shelf is too high up for her to reach, but she spots a step stool on the floor and pushes it over with her foot. As she takes a step up, she feels very self-conscious as her skirt hikes up in response to her reach. Her fingers don't quite touch the top shelf, and she steps down quickly, noting Peter's ears are tinged a bit red and his eyes are glued to the floor when she looks at him.

"Uh, here, let me," he says quietly and gets up to switch spots with her.

"I'm sorry this night isn't turning out quite like you were hoping," she says, sinking onto the desk chair.

Peter peers down at her from over his shoulder. "How do you think I was hoping it would turn out?"

"I don't know," she says. "I figure not with my friends sabotaging things."

"Yeah, I guess this wasn't quite how I pictured it going. Hey, look at this."

Violet looks up to find Peter holding a strange brass key between his fingers.

"Where'd you find that?" she asks, standing up.

Peter steps down off the stool, not seeming to notice how close he is to Violet, or else not caring, as he holds the key out to her. "It was up there under a big book."

Violet smiles. "I thought you told Savannah you don't snoop."

"I never said I don't," Peter says with a shrug.

She takes the key from him to get a closer look. It's a dull brass, almost black, with spots of purple-tinged tarnish. The head is intricate, the metal woven into the shape of a leafy crown, the stalk long and smooth, leading down to two teeth that square off at the edges.

"What do you think it goes to?" Violet asks. "The old door lock?"

"Yeah, maybe," Peter says. The locks on all the doors aren't the originals, as they'd grown weak over time. "It looks too strange to just unlock the entrance door." He steps back and hits the heel of his shoe against the stool, causing him to stumble a bit. He grabs the shelf behind him to keep from falling, and when he does, the cabinet gives way, swinging impossibly backward, as if the wall it leans up against isn't even there.

Violet reaches forward to grasp his shoulder and keep him from falling further. "Are you okay?"

Peter rights himself and pushes on the cabinet more. "Yeah, I'm okay," he says breathlessly, though Violet doesn't really hear; she's too focused on the fact that the shelves are pushed all the way back, revealing a whole other room. It's a tiny space, hazy with dust. The two cautiously step through the opening, the faded floorboards creaking beneath their feet.

Peter grabs a flashlight off one of the shelves of the cabinet and clicks it on, the beam shining with a cold, hard light through the place.

"What is this?" Violet whispers as she peers around. While the room is small, the ceiling stretches up into darkness, making her feel like she's fallen down a well.

"No idea," Peter says. "I didn't even know this place existed."

"Maybe this is why she always locks the library," Violet says. "What's that?" She steps toward the opposite wall, where an enclosed bookcase stands. The books on the shelves are locked behind black, wrought iron bars, thinner pieces of iron twisted into a style similar to that of the head of the key.

"Think this opens it?" she asks, holding the key up to the lock.

"Try it out."

Violet nervously steps up to the bookcase and slides the key into the hole. It turns easier than she thought a super old-looking key would in a super old-looking lock, and she reaches forward to grasp the handles. The metal groans as she pulls the doors wide, revealing the dusty books within.

They look ancient, the leather darkened with age, the titles faded. Except for one: a dark green book with no letters or words on the spine. Instead, a symbol of sorts is embossed in gold. It resembles a tree, though the branches reach longer, climbing up the spine like vines, and the roots do the same, cascading down to sharp tips below.

Violet hesitates for a second before reaching out to pull the book from where it sits. The cover is soft to the touch and contains another image of the tree, only now the branches and roots fill the space around it, twisting and curling in on themselves, intertwining like calligraphy.

"Interesting," Peter whispers from over Violet's shoulder.

When Violet cracks the book open, it's as if an audible sigh is released, along with dust that shimmers ethereally in the beam of Peter's flashlight. The two stare down silently at a blank ivory page.

"A journal, maybe?" he asks.

Violet turns the page carefully to reveal yet another clean one. "Maybe," she says.

The air around them fills with static and she turns another page. This time it seems to pull away from her fingers, falling on its own. With wide eyes, she watches as the next page flips without her help.

"Are you seeing this, too?" Violet asks, and instead of responding, Peter watches with the same wide-eyed expression as the pages turn faster by themselves.

The static in the air grows denser until Violet feels like she's in a room full of insects. She drops the book with a shriek and curls into Peter, hiding her eyes as the world changes around them. Peter's arms come down around her, his face burying into the crook of her neck, and they both clutch onto each other for dear life until at last, the sensation ebbs away, leaving them clinging to each other in the darkness.

Peter lifts his head first, his arms loosening as he straightens up. "Violet," he says. "Look."

Reluctantly, she looks up, surprised by the sight of the large oak doors leading out of the school. She pulls out of Peter's embrace. "What?"

"I don't—" Peter's rendered speechless when he turns around to face the hallway.

Violet turns, her eyes fixed on Peter's, which have grown impossibly wider, until at last she tears them away to settle on the hall. It's still the same columns, the same crown molding, the same rows of lockers, but that's the only resemblance this place has to their school. Alongside the two-hundred-year-old architecture are twisting vines, gnarled trees, and a blanket of fog that causes the end of the hall to disappear into a shroud of gray. It's like they've gone into a future where nature has taken over, and these are but ruins of the school the two students once attended.

"Am I dreaming?" Violet asks. "Where are we? How'd we get out of the library?"

"I have no idea, but this is rad," Peter says and surges forward eagerly toward the forest.

Panic washes over Violet as he disappears into the fog. "Peter, don't you think we should stick together? We don't know anything about this place."

"It's the school, Vi," he calls from surprisingly far away. "Just, you know, with a few more trees!"

Violet is about to tell him how absurd it is that they are standing in both a forest and their school when a cry travels back to her from the direction he disappeared. "Peter?" she calls as she runs through the fog toward him, eyes searching frantically for that blue hair of his.

She almost smacks right into him when she darts around a tree to find him standing there, clutching one fist in the other, face pinched in pain. "What happened?" she asks. "Are you okay?"

Peter sucks in a sharp breath and takes his hand away, uncurling his fingers and revealing a cut that spans the meaty part of his palm. Blood wells quickly to the surface, already smeared over his hand from having his fingers closed over it.

"I tripped and landed on a stupid rock," he says, then winces when he flexes his hand.

Violet takes it gently, turning it toward the light so she can see it a bit better. "It looks deep," she says, and he curls his fist closed again protectively.

A flash of purple catches Violet's eyes, and they dart to the left in time to see a brightly colored butterfly floating erratically toward them. As it draws closer, a tiny, shimmering body seems to materialize between the wings. Not a butterfly at all, but a tiny, winged person.

It floats gracefully past Violet, landing on a dumbstruck Peter's shoulder. The two observe in astonishment as it hops down, from one fold in his shirt sleeve to the next, until it's shimmying down his arm, then stepping carefully onto his fist. It looks down at his hand and then back up at him.

As if the tiny being is trying to communicate, it pats his knuckles, huge, black eyes shining with what seems like concern.

"What does it want?" Peter whispers.

"How would I know?"

Again, the creature pats his fingers with its own tiny ones, then swoops its arms in a swelling motion.

"I think maybe it wants to see the cut," Violet says, and the little thing nods excitedly, purple wings flitting so fast it lifts a few inches into the air. He pulls his hand back, allowing the creature to continue to float in front of them and watch eagerly as he uncurls his fingers. The bleeding has gotten worse.

Peter holds his hand back out, and the butterfly creature lands once again. Then it turns its back to his cut and, much to their astonishment, shakes its wings from side to side. The action causes a shimmering dust to kick up and settle over his palm. Peter lets out a pained gasp, and the creature flies up just in time to miss his hand clench shut once again.

"Are you okay?"

"I don't know what that thing did, but it hurt," he growls, looking up at the winged thing now fluttering above their heads and out of reach.

Violet takes his fist and begins loosening his fingers. "Let me see," she says, and gasps when she reveals his unmarred palm.

"It healed me?" Peter asks, this time looking up in wonder. The creature nods happily before fluttering away, disappearing down the hall.

"What is this place?" Violet whispers.

"I don't know," Peter says. "But hopefully whatever else lives here is as nice as that thing was."

"Where do we even go?" Violet asks, taking a tentative step forward.

Peter follows her, stumbling over a root hidden by the fog. "I mean, we're in the school — seemingly without the rest of your book club buddies," he says. "That's what we wanted, right?"

Violet ducks beneath a branch, eyes landing on a drinking fountain jutting from the wall. Such an odd thing to see among the trees and twisted vines, yet it makes her realize that Peter's right. They're definitely in the school, just a stranger version of it, and apart from that fairy thing and whatever else might live here, it doesn't seem like there are any students or faculty. They really are alone, just like they wanted.

As if Peter can read the uneasiness on her face, he takes her hand in his, and when she tears her eyes away from the drinking fountain to meet his, he smiles.

"Come on."

"Where are we even going?" Violet asks, chest filled with newfound excitement.

"I have a couple ideas," Peter replies, and starts on through the forest again, pulling her behind him, his newly healed hand warm and reassuring around hers.

"So, you don't seem like the type who would like volunteering at the school library," Violet says, after they've reached the end of the hall and turned down another.

The corner of Peter's mouth quirks upward. "What type do I seem like?"

You set yourself up for that one, she thinks as she feels her face warm. "I don't know," Violet says. "You have a sort of…reputation, I guess. One that doesn't fit with the type of person that might volunteer."

A snort escapes Peter's nose, and he looks at her. "Do you think it's true? What people say about me?"

Violet bites the inside of her cheek thoughtfully. "I don't know," she finally admits.

The smile on his face widens. "Well, then, I guess I'll just have to convince you," he says, and gives her hand a squeeze before letting it go. Violet feels her stomach sink at the loss of warmth. Luckily, Peter is too preoccupied to notice the disappointment written on her face.

"It's gotta be here somewhere," he says to himself as he steps toward the wall and starts feeling around through the vines. He inches along for several feet until at last, with a whispered "yes," he starts tearing away the foliage.

Violet watches as a large door starts to take shape out of the depths of the vines. Peter rips away the last of them, revealing the entrance to the cafeteria, and turns, a big smile stretching across his face. "You coming?" he asks, pulling one door open and slipping inside before Violet can answer him.

A smile tugs at the corner of Violet's mouth as she follows him through the door.

Even with everything they've already seen since entering this strange other world, Violet is still rendered speechless at the sight before her. Once again, she finds herself standing in a place that should be so familiar to her and yet is almost unrecognizable.

The walls and ceiling are hidden by tangled branches that overtake the rest of the room and all come together at a giant tree, which sits where a grand fireplace normally resides at the center of the back wall. The roots bubble up above the ground, so Peter and Violet have to step over them as they make their way slowly through the room, too busy taking in the scene to say anything. Blue and lavender wildflowers poke up from the moss under their feet and grow up through cracks in the tables and chairs.

Violet's eyes settle on the chair she'd sat in just earlier that day, eating her lunch and stealing glances at Peter across the room, laughing with his friends. To think that had been only a few hours ago. With the twisting vines and cracking wood, it seems more like centuries.

The sound of rustling leaves pulls Violet back to the present, where Peter is beside her, staring at the tree on the back wall. "There's something in there," he whispers as he steps toward it.

As he does, the leaves of the tree ignite into flame, a dozen fireballs shooting into the air above them. It takes several panicking seconds for Violet to realize that the tree isn't on fire and that those bright fireballs are actually birds — a flock of glowing, fiery phoenixes. Their wings spread open as they arc high into the air, feathers brushing against the vines on the ceiling before turning their beaks down and dive-bombing right for the two students.

Peter grabs Violet's hand, wrenching her back toward the entrance, and the two run, the screeching filling their heads and growing louder as they get closer. They reach the doors, throwing themselves through them, and Violet falls to the floor in the hallway, cheek scraping against a root. She looks up quickly, just in time to see the bright, glowing bodies of the phoenixes fade into the fog.

"Come on," Peter says, picking himself up off the ground and starting after them.

"Wait, what?" Violet asks, flabbergasted at just why he's running after the things they had just barely avoided being impaled by.

The question pounds in her head, and her cheek hurts a bit, but not losing Peter is much higher on her list of things she cares about, so she runs after him, trying to keep that blue hair of his in her sights. Even with how thick and overgrown the forest is, it doesn't take long for her to reach Peter, and together the two chase after the birds, their shoulders bumping into the lockers on either side of them, forest debris sometimes giving way to the marble floor for their shoes to slip on. Other times, roots and rocks jut up from cracks, forcing their way in as if the wildlife is a parasite.

They reach the end of the hall, and Peter skids around the corner, Violet grabbing the back of his shirt and yanking him back just before he careens off the edge of a cliff that has seemingly materialized out of nowhere. Loose marble chips away under his feet, and he backs up further, watching the pieces of floor fall into a seemingly endless abyss. The birds continue down the hall, and the students can only watch as they disappear into the trees on the other side.

"This is incredible," Peter finally says between heavy breaths.

Violet's own lungs fill and deflate rapidly, adrenaline coursing through her veins as she looks down again into the hazy darkness. How far down does the chasm go? A shudder travels through her, and she finds herself scooting even further back from the edge.

"Maybe we should get out of here," she says after a bit. "This place is too strange."

Peter looks at her, his eyes wide and pleading. "But we just got here," he says.

"We also just about got impaled by a bunch of flaming birds and then almost ran off a cliff," Violet replies, then wraps her arms around her middle and looks down at her shoes. "How can you want to be here for even a second longer?"

Peter steps closer, reaching up to grasp her arm and causing her to meet his eyes again. "This place is freaking awesome," he says. "Much better than our normal school. Don't you think?"

"I don't know, Peter," she says quietly. "Everything is just so different here."

Peter winces. "I'll be more careful," he says. "Besides, there's just one last place I wanted to check out. Then we can go."

Violet looks at him skeptically. "Promise?"

"Promise."

That one last place Peter wants to see turns out to be the school's swimming pool on the basement level. Much to Violet's relief, they haven't run into any more birds engulfed in fire or off any more cliffs on the way there, and by the time they've reached the pool, she's beginning to feel like it wouldn't be the worst idea to stick around for a bit longer.

Like the rest of the school, the place seems like something straight out of a fantasy novel, and the lights from the pool shine up through the water, casting everything in a shimmering, blue veil.

"Okay, now *this* is rad," Peter says, his voice echoing through the space.

Violet smiles, but still the sight of a place she should be very familiar with looking so completely wrong has her feeling uneasy. She sinks to the ground at the edge of the pool, tucking her legs under her as she looks down at the rippling water.

Peter joins her, taking off his shoes and socks and rolling up the hem of his slacks before letting his legs sink into the water. "What's wrong?" he asks as he leans back on his hands.

"How are you so calm right now?" Violet asks.

Peter shrugs. "Maybe I just do well in these types of situations."

"What exactly constitutes *these types of situations?*" she asks. "Have you been here before?"

"Well, no," Peter says. "My family used to move around a lot for my dad's work. I guess I'm just kind of used to always being somewhere new and unfamiliar."

"Don't you think this is a bit more extreme than what you're used to?"

Peter sits up. "I mean, the concept is still the same. There'd always be small hints of familiarity," he says. "My mom used the same throw pillows and art and dishes from place to place, so like even if I was drinking orange juice in a different kitchen every year, it was still the same cup I was drinking out of." Violet watches as he traces the part of his palm where the cut once was with his thumb. "The school library, no matter how different it was from my old one, still carried my favorite books. Just little things like that, I guess."

Violet looks down at the water again, then clumsily pulls her shoes and socks off and dips her feet into it. "It must have been rough going to schools where you didn't know anyone and no one knew you," she says, watching her distorted legs swish below the surface.

"Yeah. People seem to like trying to figure out the new kid. Most of the time they get it all wrong, though." Peter says, bumping his foot into hers.

Violet smiles and kicks her legs a bit harder, causing the water to ripple more. "Savannah says you're a charmer."

Peter lets out a snort from beside her, and she looks up at him. "What does that even mean?"

Immediately she feels her cheeks begin to warm. *Why did I say that?* "Uh, I don't know. Like, a flirt, I guess."

Again he laughs, though it's much softer. "Do you think I'm a flirt?"

"I don't know," Violet says. "I think you're sweet."

Peter nods as if he's considering it. "I can handle that." Again, he nudges her foot with his own. Violet's head is swirling with everything going on right now — where she's at, who she's with — and she can't think of anything else to do but nudge back.

As if following a natural progression, the nudge begins to make its way upward, first their knees bumping, then elbows, then shoulders, and before Violet knows it, Peter's face is inching closer to hers, his head tilting slightly until, once again, she feels that soft brush of his bottom lip against hers, and her eyelids flutter shut.

A loud, guttural noise interrupts their kiss. They spring apart, eyes landing on a black shape so large it engulfs the deep end of the Yellow Wood Academy pool. Murky hair fans out in the water as it begins rising, and two sinister eyes stare back into theirs from just above the waterline.

"Okay, we can go," Peter says, before scrambling to his feet and yanking Violet up by her hand.

They take the stairs two at a time and only slow down once they've reached the intersection connecting to the main hall.

"Where do we go now?" Violet asks.

Peter worries his lip between his teeth, head moving frantically like he's searching for an answer to her question. But then he freezes, eyes settling on something over Violet's shoulder, and the corner of his mouth quirks up.

"That's it," he whispers.

"What's it?"

"Look around, Vi," Peter says, and steps past her. "These are still our lockers," he says, hitting a hand against the wall with a resounding metal clang. "That door still has Mr. Harrison's name on it. It's still Yellow Wood."

"Just with fairies and sea monsters," Violet says.

"Exactly. So I'm guessing everything else is somewhat the same, too," he says. "We probably leave the same way we came."

She perks up with realization. "The library."

Violet is relieved that the staircase leading to the upper stories is right where it's supposed to be, albeit with a stream cascading down its vine covered steps. Peter utters a triumphant "yes," then grabs her hand and carefully maneuvers up the stairs, the legs of his black trousers immediately becoming soaked to the knees as they push forward. Violet is both grateful and annoyed that she's wearing a skirt because while her clothes aren't getting wet, the water is freezing. By the time they make it to the second-floor landing, she can no longer feel her legs.

Luckily, Peter is able to keep her upright, and with her hand firmly grasping his, they continue on to the top, Violet trying to ignore the fact that she just saw a unicorn laying in the middle of the art wing on the second story.

When Violet steps through the archway leading to the third-floor main hall, her gaze travels upward, and her breath catches in her throat. She feels Peter's hand squeeze hers but she's unable to rip her eyes away from the incredible spectacle before her.

In place of the ceiling is an expanse of brilliant night sky. It goes on forever, stretching farther than she can see, engulfing the world in a glittering blanket of midnight blue. A breeze blows through the place, carrying on it the scent of lilies and something sweet, something mysterious, something magical. The school around them has all but disappeared, and in its place is a vast field, the grass looking like an ocean as it ripples in the wind.

The breeze blows Violet's braid off her shoulder, and she closes her eyes, almost forgetting about the fact that there's no possible way any of this can be real.

"Hey, Violet, look," Peter says with a gentle squeeze of her hand, and she opens her eyes again. They settle on a familiar door, and her chest floods with relief. Almost there.

The feeling is quickly extinguished by the sight of a giant shadow circling the door, like a shark closing in on its prey, and though Violet has now encountered a tiny butterfly person, a flock of phoenixes, a sea monster, and a unicorn, she still finds herself taken by surprise when she realizes what it is.

"Uh, yeah, no," Violet says, shaking her head. "There's no way I'm going over there."

Peter looks at her. "But we have to get into the library."

"But there's a freaking dragon guarding the door!"

A deep voice booms across the field, shaking Violet to her core. "Come closer, children."

"A talking dragon, apparently," Peter utters.

"I don't care if it's a talking dragon. It's still a dragon."

"I said, *come!*"

Peter stumbles forward, pulling Violet with him, and together the two walk reluctantly toward the looming black beast guarding the door. To her minuscule relief — because dragon — Peter stops them several yards away from the thing, so at least they'd have a bit of a head start before being inevitably caught and eaten if the thing were to charge.

"Closer," the dragon roars, and trains its blazing green eyes directly on her. It's as if it's shooting lasers at her, burning holes into her brain and forcing her to come forward.

A few more steps and the two are terrifyingly close to the creature — so close that Violet can see the slight sheen of its scales glowing in the moonlight. It would be beautiful if not for the fact that she's absolutely petrified.

"To enter through the gate, you must answer three riddles."

Peter and Violet exchange confused glances before Peter opens his mouth. "Wait, seriously?" he asks. "We have to answer a few riddles, and you'll let us through?"

"Yes."

"We don't have to fight you or anything?"

"Answer my three riddles correctly and you may pass."

"And if we get them wrong?" Violet asks, her voice small and trembling.

The dragon straightens up, craning its long neck and unfurling its giant wings, blocking out the starlight behind it and casting the two into shadow. Only its glowing green eyes are visible in the darkness.

"If you do not answer correctly, you're mine."

A shudder passes through Violet's body, and she steps backward into Peter, his arms catching her and locking securely around her waist. How is he standing so steadily? Maybe he really does do well in tense situations.

"Okay, lay 'em on me," Peter says determinedly.

The dragon sits back on its haunches once more, its head slithering down to their level so it can stare into Peter's eyes. Then it opens its mouth to speak. "This thing all things devours; Birds, beasts, trees, flowers; Gnaws iron, bites steel; Grinds hard stones to meal; Slays king, ruins town, And beats mountain down."

A classic, Violet thinks, and she twists in Peter's arms so she can look at him.

His lips are moving silently as he repeats the riddle to himself. His brow furrows and she can tell he's struggling. *Has he never read* The Hobbit?

"Time," Violet says at last.

The creature pulls in a deep breath, its nostrils flaring as it mulls over her answer. "Riddle two," it starts, and she releases a sigh. "What can run, but never walks; has a mouth, but never talks; has a head, but never weeps; has a bed, but never sleeps?"

"A river," Violet says quickly.

The dragon hums, twin puffs of smoke escaping its snout. "An expert, it seems," it purrs. "Perhaps we make it a little harder, then." Its eyes roll up toward the sky as it decides what next to try to trick them with. Then suddenly, its head once again fills their vision, piercing green eyes now set on Peter. "A dragon's tooth in a mortal's hand. I kill, I maim, I divide the land."

Violet's heart pounds against her ribcage as she watches Peter concentrate. The longer he goes without saying anything, the more the panic grows in Violet's chest.

"Come on, Peter," she urges.

"Time is ticking," the dragon taunts.

Peter closes his eyes, lines forming in his forehead as he thinks. "A dragon's tooth in a mortal's hand," he recites under his breath. "I kill, I maim, I divide the land." His eyes open suddenly. "A sword," he blurts out.

The dragon's mouth curls into a smile. "Are you positive?"

"No, wait," Peter says quickly. "A spear."

The dragon sits back, an amused look in its gleaming eyes as it watches Peter second-guess himself, the internal struggle showing as pure anguish on his face.

"Which is it, Peter?" Violet asks.

"A spear?" he questions. "A sword. A dagger?"

"Pick just one," the dragon says.

At last, he looks at the creature. "A sword," he says, the confidence in his voice tinged with uncertainty.

The silence seems to stretch on forever. *I hope you're right*, Violet thinks.

At last, the dragon stands tall again, unfurling its wings once more to shut out the world around them.

Nope, definitely a spear.

Violet clings to Peter and squeezes her eyes shut, waiting for the inevitable strike, but when it doesn't come, she looks again to find that the dragon has disappeared, and now the library door stands there in front of them, shining in the moonlight.

"How'd you know the answer to that last one?" Violet asks, breaking the silence.

Peter pulls away from her now, his eyes searching the darkened sky. "One of my favorite books is *Storms of Time,* and the hero in it calls his sword 'Dragon Fang.'"

Violet pulls in a quick breath. "You read high fantasy?" *He's perfect.* "And yet you've never read *The Hobbit?*"

He looks back down at her and shrugs. "I couldn't get into it."

Almost perfect.

"Hey, how funny would it be if the door was locked?" he asks, drawing attention back to their current situation.

Violet was so caught up in the fact that her crush likes the same genre that she almost forgot they've been trapped in an alternate dimension, but now she lets out a nervous laugh, grasping the knob and hoping that it'll open. Much to her relief, the door gives way, and she stumbles in, holding her breath as she takes in her surroundings. It's her library. Her beloved, familiar library with the creaking floors and long oak tables and...

"Where is everyone?" she asks as she looks around. "Savannah!" she calls. "Leslie! Garrett!"

"Guys!" Peter yells as he steps in after her.

Only silence.

"They aren't here," Violet says with disappointment. "Why aren't they here?"

Instead of answering her, Peter makes his way across the library toward the office and opens the door. Violet trails behind him, frustration sitting heavily in her stomach as she thinks about the fact that they just faced a literal dragon and answered stupid riddles to get out of this stupid place and yet they're still *in* this stupid place.

Like the library itself, the office is the exact same, so Peter goes to open the cabinet and reach for the book on the top shelf, where the key was originally hidden. Luckily, it's there. With a hefty push, he sends the shelf swinging inward, revealing the dusty secret room and the locked bookshelf.

Violet follows behind, watching as Peter inserts the key and opens the doors. He quickly scans the books, finger trailing across the spines, before letting out a frustrated grunt. "It's not here."

"What?" Violet asks dazedly.

"The book that brought us here is missing." Then Peter cocks his head. "But this one is new," he says, and reaches out to snag a red book with bronze moons covering its surfaces.

"Think it'll bring us back to our world?" Violet asks nervously.

Peter sucks in a breath. "Or take us to a new one," he says. "I guess there's only one way to find out, huh?" Then he carefully cracks the book open, and though she expects it, Violet can't help but feel taken aback when the blank pages are revealed.

As the pages start to flip themselves and the room fills with static, Violet can only cling to Peter and hope that when she opens her eyes, they'll be back in the real Yellow Wood Academy library.

Their footsteps echo as the two students make their way slowly, cautiously down the dark hallway.

"Think we made it back?" Peter asks, glancing around suspiciously, anticipating some other strange, tiny creature appearing before them.

Violet's eyes search the corridor as well, only seeing the familiar aspects of their real school. Everything looks right—no trees or vines or fiery birds in sight. "I guess the only way to find out is to go to the library, right?" she asks.

Peter nods, holding a hand out to her, and she feels her cheeks heat up as she reaches for it. The moment their fingers slot together, the fluorescents above them cut out, plunging the entire first floor of the school into pitch darkness. The two stand frozen for several seconds, neither really knowing what to do.

"Violet," Peter finally whispers.

"Yeah."

"I don't think we made it back."

Before Violet can respond, a low growl rips its way down the hallway, and she jerks her head around, looking back toward the front entrance. A pair of gleaming red eyes glare back at her, and Violet feels her soul leave her body.

"We have to go," Peter utters and tugs on her, but she can't seem to move. "Violet, come on, we" — another growl erupts from down the hall — "we have to go!"

Violet's arm about rips from its socket as Peter yanks hard, pulling her along behind him as he heads for the stairs. The sound of nails scraping against the tiles fills Violet's head, and it's all she can do to keep her feet under her, legs pumping as hard as they possibly can.

She feels like her lungs are about to burst, her muscles screaming as she and Peter hurtle down the hall. He's a dim blur of blue in front of her, his one arm stretched backward, clammy hand holding fast to hers as he pulls her after him.

She can hear the snarling behind them grow impossibly louder, but she dares not turn to see how close it is as it would only slow them down.

At last, Violet finds her voice. "Stairs!" She yells, and Peter throws a hand out, catching the banister and swinging them around in one swift motion until they're barreling up the stairwell.

"Faster!" Violet shrieks, and she can hear the creature tearing after them.

They burst out of the stairwell on the third floor, the sound of their shoes squeaking loudly against the marble floor soon joined by that of scraping claws. They careen around the corner, the library at last coming into sight, and they dash for it. Peter reaches out, grabbing the handle as he flies by, and the knob promptly snaps off in his hand.

The two look at each other with wide eyes. That wasn't supposed to happen.

"What do we do?" Violet asks quickly, just as a roar echoes from down the darkened hall.

"Break it down!" Peter yells, and then starts using his shoulder as a battering ram against the door, eliciting cracks so loud they reverberate through the hall.

She joins him, throwing her body against the door. Three more hard hits and it smashes open, splinters of wood raining down around them as they scramble to the office and slam the door shut. Quickly, they pull the large oak desk in front of it, before going for the cabinet and the place where the key is hidden.

No sooner have they gotten the passageway open than the office door shudders, the wood cracking with just the first hit.

"Go!" Peter yells, shoving Violet through, and she fumbles with the key, almost dropping it as she rushes toward the bookcase.

With trembling fingers, it takes her several attempts to get the key in the hole and turn it. Each second welcomes the sounds of more splintering wood as the monster turns the door to bark chips.

Come on, come on, come on, come on.

The bookcase flies open, and the two don't waste time looking for the right book, instead grabbing each one and flipping it open, a glimpse of words on the pages causing them to chuck the book over their shoulder and grab for the next one. A blue book with a silver maze etched over the whole thing suddenly seems to jump off the shelf and into Violet's hand, just before the office door implodes. Her vision fills with blank white paper, and she begins turning the pages as quickly as she can, the room fading away, the gritty air swirling around her and Peter, and just before everything goes black, she looks back to the opening of the room and catches sight of those two gleaming red eyes.

"Violet," Peter calls from behind her. "Wait up!"

Violet's failed attempt at stifling her sobs echoes through the empty halls along with their footsteps.

She should have known better than to hope that the red book would bring them back to the real library instead of the literal nightmare they'd just barely escaped from. And while this one doesn't have a monster chasing them, it's obvious from the eerie silence and the strange, cold light cast over the whole place that this very much isn't their Yellow Wood.

"I'm not stopping for anything, Peter," Violet calls back to him, throat tightening. "We're getting out of here, now."

"Could you just wait a second?" Peter asks, and she hears his running footsteps drawing closer.

She whirls around to face him. Pieces of her hair that have fallen out of her braid stick to her face, which she just knows is splotchy and red, like it always gets when she cries. She's sure she looks like an absolute train wreck, which makes her feel even worse about the whole situation. He must think she's a total drama queen.

He gently places his hands on her shoulders and gives them a reassuring squeeze. "Look, there are no monsters chasing us—no fairies or unicorns or dragons. It's just the regular hallway. It's fine," he says. "We're fine. Just slow down for a minute and breathe."

Somehow, Violet calms herself down enough to pull in a breath, concentrating on imagining her lungs expanding fully before allowing any air to escape again. Peter leans further down, looking deeply into Violet's eyes with his own brown ones, his shoulders rising and falling along with hers as he guides her through more steadying breaths. After a few more she can feel herself calming down, her heart no longer crashing against her ribcage, and she's becoming more aware of the pressure of Peter's hands on her arms.

She knows this isn't the time or place. She knows that if Savannah were here right now, she'd smack Violet on the back of her head and tell her she's being ridiculous. She knows that she's just come down from a panic attack and that so much adrenaline is coursing through her veins right now that there's no way she's possibly thinking straight, but...he's just so cute.

This may not be the most opportune moment, but what if it's the only moment they get? And he's being so kind and so gentle, and his face is so close to hers.

And he's just so cute.

Her eyes dart down to his mouth for a split second, but that's all it takes for him to understand what she's getting at, and because he's already so close to her, it takes him just one small step closer for their lips to connect.

His hands come up to rest on either side of her face, his chest warm against hers. She can't quite breathe, but she doesn't really want to. Not if it means pulling away. Her head is swimming, heart beating rapidly against his as his mouth moves on hers, and she's never felt like this.

Her mind is reeling with thoughts of him. Just him. Not dragons, not monsters, not whatever this strange world holds. It's all about him. About this boy that she's always admired from afar.

At last, she begins to feel a bit lightheaded and reluctantly pulls away, resting her forehead against his, keeping her eyes closed because she knows that as soon as she opens them, the moment will be over and she'll have to once again face this unknown reality.

She feels Peter's hand leave her face, sliding down her arm until his fingers tangle with hers. Then he steps away, forcing Violet to come out of her dream and open her eyes to look at him.

He smiles gently. "Come on."

Violet nods and lets him pull her down the hall. They only make it past a couple rows of lockers before he stops them again, his eyes glued to the sign above the closest door. "Actually, come in here," he says, opening a door and pulling her through it.

The room is big and empty — nothing, really, but a wall of mirrors, a bar along the opposite wall, and an outdated speaker system in one corner.

"The dance studio?" Violet asks. "Why'd you want to come in here?"

"It has a bathroom," Peter says, eying the door on the opposite side of the room.

"Seriously?" she asks.

"It'll just take a second," he says. "I'll be right back."

"Is this really the time to pee?"

"Nature calls when nature calls," he says, and starts to let go of Violet's hand, but she squeezes it harder. Peter's head tilts as he looks at her, confused.

"I just really don't think we should separate," she says softly. "What if something happens?"

Peter's own expression smooths over and he takes a step toward her. "It's just the bathroom, Vi. What could possibly happen in a room with nothing but a sink, a mirror, and a toilet?"

Violet doesn't respond — just chews on her bottom lip and looks down at their interlaced fingers. "I don't know how many more worlds we have to go through, but I really gotta go," Peter says. "What if — I don't know — what if I sing a song or something the whole time, so you know I'm alright?"

Violet reluctantly nods, loosening her grip on his hand and letting it fall away. "Besides," he says as he starts walking backward toward the bathroom. "I'm kind of excited to be able to say I've peed in an alternate universe."

Violet can't help but giggle. "Yeah, who's going to believe you?" she asks.

"I mean, at least you will," he calls back, before opening the door and slipping inside. Violet is grateful when he leaves the door open just a crack — not enough for her to see, but enough to give her some reassurance.

Violet spins around now to face the wall of mirrors. She can't help but notice that her mouth looks just a little bit swollen and tinged pink. Her cheeks flood with the same color and she grins, bringing a hand up to touch her fingers to her mouth. When the slightly off-key sound of the school anthem begins, her smile widens further.

We are Yellow Wood Academy
We hail the blue and gold
No one can quell our spirit
We are forever bold

A flicker of movement in her peripheral causes Violet's eyes to shift from her reflection to the spot over her shoulder. She cocks her head to the side, studying the wall behind her. Nothing. Surely, her eyes are playing tricks on her. *There's nothing there, Violet,* she tells herself, knowing she's still feeling the effects of her earlier panic attack. It's only at this moment that Violet realizes Peter has stopped singing. Her eyes shoot to the bathroom door.

"Peter?" she calls, though with her throat already beginning to close up from the panic, it comes out as more of a strained whisper.

We're the fierce yellow jackets

She feels relief so strong she could cry, but then embarrassment over freaking out for no reason. "Stop being ridiculous," she scolds, turning back toward the mirror.

And all will fear our sting

She catches movement again, this time down by her side, and when her eyes fall to her hand in the mirror, she gasps when she sees the reflection of her pointer finger tapping against her leg. She looks up and feels her blood run cold. Instead of the reversed image of her wide-eyed expression, she's met with one of twisted amusement.

And this here is our battle cry
Forever we will sing

Her reflection lifts its head higher, mouth spreading into a malicious grin right before it lunges. Only the essence of a scream escapes before Violet's back hits the floor, knocking the wind out of her. She can't call for Peter because this terrifying mirror version of herself is on top of her, crushing her lungs, clawing at her clothes and her hair, trying to find purchase before wrapping Violet's braided hair around its wrist and yanking. Through the burning in her scalp as her reflection begins dragging her back toward the mirror, she at last manages to cry out.

"Peter!" she screams. "Peter! Help me!" She's thrashing and twisting, clawing at the hand that has a death-grip on her braid. Her vision is too blurry to see what's happening, but then a flash of blue hair appears, and the pressure on her scalp vanishes. Through the film covering her eyes, she watches a struggle ensue, until at last Peter wraps his arms around the reflection's waist and starts hauling it toward the mirror. With a loud grunt, Peter shoves the thing back into it, then throws his elbow out. It connects with the glass, causing a spider web of cracks to spread out from where he hit. One more blow and the mirror shatters, pieces raining down on the dance studio floor.

"Come on!" Peter gasps, grabbing Violet before she really has a chance to catch her breath.

The two burst out into the hall, once again running for their lives. They make a mad dash up the stairs, and when they reach the library, Violet feels a hint of relief at the sight of the door before them, unguarded. At last, Peter releases her hand, and they sink against the wall, shoulders heaving as they catch their breath.

"Are you okay?" Peter asks between gasps.

Violet is doubled over, vision still blurry, her hands on her knees as she tries to keep from having a full-on panic attack. "Let's just get out of here." She finally says, then twists the knob and steps into the library.

This time she's the one to lead the way to the office. She barely waits for Peter to step inside before she's pushing the cabinet open and entering the small room with the bookcase. The key goes in, the doors open, and the books are there as expected. Again, a new one sits among the older tomes—a bright yellow one, though, unlike the others, there are no metallic etchings on its surface. Violet turns the book over in her hands, fingers trailing over the unmarred cover.

"What's wrong? Why aren't you opening it?" Peter asks.

"The last three had designs on the covers," Violet says, finger running along the blank spine.

"And?"

"Well, it was like they were hinting at the world we were going into. What if —" Violet hesitates.

"What?"

"What if this book takes us to nothing?" she asks, looking up at him now, his face barely visible in the dim light. "What if it's just an empty void, and we're stuck there forever?"

Peter steps back further into the shadows, wringing his hands as he thinks. At last, he looks up at her again. "Well, there's only one way to find out, right?" he asks.

Violet nods and once again looks down at the yellow book in her hands. "Yeah, I guess," she sighs, then before she can talk herself out of it, she opens the book. The blank pages flip themselves faster and faster until the air once again grows staticky, and she feels Peter's hand slip into hers just before she closes her eyes.

Hands grasp at Violet, voices garbled like her head is underwater, until she breaks the surface and the world around her explodes into life. She opens her eyes to bright light. Her throat is on fire, body aching, and yet she finds herself blindly getting to her feet.

"Violet, what happened? Are you okay? Can you hear me?" It's Savannah, her face finally coming into full view, and Violet feels like she could burst into tears at the familiar sight of her best friend. At last. At last, they made it. They're back in their own world.

"Peter," she croaks, and then repeats it because the first time the word comes out in nothing more than a raspy puff of air. "Where's Peter?" she asks.

Savannah's eyebrow cocks, and suddenly she doesn't look so concerned anymore. "You mean the boy who got us into this whole stupid mess?" she asks. "He's right there." And she gestures with her head out into the library, where Violet catches a glimpse of blue hair.

"What happened, Vi?" Savannah asks carefully.

Violet ignores her, instead turning to face the cabinet and reaching out to grasp the handles on the doors. She wrenches them open and steps back. The flashlight that Peter had used initially is there, though the large book beside it is gone, and when she thrusts her arm up, having to jump to reach the shelf, she doesn't feel the key there.

"Weird," she whispers, before turning around and seeing her friend looking at her, confused.

"What's weird?" Savannah asks.

Violet looks back at the cabinet, then past her friend's shoulder, meeting Peter's eyes. He starts heading her way. "Um...nothing," Violet finally says. "I was just checking something."

"Hey, everything alright in here?" Peter asks, leaning against the doorway.

He seems oddly calm for what they just experienced.

"That's what I was wondering," Savannah says. "What was taking you guys so long anyway?"

Peter shrugs.

"Guys, Justine's here!" Leslie calls from out in the library.

"Ugh, thank God!" Savannah groans and turns away without waiting for an explanation.

Violet doesn't follow, and barely notices Leslie's words. Instead, she stares at Peter. The boy looks back at her. Something isn't right.

"Let's get out of here," Peter says, pushing off the doorframe.

As he speaks, Violet's eyes are glued to his mouth, watching his lips form the words. Something...something seems different.

She swears that the freckle on his bottom lip was on the right, not the left. In fact, it's almost like she's seeing a reversed image of him. Like a reflection in a mirror.

Violet's heart drops to her stomach. "Peter," she says, and he turns around again. "How did you know to smash the mirror in the dance studio?"

Peter's brow furrows as he thinks. At first he seems nervous, but a split second later, a corner of his mouth quirks upward. The wrong corner. "It's the only way to keep anything from coming back out," he says.

"What do you mean, coming *back* out?" Violet asks, her voice quivering.

Peter only smiles wider. "Come on, Violet," he says. "We're free now." And then he starts toward the library entrance, where the others are waiting for them.

But Violet can't move. She can only stand there, mouth open, eyes wide as she watches this other Peter make his way toward her friends, hand gripping the strap of the real Peter's backpack. He must realize she isn't following because when he reaches the door, he turns again and meets her eyes. Once more, the wrong corner of his mouth quirks up into a knowing smile, just before he slips out of the open library door.

Boys, Book Clubs, and Other Bad Ideas

by Sunny Everson

Bram's wand was the most common variety: polished maple with a single Quartz point on the end. It was neither rare nor exciting, but instead sturdy and reliable. He waved a quick adhesive spell, then took a step back to admire his work.

The notice, handwritten in ink on a piece of parchment, said the following:

FOURTH YEAR BOOK CLUB
(OTHER YEARS WELCOME)
COMPLETE YOUR CLUB REQUIREMENT
WITHOUT THE DANGER
TUESDAYS 4PM
LIBRARY

It wasn't anything impressive, but he felt a touch of pride looking at the notice. He did wonder, though, if he should have added something a little more positive to the ad, such as COME MAKE FRIENDS or HAVE A GOOD TIME or perhaps even THERE WILL BE SNACKS. (Never mind; the librarian, Madame Sanguine, had a strict no-food policy.)

So perhaps his new book club didn't sound like the most entertaining way for fifteen-year-old wizards to spend their time, but Bram figured there had to be others like himself out there — other students for whom the threat of falling off a pegasus was too great to join a sparkball team or who didn't like the particular danger of joining 4H.

Crimsonwood Academy for Wizards required all students fourth year and up to participate in at least one club per year. Now Bram was starting his first required year with no club prospects except to start his own, and what easier option than reading a book and discussing it?

(He knew, however, that the number of fiction books in the Crimsonwood library was limited to one shelf on one bookcase in the back corner. It was fine; they could reread the same books each year until they graduated.)

Yes, Bram told himself, this was going to be the perfect club for the more average teenagers of the school. One didn't need to be a hero, after all, to enjoy literature.

Bram had to admit to himself that he may have set his expectations a little high. It was nearly half past four on the first Tuesday of book club, and he was the only one sitting at his reserved table. There had been a clerical error with the table reservation as well, because instead of reading RESERVED FOR CRIMSONWOOD BOOK CLUB, the reservation card said only "bram's table" in all lowercase.

So rather than surrounded by excited bibliophiles, he was sitting entirely alone at a table that was clearly too large for just him.

It wasn't all bad, he told himself. The table had a window that looked down on the castle grounds below. He had a nice view of the sparkball field, where October Whitmore was practicing on his shimmering gray pegasus. Down on the grass, the boy spurred his steed into the air, the sunlight reflecting off his golden hair, and a daring grin on his face.

A clear view of October in action was a pleasant treat. The other fourth year was usually surrounded by his fans, both students and teachers alike. Bram had spent his education at Crimsonwood enjoying October's many triumphs from a comfortable and frequently obstructed distance.

Everyone knew October Whitmore was the Chosen One. Everyone. October himself probably knew it by then. Someday soon, likely the second he finished his education, October would be the one to take down the most powerful evil wizard of all time, the Darkmaster. It was widely believed that the Darkmaster already knew October was his prophesied nemesis and had besieged the school with curses the last few years. It certainly would have explained a lot of the strange and sudden dangers that always seemed to befall Crimsonwood.

Unlike Bram, October wasn't alone. With him out on the sparkball field was his sidekick and friend Marigold Moonfall. She was the smartest wizard of their year, and probably smarter than half the fifth and sixth years, too. Her pegasus was the color of lilacs, and her white-blond hair made her stand out against the grass. Bram thought she was probably the luckiest kid in the entire school to be October Whitmore's absolute best friend. (He had to remind himself it probably wasn't appropriate to be jealous of the girl who was orphaned when the Darkmaster brutally murdered her parents only five years ago.)

"Hey, is this the book club?" a voice interrupted Bram's thoughts.

He turned away from the window, surprised to find another student standing at his table. The boy was a few inches shorter than him, with long black hair that nearly obscured his eyes. His Crimsonwood robes were disheveled, and there was an ink stain on his sleeve.

"Yes!" Bram exclaimed with a smile. "I mean, yes, this is the book club. Please sit down."

The other boy made a face like maybe he'd changed his mind, but pulled out a chair and sat down across from Bram. "I'm—" he started to introduce himself, but Bram cut him off.

"You're Dallan Shadowend," Bram said. Of course he knew who this was. Who wouldn't know the kid who had narrowly lost the sparkball tournament two years previous? (Lost, of course, to October Whitmore.) "I'm Bram Blankley," he continued.

The other boy just stared at him, as if not recognizing him at all.

"We sat next to each other in Fortune Telling last year, and we have four classes together this year," Bram explained.

Dallan Shadowend nodded slightly. "Is no one else coming?"

Bram shrugged with a smile. "I'm sure the book club will pick up a few stragglers by next week. Here:

I thought we could do some boundary-breakers first, then discuss which book we'd like to read."

"Look," Dallan said, leaning forward, "If it's just the two of us, why don't we just do homework? We'll get the club requirement out of the way and get ahead on our studies."

"Wouldn't that be more like a study club?" Bram asked. This wasn't going how he'd expected at all. He didn't think members had to be complete book worms to join the club, but he had envisioned that they'd at least participate in the — well, the book portion of the book club.

He was going to push it further, but Dallan's attention had already moved away. He was looking out the window, where October and Marigold were racing their pegasuses in a double-helix formation. Bram was surprised by the expression on the other boy's face. It wasn't awe or admiration, but something between disgust and complete fury. His hands were clutching the table in front of him so hard his knuckles were turning white.

"Wait a second," Bram said, interrupting the boy's furious trance. "Why aren't you doing sparkball this year? Our first year, you were the only person who could keep up with October Whitmore. Even the sixth years weren't as good."

Now that he thought about it, Bram wasn't sure he'd seen Dallan compete their second or third years. But Dallan had once been good — very good, if he'd come in second after October.

Dallan turned his dour expression from the window to Bram. "What's the point of sparkball if no one can ever beat *him*? The school's golden boy." His face twisted into what Bram could only describe as a sneer.

Realization struck Bram almost as hard as the shock that followed. "You... don't like October Whitmore?"

Bram had never heard of it before. Sure, some students didn't follow October's accomplishments as closely as others, but not a soul at the school ever spoke badly about him. Until that moment, Bram wouldn't have guessed it was even possible for someone to *not* like October. He was, after all, probably the Chosen One.

The expression on Dallan's face was definitely disgust now. "What's there to like about someone who doesn't have a single flaw?"

"Isn't that usually a good thing?" Bram asked.

He decided it wasn't unreasonable that Dallan Shadowend wasn't a big fan after October had trumped him brutally in front of the entire school when they were just twelve, but that wasn't enough to explain why he actually disliked the most likeable person at Crimsonwood. The only explanation Bram could wrap his head around was that Dallan just didn't know all the fantastic things October had accomplished.

"Did you know," Bram started, an eager smile on his face, "that October's pegasus, Admetrius, *chose him* on the very first day of class our first year?"

Dallan's face looked like someone had just suggested he kiss a minotaur. He pushed his seat back and started to get up. "Look," he grabbed the first book off a stack of fiction Bram had brought to the table. "We'll just start with this. *Life Without Duty*. Sounds thrilling. We'll both read the first chapter and talk about it next week."

Before Bram could get another word in, Dallan Shadowend was already walking away, his black Crimsonwood robe hanging off one shoulder.

Bram picked up the aforementioned book and leafed through the pages. It looked drier than their history textbook, with a font size that nearly required a microscope to make out. He wondered if perhaps Madame Sanguine had accidentally shelved it in the wrong section, but no, it did say on the front, *Life Without Duty: A Novel of Morals*.

Well, if their selected book was going to take a while to get through, at least he'd have plenty of time to change Dallan's mind about October.

Bram was running late to his post-lunch Incantation class after he dropped his books on the second-floor staircase. It ended up being quite fortuitous, though; when he burst into the classroom, breathless, the only remaining seat was the one next to none other than Dallan Shadowend.

"Hello!" Bram greeted him brightly, slamming his haphazard stack of books down on their shared table.

Dallan glanced up at him and groaned.

While he wanted to launch immediately into a discussion of whether October Whitmore was the best sparkball player in Crimsonwood history due to freak athletic ability or prophesied magical ability, Professor Magnus was already starting the lesson. Despite his perpetually average scores, Bram was a diligent student.

The second half of the class brought some time for private conversation, though, when Professor Magnus had them practice their pronunciation of transmutation spells out loud (with their wands carefully stowed away, of course, so no students were accidentally turned into paperweights).

"*Recoquo chartorei!*" the students began chanting, at first in unison, then slowly dissolving into a chaos of voices.

"Dallan," Bram said as soon as his voice could be covered by their classmates', "do you know what October did with his trophy after he beat you at sparkball?"

Dallan put his face in his hands.

"He gave it to his friend Marigold. She had just broken her foot after that herd of centaurs stampeded the castle grounds, so she couldn't compete." Bram waited for his words to sink in. Dallan had to see that instead of letting it go to his head, October had humbly given the trophy away.

"I don't *care* what he did with the trophy," Dallan hissed, glowering at Bram from between his fingers.

"Actually," Bram went on as if he hadn't heard, "October was the one to stop that stampede, too. The whole herd had been possessed by a dark magician, and no one knew then who did it, but I think we all know now who it was." He raised his eyebrows.

The other boy acted like he hadn't heard, turning back to his notes.

Bram thought the answer was pretty obvious, but he offered it anyway: "The Darkmaster."

Somehow Dallan managed to look *more* annoyed. He frowned at his book and started chorusing *Recoquo chartorei* with more enthusiasm than was probably necessary.

That story about the trophy was so heartwarming, Bram had been confident it would change Dallan's mind. What if he couldn't convince him? No, no, that was impossible. He'd just need to whip out the most exhilarating October facts. No one could resist for long.

The next class Bram and Dallan had together was two days later: Ancient Artifacts.

Bram tried to wave Dallan over to the empty seat next to him, but the other boy must not have seen because he took a seat on the far side of the circular classroom. He wasn't going to be able to convince him of much from a distance, but Bram waved at him a little when Dallan looked up.

Dallan shook his head twice and mouthed some words that looked something like "weave bee cologne." Bram wasn't sure what that was supposed to mean, so he just grinned and nodded back.

He missed Dallan's reaction when Professor Oberon Wraithe began lecturing. The professor used his wand to project images onto the stone wall. Each one was a different ancient object that Professor Wraithe would describe the uses and history of.

Bram kept up by taking notes and making quick artifact sketches that looked vaguely like the real thing if you squinted a little.

"Headmaster Cromwell specifically asked me to teach you about this next item," Professor Wraithe said toward the end of class.

Bram looked up from his notes to see the professor was looking pointedly at October Whitmore.

"This is the Sword of Flames." The professor flicked his wand and the image on the wall changed to a... sword on fire. It was a little anticlimactic, Bram thought, but he went ahead and doodled it into his notes (and added some extra flames for good measure).

"The Sword of Flames was created and wielded by Crimsonwood's founder Khaxium Crimsonwood," the professor went on. "He used it to defeat an army of ghouls and goblins in order to claim this valley, the ancestral home of all goblins, where he founded his school for teenage wizards."

There was something about that that didn't sound super awesome, but Bram couldn't put his finger on it.

"It has been said that one day the *Chosen One*" — he gestured clearly toward October when he said this — "will wield the Sword of Flames to defeat the terrible Darkmaster."

"Wow," Bram breathed.

At his desk, October Whitmore had an expression of stoic determination. Next to him, Marigold Moonfall appeared to be transcribing Professor Wraithe's lecture word for word.

"Uh, excuse me, Professor." October raised his hand a little, even though the professor and the rest of class were already staring at him. "Where might the, uh, Chosen One locate the Sword of Flames?"

Professor Wraithe beamed down at him. "No one knows, October. But many of Khaxium Crimsonwood's other magical belongings have been discovered here, in the school he founded."

Instead of watching October's reaction, Bram turned to look over at Dallan. Dallan's face was drawn in a scowl, and he was leaning back in his seat with his arms crossed across his chest. Bram managed to catch his eye and used both hands to gesture excitedly in October's direction.

"SO. COOL," he mouthed.

Dallan leaned forward in his chair again and put his hand against the side of his head to block Bram from view.

The news of the Sword of Flames carried Bram through the rest of the week. He was trying to imagine how absolutely prodigious October would look wielding the sword. He was also trying to envision a prolific slow-motion scene in which October used the Sword of Flames to chop off the Darkmaster's head, but Bram didn't actually know what the Darkmaster looked like, and the mental image he currently had looked a little bit too much like his Uncle Castor in a bathrobe.

On the Monday before the second book club meeting, Bram followed his classmates across the grassy front lawn where their Herbs and Poisons professor, Professor Shrub, was waiting for them.

"Today," the professor began the lesson, "we will be pruning back an infestation of Inland Western Sneezewort." He pointed to a patch of innocuous-looking weeds growing near his feet. "Now, unlike the benign coastal varieties of Sneezewort, this particular variety is incredibly poisonous. One touch and you'll be laid up in the Medical Ward with severe abdominal pain and some persistent optic bleeding. So," he pointed to a chest next to him, "grab a pair of gloves.

"Does everyone have a partner?" Professor Shrub stood up on his tiptoes to look over the group of them. "Dallan, you don't seem to have a partner yet. Would anyone like to volunteer to be Dallan's partner?"

Bram threw his arm in the air. "I'll be Dallan's partner, Professor."

Professor Shrub smiled warmly at him. "Thank you, Bram."

Dallan did not smile warmly at Bram when he went over to join him.

"This'll be exciting," Bram told him.

"I think I'd rather be in the Medical Ward," Dallan muttered under his breath.

One of Bram's gloves had a huge rip across the palm, so he had to pull weeds with just one hand.

"Do you think October will find the Sword of Flames this year?" he asked while he pulled leaves one by one off a weed in front of him. "Or not until next year?"

"You're really annoying, you know that?" Dallan asked.

"When he does find it, everyone will know for sure he's the Chosen One," Bram went on as if he hadn't spoken. "I wonder if he'll get to bring the Sword of Flames to class. Do you think it's always on fire or does it go out sometimes?"

Dallan made a sound like a snort. "There's no way October is the Chosen One. He's fifteen."

Bram must have heard him wrong. "Of course he's the Chosen One. Everybody knows that. Even the teachers."

"And how exactly does 'everybody' know that?"

Bram could not have been happier that he asked. "Well, there's the fact that he's an orphan. His parents died of Ogre Fever when he was an infant."

"It's weird that you know that." Dallan shook his head at the Sneezewort in front of him. "What do his parents have to do with it? Other kids in our class are orphans. Ulrich Grail. Rodney Wolf." He counted on his gloved fingers as he said their classmates' names. "Even Marigold's parents are dead."

"Okay," Bram went on. "How about how super good he is at sports? Everyone says he's the best sparkball player in Crimsonwood history."

Dallan scowled and threw a Sneezewort over Bram to the compost pile. "Believe me, I know. Our first year, I practiced four hours a day to beat him at the tournament."

Bram paused. He sometimes forgot how neck-and-neck the tournament had been. "It *was* a really close game," he admitted aloud.

The other boy glanced up at him, the sunlight hitting his dark eyes just right so that Bram could see they were brown.

Bram looked away quickly. "Well, he's also a really great student," he said, getting back to the subject at hand.

"I'm pretty sure that's just favoritism." Dallan went back to scowling at weeds.

"And there's the fact that he won the Thaumaturge Tourney last year," Bram continued, "even after that dragon escaped and the labyrinth ivy was cursed to try to rip the competitors apart. Oh, and remember the students from Grimshank all turned out to be werewolves?"

Dallan had an expression on his face like he was already having some abdominal pain. "How did he even get to compete?" He turned his attention to a new patch of Sneezewort to their right. "The competition was exclusively for sixth years, but

Headmaster Cromwell completely changed the rules so October could compete."

"Well, it was a good thing, wasn't it?" He plucked a dandelion in front of him and twirled its stem between his fingers. "October was the one to catch the dragon."

"I wish the dragon had eaten him," Dallan grumbled.

"Why do you hate him anyway?" Bram asked, looking up from his flower.

"I don't hate him." Dallan pulled up a weed with one brief, angry tug. "I just think it's bullshit that everyone worships him all the time." He threw the weed into the pile, narrowly missing smacking Bram in the face with it.

Dallan's words hit a little too close to home for Bram, so he pretended he hadn't heard them. "Is he like your rival?" he asked, tossing the flower back into the grass in front of him.

To his surprise, the other boy laughed. "My archnemesis," he joked.

"Maybe it was you," Bram grinned, "who cursed those centaurs."

Dallan smirked. "I would *totally* curse some centaurs to get rid of October Whitmore, but unfortunately I didn't know how to when I was twelve."

"Excuse me. Did you just say someone's cursing centaurs again?" A voice interrupted their conversation.

They both turned to see none other than October Whitmore himself standing over them, Marigold hovering in his shadow. October somehow managed to make dirty gardening gloves look kind of chic. He glanced from Bram to Dallan with a slight frown.

Dallan opened his mouth to start saying something (probably not something nice), but Bram interrupted him.

"No, sorry," he beamed up at October. "We were just discussing our book club book."

October's handsome face relaxed and twisted into something like... regret? Guilt?

"I'm so sorry. Marigold and I saw the sign and talked about joining your book club, but we couldn't because it's at the same time as sparkball practice."

"We could change the time," Bram blushed, eyes wide.

"No!" Dallan exclaimed, eyes equally as wide. "That's the only time that works."

"Alas," October sighed and started to walk away. "Be careful with those weeds." He turned and asked Marigold, just loud enough for them to still hear, "What's that kid's name again?"

Bram whipped his gaze around to beam at Dallan. *"He was going to join our book club,"* he gasped in one breath.

Dallan sighed and rolled his eyes. "I really need to learn how to curse centaurs."

In the early morning of Tuesday, the school alarm went off. Bram shuffled with his classmates, still in his pajamas, to the dining hall, where the teachers guarded the door and Marigold summoned hot chocolate for everyone out of thin air.

After an hour waiting, Dean Undertree announced that the school's protective force field had been ruptured, although neither a culprit nor anything out of the ordinary could be found. They decided the students would continue their day like normal.

The rest of the day was uneventful.

When Bram got to the library at quarter to four, Dallan Shadowend was already there at the table labelled 'bram's table' in an almost illegible scrawl.

"Good thing I finished reading that chapter during lunch," Bram said to him with a smile, pulling *Life Without Duty* from his book bag. "What did you think of it?"

Dallan shook his head. "I didn't finish it. I was a little distracted today." He did look somewhat frazzled, Bram noticed. His hair didn't appear to be brushed, and his cloak was actually on inside out.

"Did something happen?" Bram asked him.

"Of course something happened!" Dallan exclaimed, his eyebrows furrowed. "Something broke into the school this morning. How are you not concerned about that?"

Bram shrugged. "It's probably just the Darkmaster."

"Is that supposed to be reassuring?" Dallan demanded. He looked a bit pale. "You know the Darkmaster is a murderer, right?"

Bram fiddled with his feathered pen. "I'm not too worried, I guess. If anything happened to me, October would fight the Darkmaster and save me."

Dallan's face turned beet red, and he leaned over the table between them. "Bram, not everything is about October Whitmore. The Darkmaster is very dangerous, and you or I or any other student could be seriously hurt or even killed."

But Bram just shook his head. "That's not normally what happens, though." He waved his pen around, a little uncomfortable at Dallan's sudden intensity. "It's like last year during the Tourney when the other competitors started disappearing. Or the year before when all the teachers got turned into giant spiders. If a background student like me gets kidnapped or captured, they're always found alive after October saves the day."

The expression on Dallan's face faltered. "What did you just call yourself?"

Bram had never explained this out loud; he'd thought it was just something everyone knew. "Well, October is a hero, and maybe you're his rival or something, but the rest of us are just background characters. We all fit into... How should I say this?" He considered for a second. "Categories, I guess." He shrugged, unbothered. "Mine's in the background."

For the first time, Dallan didn't seem to know what to say. "Says who?" he finally managed.

"Think about it," Bram said. "When big, important stuff happens, there're always certain people around, right? October's usually there. Marigold. Sometimes you. Maybe they're seeking it out, looking for the action. Maybe it's destiny. I don't know. I'm just not one of those people."

Dallan met his eyes for a second longer, then looked away, his expression like he might be sick. "I don't think I believe in destiny."

If Bram was struggling this much to convince Dallan of October's awesomeness, it was going to take a lot longer to bring him around on destiny.

"Look" — Dallan grabbed the book from between them — "the book you chose is shit. It's really hard to read. I'll try to finish chapter one by next week."

Bram almost reminded Dallan that he had picked the book himself, but instead he just smiled at him and watched the other boy turn and leave. It was nice knowing he'd have book club to look forward to each week, and that someone else was planning on being there, too.

Over the next few days, Bram noticed his classmates seemed as uneasy as Dallan. It was hard not to get caught up in the anxiety hanging over them. He kind of wished the Darkmaster would just get it over with and do whatever dastardly thing he was planning.

His week wasn't all bad, though. With his weekly letter, Bram's father sent him an ornate brass magnifying glass to make reading *Life Without Duty* easier.

He hurried down to the dining hall for lunch on Friday, excited to show it off to Dallan. He recognized his long dark hair and messy robe from across the room, sitting alone at a table in the corner.

"Dallan, check it out!" Bram exclaimed, hurrying around the table to sit across from him. "Oh," he exhaled when he saw his friend's face.

Dallan was not well. He had a bit of a black eye and a split upper lip, and the front of his robe was ripped.

"What happened?" Bram gasped, feeling like someone had punched him in the stomach.

The other boy didn't meet his eyes, scowling and looking in a different direction. "I challenged October to a duel, and he kicked my ass."

Bram thought immediately of every time he had said October was Dallan's rival, and the sensation in his stomach grew worse. "But why?" he gasped.

Dallan finally looked at him, his expression icy. "Because I actually thought I could beat him."

"No," Bram said, struggling to wrap his head around the situation. "Why did he kick your ass?" There were rules for dueling, and the first was clear: duel to disarm, not to harm. Otherwise, it wasn't a duel at all—just a fight. He couldn't reconcile the bruised Dallan in front of him and the sunny, smiling hero he'd venerated for years. Didn't October only beat up bad guys?

Across the table, Dallan's expression soured further. "Look, I know you're obsessed with him, but

October's just a dumbass teenager like the rest of us."
He grabbed his bag and got up, the food in front of
him untouched.

"Wait." Bram caught Dallan's hand to stop him,
then let go with a blush. He felt like he needed to say
something, but the words, whatever they were, didn't
come to him. Instead he held up the brass magnifying
glass. "For the book," he mumbled.

For a second, he thought Dallan was going to walk
away without taking it, but after a pause he did.

"Thanks," Dallan muttered. He glanced up and
met Bram's eyes for a moment, then left.

The weekend passed. Two second year students
disappeared from their beds on Saturday night.
Everyone around him was talking about it, but Bram
barely noticed. He felt like his head was filled with
fog, and he spent most of the weekend in his dorm,
trying to start chapter two of *Life Without Duty*, but just
staring at the paragraph in front of him.

He was ravenous when he woke up on Monday
morning, having barely eaten at dinner the night
before. He dressed and headed down to breakfast
early.

The halls were eerily quiet. There were other
students awake and about, but they all seemed to be
in groups, hurrying wordlessly toward their
destinations.

Bram came down the staircase from the second floor and saw a crowd of first years standing at the bulletin board. They were whispering back and forth like a pack of mice. He was only three years older than them, but he was struck by how young they all looked. A girl in the middle of the group burst into tears, and the group hurried into the dining hall while trying to comfort her.

He paused to look at the new announcement on the board.

All students will return directly to
their dormitories immediately
following dinner beginning Monday.
If you have any news on the
whereabouts of the following
students, please report to
Headmaster Cromwell at once.

Listed beneath the message were the names of not two, but five total students.

"Those are all first years," a voice next to him observed, and Bram turned to see Dallan next to him. He was pointing to the bottom three names on the list.

"They must be terrified," Bram said quietly.

"Why aren't the teachers doing anything?" Dallan asked, watching Bram's face intently like he might actually know what was going on.

But he didn't. "They're probably scared, too." He looked from the announcement to Dallan's face. "They did get turned into giant spiders that one time. I bet they're not very excited to help anymore."

"What you said the other day was kind of bullshit," Dallan interrupted him. "You really think we're all stuck in... categories? Archetypes?" Bram noticed how close the other boy was to him. Their shoulders were nearly touching.

On one hand, Dallan had already played into the rival category once that week, challenging October to a duel without provocation. But on the other, October had broken out of the perfect hero paragon when he'd responded to the challenge with such force. Dallan's black eye was almost gone, leaving one side of his face with a yellow tinge.

"I hope it's real," Bram admitted, "because that means October will solve whatever's going on and bring these students back."

Dallan took a step back, scowling. "That's messed up. Just because he's everyone's favorite doesn't mean we should all sit around and wait for him to save the day again." He stalked away into the dining hall.

Bram was left with Dallan's words and the list on the wall. Was it messed up? And was Bram really so confident that October Whitmore, a fourth-year wizard-in-training, was enough to stop a loose murderer?

On Tuesday, another student had gone missing overnight. Classes were subdued; even the teachers didn't feel like talking very much.

Bram headed straight to the library after classes ended and used the time until book club to start his paper for Star Gazing. He was halfway through the third page when he finally looked up from his schoolwork to see what time it was.

4:25 p.m.

Dallan had shown up for the first book club even later than that, but this time his lateness sent a jolt through Bram. Maybe it was three and a half years of Fortune Telling classes, or maybe it was the fact that a serial murderer was kidnapping his classmates, but Bram had a sensation of dread growing in the pit of his stomach.

He tossed his schoolwork haphazardly into his bag and hurried from the library. He headed up the front staircase toward the fourth floor where the fourth-year dormitories were, glancing into classrooms as he passed.

Bram didn't know which hall Dallan's dormitory was on, so he wandered slowly down each, checking the names on the doors. He was halfway down the third hallway when a door on his left swung open and nearly smacked him in the face. It was Dallan, looking surprised to see him there.

"You're late," Bram said, blushing and shuffling his bookbag. "I was worried you'd..." He shook his head, not finishing that thought.

He noticed then that Dallan didn't have his books or schoolwork. He wasn't wearing his Crimsonwood robes, and his sleeves were rolled up to his elbows. He had his wand (walnut and obsidian) in his hand.

"Are you going somewhere?"

Dallan closed the door of his dormitory and locked it with a wave of his wand. "I'm going to save the missing students," he said when he turned back around. He started down the hallway.

Bram followed, surprised someone shorter than him could walk so fast. "What are you talking about?"

"October and Marigold went to find the Darkmaster," Dallan said over his shoulder. "They left sometime after lunch." He was shaking his head disapprovingly. "They don't even care about the missing students."

"I don't understand." Bram caught up to Dallan and grabbed his shoulder, pulling them to a stop. "Why you? Why not just wait until October deals with the Darkmaster?" He was worried, and he couldn't tell if he was more concerned about October facing off against a known murderer or Dallan's safety. "Is this something about being his rival?"

"No," Dallan scowled, then met Bram's gaze with a determined expression. "October's only going because he thinks that's what heroes do. Because that's what the Chosen One would do." He shook his wand at Bram. "He doesn't actually care about those missing kids. I'll save them. I'll show you."

Bram felt like he'd lost an argument he didn't even realize he'd been having. "D—do you even know where they are?" he asked.

"October and Marigold were looking around the dungeons yesterday. I think they found something in the old locker rooms." The look of determination

247

hadn't left his face. "They can deal with the Darkmaster. I'll just find the missing students and bring them back."

Bram closed his eyes for a second. He felt like there was something he was supposed to say to make Dallan give up on his plan, but he couldn't find the words. "This is a bad idea," he finally said, opening his eyes, but Dallan was already gone.

Bram didn't sleep.

Neither Dallan nor the others had returned by dinner, and overnight he had no way of knowing if they'd made it back safely or not. He tried reading from *Life Without Duty*, but every time he heard a sound in the hall, he went to his door and peeked out.

As soon as light started creeping through the window, he jumped up and threw on his robes.

He was going to grab a seat at a table near the entrance of the dining hall and catch Dallan when he came down for breakfast. Bram would be overcome with relief to see everyone safe, and Dallan would be flattered that he was so concerned.

Bram left his room without remembering to lock it and hurried down the hall. He could hear his neighbors' morning alarms starting to go off. He turned and pounded his way down the stairs to the entrance hall.

He nearly ran right past it, but something caught his eye, and Bram jerked to a halt.

The announcement on the wall that mentioned the curfew and listed the missing students had gotten longer. There were two third years and one sixth year who had also gone missing, but it was the three bottom names that caught Bram's attention.

October Whitmore
Marigold Moonfall
Dallan Shadowend

Bram felt like his intestines had turned to ice. *They hadn't made it back.* Either Dallan hadn't found anyone yet or the Darkmaster had taken all three of them hostage like the other students.

He turned away from the bulletin board without looking where he was going and nearly ran right into someone.

"Excuse me," he uttered, then saw who it was.

Headmaster Cromwell was wearing his traveling cloak (well known for its embroidered toads along the hems). He was tall and willowy, appearing as though a good wind might send him flying away. He had a long, red beard shot with streaks of gray. He glanced at Bram only briefly, then hurried into the dining hall without a word.

Bram didn't linger either. He took the stairs two at a time, pausing on the landing to pull his wand from his pocket. It was four more flights down to the dungeons, and down two halls to the right to the locker rooms.

The school had supposedly once had a series of subterranean cave-lakes that were used for some classes and competitive sports. As frightening as falling off a pegasus sounded, the student body as a whole liked cave swimming even less, and over time the subsurface sports went to the wayside.

Which meant the dungeon locker rooms did as well.

Bram paused at the door to catch his breath. When he pushed it open, it made a terrible *screeeeech*. Instead of lights in the ceiling, the locker room had old-timey torches on the wall, all of which were lit. It was eerie, but probably just a lingering old spell that prevented them from ever going out.

The lockers that lined the walls were all made from what was probably once beautiful dark wood, each about six feet tall and maybe two feet wide. Unlike the torches, they were clearly not charmed, because they were in a terrible state of disrepair. Over half the doors had fallen off.

With his wand held aloft in a defensive pose, Bram made his way slowly through the room. He passed all the lockers without seeing a thing out of the ordinary. At the end of the room, there was a small hallway to the right. He inched his way down the hall.

The torches were a little dimmer here, casting long shadows between the shower stalls. He crept past each one, certain the Darkmaster was going to jump out at any second.

The fourth stall did not have a shower. It ended in a wide, dark hole where a chunk of the wall had swung open.

Bram swore under his breath.

He knew it would be harder if he hesitated.

"*Lucerna*," he whispered. The quartz point at the end of his wand lit up with warm, yellow light. With it held out in front of him, Bram inched into the shower and the gaping dark beyond.

Bram had imagined the epic battle between October Whitmore and the Darkmaster dozens of times. Every time, he had envisioned the Darkmaster hiding in some macabre setting, like an abandoned forest cottage or, yes, even an underused dungeon locker room.

His expectations were consistently being subverted. Less than twenty feet into the creepy hole in the shower wall, Bram turned a corner and found himself in a cozy sitting room. There was a fire in the hearth — presumably also a spell. The walls were almost entirely covered in bookshelves, with hundreds of books with finely bound spines. It was pretty much exactly how Bram had always imagined the teacher's lounge would look: part smoking lounge, part library.

There were no doors out of the room.

Well, his friends weren't here, so there had to be some way to get beyond the teacher's-lounge room. He started looking closer at the bookshelves for clues. Perhaps one of them was a secret doorway.

Bram stopped. There was something strange about the books.

Instead of a title, each book had two words printed down the spine: names. And not just any names. *Hester Hallewell. Trent Jinx. Frewin Riddle.*

Those were all current sixth years.

Bram scrambled down a few more bookcases. He crouched down to read the last few. Sure enough, there next to *Anita White* was a thick, gold book with the words *October Whitmore* stamped in iridescent leaf. He pulled it out and turned it gently over in his hands. Yes, this was exactly how he expected a memoir or history book about October to look. He wondered what was in it, if it was some kind of magical record of October's adventures. Could he perhaps flip to the end and read the part where the hero saved the day and was recognized for what he was: the Chosen One?

He started to flip the book open, but another thought wiggled its way into Bram's mind, and once there, it grew. He looked away from *October Whitmore* and up at the bookshelf in front of him.

Was his own book there?

He put the gold book back without looking to make sure it was in the right spot, scanning the name-titles as he stood. There was *Dallan Shadowend*. It wasn't as hefty as the October book, but it was over an inch wide with a handsome green cover. (Not black? He had definitely expected Dallan's book to be made with a pitch-black fabric the color of his hair.)

He moved to the top of the shelf. *Zohar Alore. Idyora Arick. Oxeor Bickford.*

There.

Bram Blankley.

His hand hovered in the air off its spine. The book was much bigger than he'd expected. He had expected a slim spine with a brief and pleasant but mundane life described within. He hadn't expected a book about as thick as Dallan's, with a cover of soft red leather. His name was pressed into the spine in gold leafing. (This library really thought he was a gold leafing kind of guy?)

The suspense was killing him, so he gingerly slid the book from the shelf. Thank goodness the edges of the pages weren't leafed in gold as well. But he did notice the pages were very thin—there were so many of them—and when he flipped it open to a random page, the font was nearly as small as *Life Without Duty*. What did this book know about his future that he clearly didn't? Was the book aware how mediocre his grades were?

The text was tight and neat, but somehow the words were illegible to him. If he squinted hard at them, he could make a word or two out... *Bram* and *Crimsonwood* and *spell*, but that could be about any part of his Crimsonwood education.

He looked up with a sigh. Should he just flip to the end and squint at that to get a few-word peek into his future?

Before he did, though, another book in the middle of the shelf jumped out at him.

Marigold Moonfall was the biggest book on the shelf. The cover was in a shade of purple almost identical to Marigold's lilac pegasus, and the leafing of the title was practically glowing. It was half-again larger than

October's book, to the point that picking it up would be difficult.

He knew Marigold was probably the smartest wizard in their year, and also a fantastic sparkball player, but what else was transcribed there? A sidekick's view of all of October's accomplishments? If he was being honest with himself, Bram was a little offended that Marigold's book outshone October's. He wasn't sure if he could both hold her book and flip through it, but he *had* to know what was going on in it.

Bram let his own book fall shut and reached up to gently slide it back between its alphabetical neighbors.

There was a sound in the room behind him. He whirled around so quickly he nearly fell over.

Just as he'd slid the *Bram* book back onto the shelf, one of the other bookcases had swung open to reveal a door.

He stood still, trying to connect the dots on what was happening. The room was some kind of puzzle, and visitors to it had to solve it somehow to move on. Picking up one's own book didn't open the door, but somehow, *putting it back* did.

How many people, he wondered, had sat in those chairs, pouring over their own books for hours? Days?

The books and their name-titles were still quite entrancing, but Bram couldn't risk picking one of them up if it meant the door might close. His friends must have found this door and continued on.

So would he.

The next few rooms were not as comfortable, nor as perplexing. It seemed not all of the puzzle-rooms reset themselves. He passed into a room where a series of gigantic pendulum blades had come down from the ceiling and were now resting, perfectly still, in the center of the room.

In another room, the floor was a checkerboard of large gray, black, and red tiles. One tile just inside the room was sunken slightly. In the wall behind it were a few crossbow bolts.

Bram swallowed his anxiety. As far as he could tell, stepping on certain tiles would set off a trap — perhaps more airborne bolts, perhaps something else.

He had a cheat to get through it, though. Whoever had solved the room before had left little Xs on some of the tiles. Bram put his foot on one, the rest of his body tensed to crouch if necessary. Nothing happened, and the tile held true. He hopped his way slowly across the room, and nothing flew out of thin air to impale him.

The next room was completely empty, with only the door he had come through and another open door on the far side. Whatever had been there before, it wasn't now.

There were several more rooms of simple, sprung traps.

He entered yet another room, and for a second thought it was entirely empty and without an exit or puzzle at all. But he spotted something on the wall opposite from him, and he stopped in his tracks to look at it.

There was a ring of gemstones the size of his palm in a circle. Jasper, Citrine, Amethyst, Tiger's Eye, Quartz, Fluorite, Selenite, and something that was either Tourmaline or Onyx. In the center of the ring of stones were the words:

A treasure beyond;
The greatest of these
Will show you the way.

Bram frowned. It was a riddle, and he was never very good at them. The others must have figured it out, though, because they were nowhere to be seen.

The greatest of these, it read. The puzzle thought one gemstone was greater than the others. Bram lifted up his wand and looked at the Quartz point on it. Well, Quartz was far from the strongest or most powerful wand-stone. It was so average that over half of all wizards had Quartz points on their wands.

He looked at each of the stones, trying to remember the first-year class that had taught him about wands and stones. He couldn't remember anything at all about Jasper or Fluorite, and wasn't Citrine something about cleaning? He had to be remembering incorrectly, but if nothing about the stone stood out in his memory, it couldn't be the greatest, could it?

He remembered Selenite was associated with clarity and peace, which was a good bet for "greatest." Amethyst was for balance, if he remembered correctly. (Marigold's wand had Amethyst on it.) And

Tiger's Eye, Bram knew with absolute certainty, was a symbol for warriors and willpower. (October's wand had a Tiger's Eye.)

The black stone was a puzzle, though. Tourmaline was a protective stone, but if it was Onyx it would be for determination.

It was probably Tiger's Eye, he decided. Not only because that was the shiniest and most exciting of the stones there, but also because Bram was quite certain that was the stone October himself would choose when solving the puzzle.

He nodded to himself. No point agonizing over it further, because he wasn't likely to draw a deeper conclusion, even if given the time. He put his wand in his left hand, raised his right, and crossed the room to press the stone.

About two feet in front of the wall of stones, Bram happened to glance down at the floor. His heart sank in his chest. He hadn't noticed it before, but the floor in front of the wall was a trap door. If he pushed the wrong stone, would it open up? What kind of terrifying trap would he fall into?

Bram tried to stop so he could consider his choice more carefully, but his momentum got the best of him. His left foot caught on the back of his right foot and he fell forward against the wall, his outstretched hand slapping one of the stones.

There was a sound of stone sliding against stone, and Bram instinctively clamped his eyes shut, sure he was about to fall to a terrible fate.

But he didn't fall. When he opened his eyes, a doorway had appeared in the wall to his right. Beyond it was a stone staircase leading down.

He stood back up straight, but paused. His hand was still slapped squarely over the Quartz stone in the wall.

Bram chuckled. "Well, that's a lie," he told the riddle on the wall.

He braced himself for more traps, but none came. It was, by all appearances, a totally normal staircase. It twisted around in a circle like many of the castle staircases, spiraling down several more stories. He held his wand alert in front of him, but the stairs were well lit with more charmed torches. With only a few steps left before it leveled out, Bram paused and peered around the curve.

He heard voices. They were just far enough away that he couldn't make out who it was or what they were saying. He held his breath for a moment, trying to listen harder. Surely if it were the Darkmaster, he'd be able to tell by his nightmarish tenor, right? But the voice didn't sound out of the ordinary. In fact, it sounded... younger?

Bram crept from the stairwell, his eyes darting back and forth for potential threats. The hallway continued straight to what looked like a large, empty cavern, but the voices were coming from a second, smaller hallway immediately to his left.

"Hey, look, it's that one kid!" exclaimed a voice that Bram definitely recognized. At the end of the narrow hall was an iron door with a small, barred window cut in the top. A particular sunny, blond face was staring out at him with exaggerated excitement. "I told you I heard footsteps."

"October," Bram breathed a sigh of relief.

October's face was shoved aside, and another replaced it. (Or at least, part of another face, because Dallan was too short for anything more than his eyes and forehead to appear in the barred window.)

"Bram!" (It was hard to tell what the expression on his face was with only half of it visible.) "Are you okay? How did you find us?"

"I went to the locker room and just kept walking." Bram was shaky with relief to have found him, apparently unharmed. "Are the others in there? Marigold?"

"I'm here," her voice answered, and she came to the door next to Dallan, "but none of the others. The Darkmaster must have them." She tugged at the bars in front of her, too close together for any of them to reach through. "Bram, the door has an advanced lock charm on it from the inside. You should be able to cast a basic unlock spell from your side."

Bram nodded. "Stand back, just in case." They all shuffled out of his sight. He exhaled and held his wand out. (Releasing charms had taken him months to master his second year. He'd only really worked them out after he'd locked himself out of his own dormitory.) "*Potens clavaam!*"

There was a metallic clicking sound, and the door swung open. The three of them burst through the doorway and nearly bowled Bram over.

"I don't know how you survived this far, but excellent job, mate!" October slapped him on the shoulder with a grin.

"I can't believe you came after us," Dallan breathed next to him, the bright expression on his face making Bram wish the others weren't there.

"What was the answer to the riddle?" Marigold asked, interrupting his thoughts.

Bram shook his head and shrugged. "Quartz, apparently, but that doesn't seem right."

But Marigold was nodding. "It's a trick question. The majority of wands are made with Quartz stones. The answer was either a play on words—that the 'greatest' number of wands have that gem—or that the majority is stronger than the rarer stones." She had an expression on her face like she had just learned a valuable lesson, but Bram didn't entirely follow what she was saying.

"He picked Tiger's Eye, didn't he?" Bram asked her, gesturing to October next to them.

She rolled her eyes. "He hit it before I'd even finished reading the riddle a second time."

"I picked Onyx," Dallan admitted.

"I thought that was Tourmaline," Bram told him with a sheepish grin.

October had lost interest in their conversation already and was headed back down the narrow hallway.

"He's right," Bram said, "Let's get out of here before the Darkmaster finds us."

"Right after I find my sword," October said and disappeared down the larger hall. Marigold had already started after him.

"They didn't even come down here to find the Darkmaster," Dallan explained with a scowl as they followed. "They're looking for the sword."

"I will face the Darkmaster, and vanquish him, right after I have the Sword of Flames," October said boldly, bursting into the cavern with his wand held high.

"We could leave them," Dallan suggested, not bothering to lower his voice.

As much as he would rather return to the safety of the upper castle as soon as possible (he was missing class!), Bram shook his head. "We should stay together for now."

The cavern was indeed large, its ceiling as high above them as the room with the stones and riddle. It appeared to be a partially finished cave. The floor was smooth and polished flat, but there were stalactites still hanging down from the ceiling, some of them meeting with a handful of stalagmites at the edges of the cave. There did not appear to be an exit or way in.

"It must be here," October declared, looking around.

"So, if the Darkmaster didn't make all of this, who did?" Bram asked.

"I think it was Khaxium Crimsonwood," Marigold answered, keeping only a few steps from October's side at all times, "to hide the sword and keep it safe for the Chosen One to find."

"Did you hear something?" Dallan interrupted. Bram took an instinctive step closer to him, glancing uneasily toward the walls.

There was definitely a sound, and it was not near the walls. All four of them looked up.

There didn't appear to be anything there. Then the sound came again — the sound of movement. This time it was behind them. The students turned as one.

A shadow had dropped down from the ceiling and landed with a clicking of talons. It had the body of an extraordinarily large bird, but a face that was almost a human woman.

Its eyes were an unnatural glowing green. The blazing green was eerily familiar to Bram, and it took him a long moment to place it.

The centaurs. The creature in front of them had glowing green eyes just like the possessed herd of centaurs that had ravaged the campus their first year.

"It's possessed," Bram whispered, at the same exact moment Marigold said, "It's a harpy."

The harpy's mouth opened in a very un-human way, and a voice echoed out of it without moving, like a speaker amplifier.

"At last I have you, October Whitmore," a deep and legitimately bone-chilling voice boomed from the harpy's open mouth. "Prepare to meet your doom," the Darkmaster exclaimed.

Bram had previously thought that he understood fear. He'd had a series of nightmares as a child about getting lost forever in his Grandma Blankley's very cluttered house, and he definitely knew the blood-curdling terror that came when he sat down to take an exam and realized he hadn't studied nearly enough.

But this was different. He was facing down not only a large, dangerous creature, but also the greatest evil wizard of all time. Everything else in the world fell away, and his body boiled down to just breath and deep, instinctual horror.

Somehow, he'd imagined a battle with the Darkmaster would be dazzling and photogenic. He'd never predicted how much great fear felt almost exactly like an urgent need to vomit.

The harpy's mouth closed for half a second, then reopened, a red glow growing from deep within its throat.

"Harpies can shoot fire!" Marigold cried, already diving away.

Bram would not have moved quickly enough if Dallan hadn't given him a good shove. They both fell to the ground, out of the creature's shot. October, however, had stood his ground and batted the fireball away with a muttered spell and the flick of his wrist.

"Try me, villain!" October yelled at the creature.

"Don't stare!" Dallan cried, tugging Bram to his feet. "Fucking run!"

Bram stayed close behind Dallan, trying to both keep his head down and keep an eye out for oncoming fireballs.

The next few shots of harpy fire had October scrambling for cover, and the beast turned its maw on the other fleeing teenagers.

"Look out!" Marigold's voice tried to warn them.

Bram turned to look, and the fireball was shooting right for him. His schooling took over, and he raised his wand and uttered the first spell that came to mind.

"Recoquo chartorei!"

In a brief flash of white light, the fireball transformed into a golden, bird-shaped paperweight and fell from the air at his feet.

Bram gasped, a bit surprised to still be alive. He scrambled after Dallan, who was watching with an expression of bewildered surprise from a few paces away.

"That was awesome!" Dallan exclaimed.

They took shelter behind a stalagmite and peered around it to see how the others were fairing.

Marigold was also hiding partially behind a stalagmite on the far side of the cavern, but was firing a series of wicked-looking curses back at the harpy, none of which seemed to have any effect.

October was still standing exposed to the harpy's fireballs, but he successfully deflected each and every one, although the averted fireballs were still potent. Bram and Dallan ducked their heads as one flew by and exploded on the wall behind them.

"Look!" Dallan exclaimed, pointing behind October, where there appeared to be something on the wall.

It was a sword, mounted with the blade pointing toward the floor and the hilt toward the ceiling. It looked relatively boring and un-spectacular, except for the very sharp and skinny end of the blade.

"October, look!" Bram yelled at him. "The sword!"

Despite the harpy's ongoing attacks, October turned his back to the Darkmaster's puppet.

"Aha!" he bellowed.

"Watch out!" Marigold cried and lunged from behind her stalagmite to deflect another fireball. It bounced away from her and directly toward where Bram and Dallan were crouched.

The fireball hit the front side of the stalagmite and exploded.

Bram was thrown back against the floor, his ears ringing. He felt a shower of decimated stone bounce off him. It took him a moment to get his wits back, and when he did, he crawled backward until his back hit the wall.

The harpy had turned toward the two of them.

"I shall destroy your weak friends first," the Darkmaster exclaimed and started to cackle a laugh, but the harpy's mouth closed again, and the sound cut off. When the mouth opened again, it was glowing with growing fire.

"Get the sword!" Dallan cried.

"I'm trying!" October called back from across the room. He was grabbing the hilt of the sword and trying to tug it down off the wall, but it wasn't budging.

The harpy made a hacking sound, and another fireball flew from its mouth, aimed to kill.

"*Recoquo chartorei!*" Bram yelled a second time, then threw his arms over his face to keep from being bludgeoned by a glass and silver paperweight in the shape of a rainbow.

The harpy was still facing them, taking a labored step closer and preparing to shoot another fireball.

"Help!" Bram cried.

"It won't come loose!" October was still tugging at the sword, pushing against the wall with one foot for leverage.

"Move!" Marigold exclaimed and shoved him aside.

Her hand closed around the hilt of the sword and it swung away from the wall in a single smooth motion.

"Hey!" she yelled at the harpy, and it rotated to look at her. "Remember me?" She hefted the sword into the air in front of her.

With an audible *woosh,* flames exploded to life up the length of the blade.

"Holy shit," Dallan swore.

"You killed my parents!" Marigold screamed and sliced the Sword of Flames once across the harpy.

The creature's body disintegrated into dust with a final, heart-shattering scream that would probably haunt Bram's nightmares for years.

The scream echoed out, leaving the room filled with silence.

Bram broke it by saying, "This is definitely the coolest thing that's ever happened to me."

They made the trek back up from the cavern in silence. Bram kept glancing pointedly at Dallan, but even the other boy didn't seem to know what to say. Neither October nor Marigold seemed capable of making eye contact with one another.

The dungeons were quiet around them, but they could hear the sound of many footsteps and hushed voices upstairs in the entrance hall. Bram took the lead up the stairs, a part of him furtively hoping they hadn't missed lunch because he was ravenous.

There were students exiting the dining hall and hurrying up different staircases toward their next classes. They all seemed to be in groups with their heads kept low. They didn't know yet that the Darkmaster's presence in the school had been removed.

When Bram reached the top of the stairs to the entrance hall, no one noticed or batted an eye. When the others came up behind him, though, every student within eyeshot seemed to notice all at once and turned to stare (some students on an upper staircase even cheered).

In much less time than it could have possibly taken for word to spread, Headmaster Cromwell strode purposely toward them between the gawking students.

"October, thank the stars you are safe!" The Headmaster took October affectionately by the shoulders, but stopped shy of embracing him. "I knew you would figure out how to break free from the Darkmaster." For the first time, Headmaster Cromwell noticed the other three were also there, looking a little dusty and singed. "And you saved your classmates. Good boy."

"And the other missing students?" Dallan asked, glowering at the Headmaster from beneath his dark hair.

"Have already been located," Cromwell answered, barely sparing Dallan a glance before turning back to October. "They were cursed, but they will recover."

The Headmaster paused meaningfully. "Tell me, October, did you do it? Did you find the Sword of Flames?"

October met Cromwell's eyes with an expression of pained admiration.

For half a second, Bram wondered if October would lie. This was his mentor, after all—the Headmaster who had tutored him personally and bent all the rules for him.

"No, sir," October admitted. He stepped back and turned so that Marigold was no longer hidden behind him. She still had her wand out in one hand and the Sword of Flames (not lit) in the other. "Headmaster Cromwell, Marigold found the sword. *She* is the Chosen One."

The Headmaster didn't reply — just gaped in shock.

"Don't worry, though," October went on, putting his hand on Marigold's shoulder. "She's already a formidable warrior, and she will surely be the greatest wizard of our age."

Marigold teared up at his praise and nearly stabbed October when she went to hug him with the sword still clutched in her hand.

"Do you think this means we'll get to have a sword fighting elective next year?" Bram asked Dallan, letting the excitement continue without them.

Dallan turned his full attention to him, and a smile tugged at his lips. He crossed his arms across his chest. "I bet you feel pretty embarrassed about all that 'categories' bullshit. Especially after all this hero stuff you've been doing today."

Bram opened his mouth to defend his theory, but stopped. In the first puzzle-room, his book had been the same size as Dallan's. (Marigold's massive tome now made a lot more sense.) Maybe he wasn't such a background character after all.

"I think the biggest thing I learned today," he told him, "is that I need to study a lot more."

Dallan laughed, and the sound brought a warmth to Bram's cheeks.

He turned to sneak into the dining hall to see if there was any lunch left to be had, but Dallan caught his hand and stopped him.

"Hey," Dallan said, "since we both missed book club yesterday, we should probably reschedule for this afternoon."

Bram paused, the expression on Dallan's face making it hard for him to formulate a response.

"Friends!" October interrupted with a bellow. "Come celebrate with us!" He and Marigold were beckoning for the two of them to join them.

Bram glanced from the two heroes to the boy at his side and smiled. "Sorry, October. We've got a book club thing."

Boys, Book Clubs, and Other Bad Ideas

by Maria Berejan

The gates to the Afterlife Library towered before Paige, more darkly imposing than usual. In the three years she'd worked there, she'd never been late, and her job wasn't one that lent itself particularly well to being late to, but time wasn't on Paige's side this morning.

The sentry—a gray hawk of a woman with a permanent grimace affixed on her face—scowled at Paige with beady eyes and tapped her wristwatch slowly as Paige hurried past. Paige scowled, checking the time; she wasn't late *yet*. A few seconds here or there wouldn't end the bloody world, Paige thought darkly, though it would perhaps mark the end of Paige's honor; after the countless[1] applications it had taken to secure this position, she'd vowed to be the best damn worker the Library had ever seen. With a huff, she upped her speed from mercenary march to just light of jogging and kept her head bowed, hoping nobody would notice. She was almost there; she could spy the dim outline of her desk through her veiled lashes, the small wooden name card in one corner pronouncing her role: *Paige Vanth, Death Day Coordinator.*

---

[1] In fact, Paige knew exactly how many applications she'd sent: 632. The minutes Paige had spent agonizing over each one after it was sent: countless. Paige's level of satisfaction at finally procuring a role, introductory as it was: boundless.

Her coworkers were just starting to take their seats now, and as she stepped into the room, she breathed a quick sigh of relief; she was right on time.

Before her thought even finished forming, her body collided with something solid from the side, and she stumbled, limbs flailing, barely catching herself on the corner of her desk. Her assailant was not as lucky, collapsing to the floor, followed closely by an impossibly large stack of books.

"Sorry, I—" Paige's voice shriveled in her throat as she saw who she'd run into. Flowing locks as dark as cooled lava rock, eyes as red as the sun setting on the horizon, tall and lean as a willow branch and strong as heavy summer wine.[2] Paige internally groaned, already feeling her ears flood with warmth—of course it had to be *him*. In her years of fantasizing, she'd somehow neglected to imagine meeting her crush for the first time with her legs sprawled against his on the marble tile.

"Hard to see past these bloody things," Luciferus groaned as he pulled himself up. "I told those damn gremlins they were piling them on too high."

"No, really. My fault," Paige said, her voice coming out slightly squeaky to her ears. She tried valiantly to clear the echoes of his husky voice from her mind, though they lingered. In an effort to appear helpful, she reached for the closest book and swallowed a gasp when she realized it was a Life Tome. Three years of working here and yet this was the first time she was

---

[2] This is what we call "an extreme case of rose-tinted glasses."

seeing one up close. She resisted the temptation to flick it open; there were more important matters at hand right now.[3] "I'll help clean up. I'm sor —"

"It's ok, really." Luciferus surveyed the mess before him and sighed before fervently stacking the books back up. He reached for her hand — or rather, the book in her hand — and seemed to think better of it. "Actually, would you mind helping me deliver these? I fear if I stack them all up again, I'm tempting fate for another failure." He flashed a wry smile, and Paige's heart did a painful pitter-patter.

"Um," she said, sparing a glance at the clock just as a hefty stack of tomes got deposited in her hands. "I guess —"

"Great. Thanks for this. Just follow me, ok? Keep up." Luciferus said, hefting his own pile up and setting a brisk pace across the room, leaving Paige blinking at his diminishing form. Paige huffed and jogged behind him, barely dodging desks and coworkers as she struggled to catch up.

The arched entrance to the Deceased Division dawned on them, and as they moved closer Paige got a glimpse of the maze of bookshelves beyond. They seemed endless, and for all she knew they very well could be; only Elder Librarians and Deaths were permitted to step foot inside and care for the life stories of the deceased. The temperature plummeted as she passed the dark stone, cold as a cave.

"Delivery." Luciferus' drawl sounded from ahead,

---

[3] Namely, regulating her blood pressure.

and Paige turned her eyes forward to where two librarians scowled at them over oval glasses. Luciferus was already nudging his pile of books onto the desk, his back to her.

She followed his lead, carefully depositing her stack in front of the waiting librarian, and then took a step back, surreptitiously stretching her wrists and regulating her breath. She had no desire to seem weak in front of strangers, but those books were *heavy*. She glanced at Luciferus, who seemed deeply engrossed in conversation with one of the librarians, and frowned; a thank you was probably too much to hope for. She squashed her disappointment and turned to leave.

"Hey—wait." She looked up to see Luciferus matching his stride to hers and she almost faltered.

"Look, sorry for being a bit short back there. Those ladies get awfully cross if they're left without books to sort for too long," he said, half a smile crossing his face. "Thanks for your help, though. You're Paige, right?" he said, and at that Paige did trip.

She righted herself quickly and continued walking, hoped he hadn't noticed.[4] *He knew her name. Oh, Satan. Pull it together, Paige. You've got a PhD, for fuck's sake. You can talk to a boy.* A nugget of hope lodged itself in her throat.

She closed her eyes for a second, pulling in a deep breath, and then, with squared shoulders, she turned a bright smile in Luciferus' direction, noting his

---

[4] He had.

expression seconds later. *Too bright; dial it back.*

"Yeah. How'd you know?" she asked.

He chuckled. "You've only been working here, what, two years now?" *Three,* she mentally corrected, but what did that matter right now? *He knew her name.* "Of course I know your name, though I guess I've never introduced myself before. I'm—"

"Luciferus." Paige said, and then clamped her mouth shut.[5]

"Right." Luciferus smiled. "Listen, sorry, I've got to go... Death doesn't wait, and I've more Life Tomes to file. But"—he paused, giving Paige a long look that left her feeling naked and short of breath—"well, would you want to have a drink sometime?"

"A drink," Paige parroted, her brain working overtime to decipher this phrase.

"Yeah, as a thank you. With me. Or with some buddies, if you'd rather?"

"No. I mean yes! Yeah, of course. Drinks sound great. With you," Paige babbled.

"Great—tonight then. Six? Meet out front," Luciferus said with a grin, before peeling off to the left. "See you then, Paige."

"Right. See you," Paige said, watching his form retreat.

She looked around, feeling as if she were the center of attention,[6] and surreptitiously sat down at her desk

---

[5] To be fair, everyone knew of Luciferus, the youngest in a long line of Lucifers. This one, it seemed, had only inherited part of the fiendishness, but 100% of the charm.

[6] She was far from it, as usual.

and set her bag by her feet. Her eyes stared at the small stack of Death Agendas before her, but her mind danced worlds away. She was having drinks *tonight* with Luciferus. Maybe there was something to dream about after all. With one last glance toward where Luciferus had disappeared, she wistfully sighed and set to work.

On a normal day, she quite liked her job.[7] Sure, it could be mindless and dull at times, but there was a certain calm she enjoyed about the monotony of checking dates and filling calendars. She took her job seriously, even though one didn't exactly need a PhD to do it.

The hours passed in a blur that Paige couldn't rightly describe if asked, and by six she was itching to get out. She sprang up as soon as the clock struck six and, only slightly breathless, she met up with Luciferus in front of the Library.

"Hey! Ready to go?" he asked, smiling up at her from the bottom steps, and she couldn't help but smile back.

"Yes, let's do this," she nodded, hoping she didn't sound too eager, but eager enough. She was more than ready.

---

[7] As a Death Day Coordinator, Paige had the not-very-prestigious-but-incredibly-important responsibility of taking her portion of the names of those dying the following day (total:150,000, +/- 10,000) and dividing them amongst the Deaths. She liked to coordinate the death lists by each Death's particular death-type preference, when possible, and always attempted to add in a bit of randomness to the locations for good measure and a change of scenery.

The next morning, bleary-eyed and barely awake, Paige stumbled into work, aching in places she never thought she could ache and with a headache that rivaled those only her Great Aunt Mary could bring about. The night before was a blur of good wine and — after a few goblets — great conversation that she hadn't wanted to end; it showed clearly in her baggy eyes and throbbing everything.

She sat down in her chair, stifling a groan at the sudden reverse vertigo she felt — wasn't that supposed to be when you got up too fast, not when you sat down too heavily? — and discreetly opened her satchel, rooting around for water or pain potions hidden away in the corners. Her hand came back empty, and she sighed, righting herself where she sat. As she pulled her chair in, she stubbed her foot on the corner of something beneath her desk.

She cursed and stiffly bent down, squinting her eyes to see what she'd hit. Sitting there innocently and inexplicably on the floor was a thin — but apparently very pointy — Life Tome.

She stared at it, trying to get her sluggish brain to compute where it could have come from; it stared back, offering no answers. She reached forward and picked it up.

"Hey, Paige!" Luciferus' dulcet tones startled her once more, and she froze, hoping that if she didn't move, she wouldn't do anything too embarrassing.

"Hey," she said, trying to minimize saying words so her brain wouldn't explode, but still hoping to come off as cool, nonchalant, entirely approachable, and not at all weird. She shoved the Tome in her satchel before he could see.

"That was fun last night, eh?" Luciferus said, all charm and crisp, cool voice. Nobody should have a voice like that when fighting a massive hangover, and Paige couldn't comprehend a universe in which anyone that drank the volume of wine he'd drunk last night did not have the monster of all hangovers right now. Thoughts of last night had made her feel better, but watching Luciferus in all his unhungover perfection made her feel so much worse.

"Yeah, that was incredibly fun. Thanks for inviting me," Paige said. Fun? What kind of librarian couldn't think of a better word than *fun*?

"Of course! I've been meaning to for a while now," Luciferus said, causing Paige to immediately deploy regulatory anti-short-circuit elements[8] to her brain. "Anyway, we should definitely do that again! Tomorrow night, maybe?"

"Yeah, absolutely. Tomorrow. Sounds grand," she said. Who says grand nowadays beside her Great Aunt Mary?[9] Paige mentally slapped herself.

"Grand," Luciferus said back. "I like it." He grinned, and Paige added "grand" to the list of her all-time favorite words to date.

---

[8] They consisted of the following: *Does not compute; do not dwell on it.*

[9] In fact, not even Great Aunt Mary, who had given it up recently with the second coming of "swell."

The clock chimed, startling them both to reality.

"Work beckons. I'll catch you later," Luciferus said, giving Paige a playful salute, and headed off. Paige sighed, taking a moment to get her thoughts in line and her breathing restarted, and then she set her satchel at her feet and got to work.

By the end of the night, her headache had mostly dissipated, though the aches in her body had gotten worse. She sat up straight, stretching her arms over her shoulders, and heard a distinctive pop before a small amount of relief flooded her.

She looked around, but the desks around hers were empty; she must have been so engrossed that she had missed Luciferus and the rest leaving for the day. Ah, well, it was likely for the best. She figured she had hit her quota of sober conversation without serious social blunders; any longer would be pushing it.

She filed the Death Agendas for tomorrow, passed on her list of names to the Deceased Division so they could keep track of the movement of Tomes, and then headed home. As soon as she got through her front door, she shed her coat, put the kettle on, and went to draw a bath with rose-scented bath salts.

Within moments her bath was almost overflowing, errant steam engulfing her whole bathroom and making it feel like she was stepping foot directly from some nondescript winter residency into the humid embrace of the Amazons. She shimmied out of her toga and giddily went to collect her large mug and, finally, her guiltiest pleasure — the latest installment in a series of fantasy books[10] by her favorite author, P.D. Witte.[11] Yet when she reached into her satchel, what met her hands first was not the familiar feel of the soft paperback she was currently reading, but instead the sharp, pointy corner of something jabbing her directly in the thumb.

"What the—?" She opened her bag, peered inside, and stopped short when she saw the Life Tome on top.

Her brain rewound through the events of the day, and with the last few cognizant brain cells she had left, she remembered sneakily depositing it there while the majority of her being was focused on interacting with social cues from the hot demon before her. Damn social cues always got her in trouble, and this time she was in deep. She wasn't supposed to bring these home. Hell, she wasn't even technically supposed to see them up close; she just dealt with the death days, not the life stories.

She couldn't believe she'd forgotten about it. She frowned, setting it aside, and rooted back in her bag for her book, but paused. It wasn't every day she had this kind of access; she may likely never see another Life Tome up close in her life.

The nagging part of her brain that sounded

---

[10] Fantasy books, while a guilty pleasure for many in general, are guilty for Paige in particular because demons do not write books beyond those needed for lecture and life, and thus do not find purpose in anything written by humans. Paige's mother would *not* be proud.

[11] This particular copy was well-thumbed-through; Paige liked to think that through some magical force of nature, every reread would bring P.D. Witte closer to finally releasing the next novel. Alas, so far it had proved fruitless, but Paige was persistent.

suspiciously like her mother insisted she leave it be. She nodded to herself even as she picked up the Tome, using one long finger to flip through the pages; they were sturdy enough to withstand moisture. Life Tomes were built for endurance.

Her mother's voice screeched in her head, and she took a deep swallow of burning tea to drown her out. Book in one hand and mug in the other, she stepped forth into the sweet embrace of rose-scented heat before she could rethink her decision, and finally, after sinking almost nose-deep into the steaming hot water, she sighed deeply and relaxed. Satan, but this felt good. She needed to remember to take baths more often; they were better than sex.[12]

She took a deep gulp of her masqueraded brandy and finally turned her attention to the Life Tome. She studied it, but it looked like any other leatherbound book, though it felt solid and deceptively heavy in her hands. She flipped it over and inspected its spine. It simply stated, "Peter Dewett #5271."

"Well, alright then, Peter Dewett the 5271st. Let's find out your life story," Paige said, and flipped the book open, but then paused. "Just so you know," she whispered to the book, "you're my first. And I'll treat you with respect."

Then the page flipped, and the story began.

---

[12] Paige had never had sex, but she'd read enough to be confident in her estimates.

Peter Dewett lived a relatively unremarkable life, but it was exceptionally remarkable in all ways to Paige, for it was the first human life she'd ever read about. It was funny, she realized, that she spent her whole day scheduling human deaths, and yet she knew next to nothing about what they did and how they lived.

The Life Tome was an incomplete story; it did not portray the day to day, but rather the most singularly spectacular moments of Peter Dewett's life — the moments that defined the person he was. Paige read about his birth, his first cold that forever introduced an aversion to cough syrup, his first playground bully, the break in his finger that stopped dreaded piano lessons but also gave him a fear of heights. The first time he won a contest; the first time he lost a friend. Childhood pets. The book that made him love reading. The death of his brother, and the resulting emotional decline of his parents. The first love of his life, and then the second. The first story he published. The many rejections he faced.

The more she read, the more she had to continue; the life of Peter Dewett grasped her interest with talons so deep she could not pry herself away.

She resurfaced hours later to discover she'd been drinking air out of her mug and her bath had turned icy around her. She put the book down long enough to rinse off the soap suds that had coated and condensed on her body, and then she dragged herself out, still dripping; hastily wrapped herself in a towel; and settled into the nearest chaise to continue reading.

In the recesses of her mind, Paige heard a distant thud, followed by a jabbing pain in her foot. She squinted salt-crusted eyes and groped around her, disoriented for a moment. Her hands touched threaded towel, remnants of damp still around the edges, and her foot met with cool, rigid leather. *The Tome.*

Paige groaned, her muscles stiff and uncooperative. She must have fallen asleep while reading.[13] She reached to the floor, collected the precious book, and sighed in relief at the sight of pristine pages, unbent from her carelessness. Yet when she flipped it around, she paused; the book had fallen open near the end, and rather than writing on the page, there was a portrait.

Paige studied the features, tracing them with a long finger. Peter did not look like how she'd pictured him, yet as she gazed upon him, she felt a familiarity in his features. This was Peter Dewett; it suited him. She found the spot she last remembered reading and slowly flipped through the rest; she yearned to continue.

And then she saw it. Tucked in the midst of a paragraph surrounded by irrelevance was a name that meant a great deal to Paige: P.D. Witte — her favorite author.

---

[13] This was, indeed, a common occurrence for Paige, though usually it was done in the comfort of her blanketed bed, where no books came to harm.

Paige stared at the name and then frantically at the words around it, trying to find meaning in what she was reading. There it was, in black and white: *"Peter Dewett at age 25 begins writing under the alias of P.D. Witte."*

Paige stared at the text, her thoughts storming. Could it be? If this was really him, then this Tome was her holy grail. She could read about all the books he had yet to publish and know when they would come. She could —

Her alarm went off, a persistently grumpy foghorn from the other end of the room, startling her from her thoughts. She went to turn it off, wanting nothing more than to return to the book and devour it, but she stopped short. No, she had to get to work. Her conviction stood; she had never been late, and she wasn't about to start now, not even for this.

She got dressed quickly and slipped the Tome deep into her satchel, making sure it was well covered and secure. Beside it, Witte's fantasy book was tucked in, and for a moment she stared, overcome by the thought that she was reading the intimate details of the life of its author. Surely a Life Tome had never touched covers with anything its subject had created before. Paige felt a surreal giddiness at the sight. She shook her head, closed her bag tight, and marched out of her home. It was time to get to work.

Paige buried herself in her tasks, stacking Death

Agendas high as she filled in names on each page, working her way down the list of deaths for tomorrow. Periodically the Agendas disappeared, carted off by assistants or Deaths, but she didn't stop to notice. She had to focus; otherwise, her mind soared with impatience. She was acutely aware of each second that brought her closer to being able to read more of Peter Dewett's life.

She crossed another name off the master list after writing it into the appropriate Death Agenda and unfurled more of the scroll. One hundred fifty thousand deaths per day made for a very hefty list to get through, but she was making good progress. She skimmed down the next section and stopped short. The name that had engulfed her thoughts stared back at her, the black ink looking particularly sinister on the weathered, yellow parchment.

Calm down, Paige. She consoled herself rationally, even as her breaths turned shallow and her vision hazy. *It could be another Peter Dewett. After all, there're at least 5270 others. Doesn't mean it's yours.* She traced the line to its end, taking in the suddenly foreign-looking squiggles that clearly pronounced #5271. *Fuck.*

She had to get out of here. She had to check. She uncurled her hand from its death grip on the parchment and grabbed her satchel, making a beeline for the bathrooms. She barricaded herself in a corner stall, shuffling about to make noise for the attendant and cover up the crinkle of pages as she carefully extracted the Life Tome and flipped to the end. Her eyes dashed across lines, word after word, until she saw it—death date: tomorrow.

She stared, feeling as if her limbs had turned to stone even as her head flushed with uncomfortable heat. She stifled a sob.

"Everything ok?" she heard the attendant call out. Paige gave a noncommittal groan and flushed, hoping the attendant would take the hint. A few short hours ago she didn't even know of the existence of Peter Dewett, but now it was a name sure to plague her for the rest of her life. She'd never met him and likely never would, but her every thought obsessed about him just as she'd been obsessing about P.D. Witte until now. And if he died right now—Paige's heart stalled at the thought—he'd never finish his next book!

Paige scratched the tears out of her eyes and squared her shoulders; she had no idea what she could do, but it was clear she had to do *something*.

Think, Paige, think! There had to be an option, a way to stall this somehow. She could scratch the name off of the list and not put it into the Death Agendas—but her list was generated from the Book of Souls itself.[14] If anyone checked—and they would, probably within the week, to make sure the Life Tome had been correctly moved from the Living Section to the Deceased Division—they would no doubt follow the irregularity back to her. At best, she'd plead innocent and never get a promotion again; at worst, she'd be

---

[14] A carefully curated master record of every life and death there had ever been and ever would be. Nobody really knew how it worked, but it did.

sacked on the spot.[15]

Could she simply erase him from existence? She had the Tome. The only records were the Book of Souls and any inventory lists from the Living Section. Even as she thought it, she knew she couldn't. Life and death were precious transactions; nobody was meant to live forever. Paige shuddered to think of what ramifications keeping this Tome to herself might cause.

Her fingers traced the date, feeling the raised ink on the smooth surface of the parchment against her skin. She couldn't make Peter live forever, but maybe…maybe she could extend his life? Simply push out his death, and give them both just a bit more time.

Surreptitiously she pulled her satchel close, shuffling through its contents while letting out a few coughs for the sake of the attendant. She encountered a myriad of pens, a tin of rouge, and some napkins, as well as her lunch of pomegranate and citrus salad. She took a pen and contemplated the rest, none of which were particularly useful,[16] but they'd have to do.

She carefully selected a pristine lemon slice and put the rest away, then took a deep breath. Was she really going to do this? She wasn't sure how it would affect Peter — or if it would have any effect at all. It was a big risk to take. She gnawed on her lip, uncertainty weighing like a boulder in her stomach. But she had no other choice; she either had to try or she had to let

---

[15] The latter was far more likely than the former. Paige attempted to ignore this fact.

[16] Demons were not fond of Wite-Out, sadly.

Peter die. And if she tried, she had to really *try*.

Paige didn't make a habit of defacing books often, but she'd learned a few tricks while pursuing her PhD[17] at the illustrious Redwood Academy of Bibliothecography.[18] She dribbled a single drop of lemon juice on her finger and swiped it across the date, careful to rub only on the ink. If she let it sit too long, it could corrode the parchment underneath. She used a clean finger to brush at the ink lightly until it began giving way. She took a few deep breaths and blew on the page, making sure it was dry, before picking up her pen. Yet just as she put nib to parchment, the letters came back, looking as if they'd never left, and very clearly spelling the same date once more: tomorrow.

Defeated, Paige sank back, head in hands. Clearly, undoing the death date from the Life Tome itself wasn't an option. Likely it pulled the data directly from the Book of Souls through whatever magic orchestrated everything. That left one option, then: she had to go to the source.

She shivered, the thought of touching the Book of Souls — never mind altering it — sending a cold sweat down her back. Satan forgive her, she was about to break every rule that librarians held sacred. She took a deep, shuddering breath and exhaled, thinking through the options one last time but coming up

---

[17] Namely, how to erase ink with just about anything. You know. Just in case.

[18] So named for all the red wood used in its construction. Demons were not the most imaginative lot.

empty. This was her only choice, and she was already in too deep to stop.

She went to put the Tome back into her satchel, but thought better of it; she might need it close by, and there was no way she was getting close to the Book of Souls with a mammoth bag in hand. She shoved it in the folds of her tunic instead, along with the pen and the bit of lemon, and flushed one more time for good measure. Then, unlocking the stall door, Paige swiped her hands under the running faucet and quickly fled past the concerned attendant. She caught a glance of herself in the mirror and blanched at the pallid complexion she saw, but shook her head and resolutely marched forward, ignoring the acid in her throat.

"Hey, Paige," she heard as she barreled her way down the hallway like a brazen torpedo, and she stopped short just before she ran directly into Luciferus. He placed a hand on her shoulder, steadying her before she took them both down again. "Are we still on for toni—hey, are you okay? You look a little pale," Luciferus said, and by gods she loved his stupid, beautiful face, but could this boy have worse timing if he tried?

"I'm—yea, I'm fine. Uh, just a bit, er, under the weather," she said, brushing his hand off of her shoulder while clutching the Life Tome close to her chest. It looked weird, she realized; he probably thought she was clutching her boob in agony, and her face flushed at the thought, but she couldn't help that. Not now. She just hoped he had a short memory. "I'm sorry, Luciferus, but I've got to go. Urgent, uh, business. Yeah," she said, her voice high-pitched with the strain of lying. She had never been the imaginative type. She wished the ground would open up and swallow her whole, or better yet, swallow him so she could just go on her way, but the ground remained firmly solid, and — Paige glanced at the clock above her — she didn't have *time* for this shit. "Tonight — I'm not sure. Rain check?" she said, already inching past him.

"Yeah, sure, whatever you need," Luciferus said, and that was all the confirmation she had time for.

"Great! Sorry about this. See you later!" Paige garbled out, rushing past him and leaving him to blink at the empty spot she'd just consumed. She felt a twinge of regret, but resolutely squashed it. This boy could wait; she had another one to save.

She stashed her satchel at her desk and picked up the list of names. She peeked around, hoping she hadn't attracted attention.[19] Using every ounce of subtlety her body was capable of, she squirted a bit of lemon juice over the list — just enough to muddle some letters.[20] Then, with list in hand and tunic clenched tight, Paige headed down the hall before she could think better of it.

After a few sharp turns and a jog up a rather imposing staircase, Paige shouldered a heavy wooden door open to a cavernous room, seemingly comprised

---

[19] As usual, she had not.

[20] She made sure to only do the names she'd already documented in Agendas; she had a PhD for a reason.

entirely of towering, maze-like bookshelves and precarious stacks of scrolls. Dim candles illuminated nooks and turns, and various assistants milled to and fro, carting knowledge in every direction. The Book of Souls lay entrenched in the innermost section of this room, Paige knew, studiously looked after by Elder Librarians day and night. She took a deep gulp of air in and exhaled slowly; this would be the tricky part. She straightened her spine, tucked her chin up, and resolutely marched forward.

As Paige drew close, she watched two librarians puttering about near the pedestal that held the Book of Souls. Her fingers twitched nervously as she neared.

"Excuse me," she said, clearing her throat. The closer of the two librarians turned to her, the other glancing their way. "There's been an accident and unfortunately, the list of deaths — " she said, presenting the ruined list forward and hoping she looked appropriately distressed.

"Dear me, you've right mucked it up," the librarian said, the corners of her mouth turned downward as she peered at the smudged ink. "This is for tomorrow?"

Paige nodded, shoulders hunched forward meekly. "I don't suppose I could peek at the Book of Souls to cross-reference some of these?"

The librarian tutted. "You could try, but it'd take too long to get them all righted." She handed the list back to Paige. "Better start. I don't think we've yet sent the copy to the Deceased Division; I'll see if I can track that down for you," she said, wandering off to the left.

One down. Paige headed for the Book of Souls, ever aware of the second librarian's steely gaze on her back. She carefully opened it, flipping pages delicately as she ruminated. There had to be a way —

A crash came from the right, followed by crinkling of parchment, and Paige jumped.

"*Bloody* interns!" the second librarian cursed, her face transforming to a stony mask of wrath. She gave Paige a deep glance, clearly denoting "*stay put and touch nothing*," before descending down the rightmost aisle in sharp, furious strides.

Paige glanced to the left — coast still clear — and lurched forward, hunching over the pages as she hurried to find her target. Finally, there it was: Peter Dewett, 5271, Day of Birth April 24th, 1989, and Day of Death set to tomorrow, 11:37 am. Paige's fingers flew into the folds of her robe, swiping the lemon and then swiping at the line.

Nothing happened.

She swiped harder, her stomach lurching at the thought of her finger going through the page, or of nothing happening and this being for naught. It *couldn't* be. It had to work.

It didn't. Paige stared at the page with dismay. The path to the left was still clear, but not for much longer, she had no doubt. She could hear the second librarian giving the interns hell to the right; mere steps backward and Paige would be clearly visible, attempting to desecrate the Book of Souls. Thoughts of the future of her illustrious career flitted through her mind before catching fire. She was running out of time.

In desperation, Paige grasped her pen and brought it up. She didn't know how the Book of Souls worked—nobody fully did—but if erasing hadn't worked, the only option she had left was to rewrite it herself. Changing 2020 to 2040 couldn't be that hard, surely. Twenty years for a single stroke of a pen?[21] She'd take those odds.

Paige brought the pen down on the paper, feeling like she was drawing a sword on her own neck, and with one quick jerk she drew a single, stubby line.

The pounding of her heart beat an angry rhythm in her skull, and her fingers trembled so much she could hear her nails clattering against the pen. *Breathe. Just breathe,* she reminded herself. That was it; she'd done it—

Except that, as she gulped air and tried not to impersonate a fish, the ink absorbed into the sheet, and the date disappeared.

She stared dumbly at the blank bit of parchment, pen still aloft, wondering what to do. Then, before her eyes, a new date formed, looking for all intents and purposes as if it had always been there.

Three years. She had bought Peter Dewett three more years.

Paige released the breath she hadn't realized she'd been holding. A sudden wave of nausea hit her, followed immediately by lightheadedness. Her limbs

---

[21] A small part of Paige's mind thought eagerly of all the new Witte books she'd get to read. She squashed it; now was *not* the time.

felt like iron, weighing her down into the earth, even as her ears threatened to burn off. She needed to sit. She needed to breathe. She swiped the sweat from her upper lip and hid the pen in her tunic, just as the first librarian rounded the corner to her left.

"Here you go, lassie," she said, handing a fresh scroll to Paige. Paige took it numbly, hoping it didn't slip through her wobbly fingers. "See if you can copy those out, and then pass this list on to the Deceased Division, if you wouldn't mind?"

Paige nodded, flashing a smile in thanks and turning before the librarian could tell it was fake. She fled from the room, letting the thick door close heavily behind her, sealing her from the thought of what she had just done.

Rather than head down the stairs, she took a right, getting lost in the passageways until she found a broom closet she was sure she'd be alone in. Once ensconced within, she carefully pulled the Life Tome out of her tunic, wiping the damp from the cover and turning to the end. Where there had been a Death Day before was now empty space; the story would continue now in real time.

Paige sat there clutching the book to her chest for a good while, until her breathing returned to normal and she felt confident that chances were high she would not burst into tears as soon as she left. She hid the book once more and headed back to work, feeling as if nothing was quite the same anymore.

That night, Paige sat down and read the rest of Peter Dewett's life. She wanted to know exactly who she'd rescued. She read about his work, his life. His first book, and then his second. A few more after that. His moderate rise to recognition. The death of his wife, whom he loved dearly, and his descent into a wretched depression that curdled all creativity. And finally, she read of his ascent, step by step, back to normalcy. Small moments of laughter and hope. Snippets of a creative mind. Community.

A new book idea. A beautiful one — one that many, especially Paige, had waited for. A book that could impact lives. He'd just begun to write it, the glimmer of the story just taking shape.

Paige desperately wanted to read it. If she hadn't prolonged his life, this book would never have been written. Surely three years would give him time to complete it, to add to his legacy in a positive way. Was it so bad, what she had done?

She stared at the Tome for a very long time that night. And she thought.

Three years passed in the span of a few heartbeats.

In the first beat, Paige threw herself into work. Every day, she waited for the call to come — that they'd discovered what she'd done. She was sure to be fired, incarcerated, or perhaps something worse. Paige kept her head down and worked while she waited. Yet the call never came. She exhibited, for all intents and purposes, a remarkable work ethic and the qualities of an exceptional employee. It surprised no one but Paige herself when later that year she got a promotion, and the following year yet another, landing at the rather auspicious position of Curator.[22]

In the second beat, she focused on her budding relationship with Luciferus. As the days passed, she and Luciferus drew close, spending more and more time together, until they were near inseparable. Their habits knit together, as did their thoughts. Things got so serious that one day, Paige brought him over to her parents to formally introduce them. The next day, Luciferus asked Paige to move in with him.[23]

On both accounts, her mother was very pleased.

In the third beat, Paige fell in love. She'd thought she had been in love from the beginning, but as time passed, her feelings intensified. Before had been a giddy approximation of what she felt now. Every morning she woke breathless, staring at the man beside her, a lump in her heart. She went to work and marveled at doing a job she so thoroughly enjoyed.

At the end of the night she wandered the halls, taking her time to lock up. And ever so rarely, on nights when her parents were sure not to call, and Luciferus was out, and the Library was dead silent, a

---

[22] Wherein she worked directly with the Book of Souls and numerous departments to coordinate the daily creation of Birth and Death lists and the general shuffle of Life Tomes from place to place.

[23] She accepted only after figuring out how to hide her fantasy book collection from him. Some things she just wasn't ready to divulge yet.

mere whisper carrying like a windstorm across the marble halls — then, Paige would quietly sneak to the Living Section, heart thundering in her chest, and make her way carefully down the rows until she reached the familiar Tome she was after — Peter Dewett #5271. She had replaced it the morning after she'd changed his Death Date, blaming its discovery sneakily on an intern. Now she'd take it down carefully, caressing it like one does an old friend, and after making sure she was alone, she would sit and catch up on his life. And finally, she would breathe, the guilt harbored in her heart diminishing the smallest bit, while the love she harbored blossomed.

Paige felt like an imposter. She didn't deserve what she had in life, not after what she'd done. She didn't regret her decision — she couldn't — but she knew it hadn't been right. She carried the guilt with her daily. But it would all be over at the end of three years. Peter would publish his book, and then he would die, and the world would be rightened, back to what it had always been meant to be. Just three years.

Yet as time passed, she felt frantic. Her mind lingered on Peter, and she couldn't pull it away. The days trickled by, and with them Paige's guilt grew, even as her willingness to let Peter die withered. She was in love with him, as one loves great characters in books — or perhaps more so, because this book was the greatest book she'd ever read, and this Peter was more than a mere character. She wasn't ready to let go — not yet. She'd thought three years would be enough, but it wasn't. His book wasn't complete.

The week before his second death, Paige lay awake, mind raging war. She shaped each possibility, imagining and obsessing, replaying and viewing the outcomes. She couldn't desecrate the Book of Souls — not again. It went against every moral she held. Yet the thought of letting Peter die froze the blood in her veins. He had more to do; he wasn't done. The book was almost complete, but not quite. If he didn't finish, was the guilt she'd harbored for the last three years worth it? Try as she might, she could not answer.

Two days before Peter Dewett's death, Paige walked into the Afterlife Library with shoulders drooped and shadowed eyes. She climbed up the stairs, pushed the wooden doors open, and walked to the Book of Souls. This time there were no librarians to contend with; she was it. She opened the book, found the name, and traced the line to the Death Date. Then, with a simple flick of her wrist, she crossed it out.

The Book thought and spat out another date. Sixteen months.

Paige breathed a sigh of relief, her eyes heavy and tired. She felt her guilt with every beat of her heart, but she was used to it by now. Sixteen more months, and then he would die, and everything would go back to the way it was meant to be. She could do this. Just sixteen months.

Paige closed the book and walked out of the library early for the first time in her career. She went home, and finally, she slept.

Sixteen months passed as sluggishly as a humid summer breeze barely ruffling the grass. This time, Paige had no doubts; she knew the levels she would stoop to for Peter. She didn't lie to herself any longer.

She knew from the beginning she would not hesitate this time. Still, she waited to see how his life progressed, reading his Tome as often as she could.

Peter finished his book. The day it came out, Paige devoured it, shutting herself in a closet so Luciferus wouldn't see. It was a gem of a book, and Paige spent months thinking about it afterward, quoting little snippets of it in her mind. Peter began work on another book. He was happy again, or beginning to be; he had met someone. He was thriving. He deserved more time.

A month before Peter's Death Day, Luciferus proposed. He caught Paige mid-bite on a honeyed pear salad, and she sputtered.

"Why?" Paige asked before she could stop herself.

"In case you haven't noticed, I kind of love you?" Luciferus replied, eyebrows pinched. One side of his lips quirked up.

Paige stared at this kind, beautiful man before her and paused. "What do you love about me, Luciferus?" she asked, needing to hear it, needing to know. She clutched her fork tight, her fingers already beginning to numb.

"Well" — Luciferus sat up, some underlying current

telling him this was important—"I love a great many things about you, Paige. It would be easier to list the things I *don't* love about you rather than what I do, and those are few. Quite simply, I love your soul. You're beautiful and smart and kind and funny. You're honest and caring. But beyond all that, I discover new things about you every day, Paige, and I love every one of them. I want to keep doing that. I want to know everything about you and weave the rest of my life with yours."

Paige's mouth went dry and bitter despite the honey she'd just consumed. "One day you might not like what you discover," she whispered.

"Like it or not, it will be a part of you." Luciferus shrugged. "And I've become very fond of you. None of us are perfect, Paige," he said, brushing his fingers through her hair. "But I know enough to know I love you, and I want to keep loving you every day for the rest of our lives."

"I see." He didn't know, not at all. He didn't know what she'd done—what she was planning to keep doing. He didn't know that, after four years of giving in to her desires, she had grown used to being selfish.

"Yes," Paige said. "Yes, I want to spend my life with you." Because she did want to. And she hoped, even as her guilt grew, that he would never find out just how selfish she'd been.

The next day, she crossed out Peter's Death Date in the Book of Souls once more. This time, the result came slower.

Five months. Paige swallowed. She felt like the

threads of her life were unspooling; as she deepened one love, she was close to losing another. She'd keep it together, somehow. She'd take it one day at a time. Just five months.

Paige took things one day at a time, until the days ran out.

The ceremony was planned for the 15th of May. Peter Dewett's death was on the same day. It would be fine, Paige told herself, to simply let him die. He'd had his time, as had she. There were other things to focus on now—important things.[24] This couldn't continue.

Luciferus noticed her wan appearance more times than she'd have liked him to. Each time, he offered a supportive embrace and an open ear, but she waved away his concerns. After all, what could Paige tell this man who proved daily he was too good for her? That rather than focusing on the happiness he brought her, she was heartbroken over a death that hadn't even occurred yet? Death was an inevitability of life; there was no point to her sadness, no reason to indulge in it. She told herself this every moment of every day, whispering it in her mind, but still the chasm in her heart deepened.

On the evening of the 13th, she could take it no longer. One more time—that's all. Luciferus deserved

---

[24] Organizing a wedding was no small feat, after all, even when the groom did partake in the planning—and boy did Luciferus partake.

her full attention and happiness, and it was clear she could not deliver it in this state. She would prolong Peter's life one last time—just enough to set right by her life—and then she would let matters unfold as they inevitably would.

It was already late, the evening shadows long erased by the black canvas of night. She tiptoed out of bed, freezing as Luciferus groaned. She waited a few heartbeats, to be certain he was still asleep, before padding down the hall. She slipped on sandals and a shawl, grabbed the Library keys, and stole into the night.

It wasn't hard to get in; the sentries were used to her odd hours, and she'd built a reputation for herself these past few years of being trustworthy and honest.

The Book of Souls waited for her in its usual spot, and Paige went to it as one does to a butcher's block. She brandished her pen, her stomach dropping in disgust even as her body thrummed with adrenaline. Her fingers trembled, and her breath came sharp. She needed this release. *Just one last time*—

She slashed Peter Dewett's Death Date with practiced skill and waited. The ink pooled darkly on the page and slowly seeped into the parchment. The Book thought for an eternity, and finally, it gave its answer.

May 15th.

Paige stared, eyes taking in the letters but not comprehending the meaning. Had she done it wrong?[25] She tried again, pressing firmly on the pen, until the nib creaked and she could see a blot of ink begin to pool. The page consumed the ink like desert does water and spat nothing back. The date remained unchanged.

Paige cast her gaze about, snatching a new pen, and then another,[26] scratching at the page with increasingly frantic movements, but each one proved of no avail. The date would not change.

"Miss Vanth?" she heard, what felt like both a lifetime and an instant later. She turned to the voice with slow, numb movements. The pen was no longer in her hand. Before her stood an intern, looking upon her with confusion. "Miss Vanth, I thought you were out for the week, what with your wedding tomorrow?" He set his satchel down on a nearby chair, and a small puff of dust mushroomed up, glittering in the early morning light. Had she been here for so long?

"I'd just—forgotten something," Paige said, clearing her throat. It felt like she hadn't had a sip of water in a hundred years. She took measured steps toward the door, and then paused. "Do you happen to know who is making the death lists for the day?" she asked, hoping her voice didn't give anything away.

The intern looked up from his satchel. "Oh, needn't worry about that, miss. We finished the whole week's

---

[25] Was there a wrong way to cross something out? A PhD had not prepared Paige for this.

[26] She didn't know why the Library had bright pink pens available, but she tried that one, too.

worth yesterday!" he said brightly. "The Elder Librarians wanted to get on top of them through your absence. We delivered them to the Deaths and everything." His face beamed with pride.

"I see," Paige whispered, and took the last step out of the room. That was it, then. It was done; Peter's death was solidified, and there was nothing more she could do to stop it.

She walked home in a fog, every step taking her deeper into despair. By the time she passed the threshold, her feet could barely support her, and with the next step she collapsed. She placed her cheek onto the cold marble of the floor and wept the tears she'd kept to herself for four and a half years.

"Paige? Paige! Are you hurt?" Luciferus' voice came from above, but Paige didn't have the strength to respond. She felt herself enveloped in warmth, and then she was moving, carried through the air. She felt soft bedding under her hands, soaking up her tears; soft murmurings in her ear; a comforting weight supporting her. She tried to speak, but no words came. Instead, darkness prevailed, and she welcomed it.

She awoke to the smell of rose. A warm mug of tea was held near her nose, Luciferus' hand on the other end.

"Evening, love," Luciferus said. His normally

boisterous voice was subdued, and his eyes were slumbering embers instead of warm fires. The room around them was black with night, their faces illuminated only by the flicker of candlelight. Paige took the cup and sipped, the scalding liquid heating her body back to life.

"Paige, I—"

"I'm sorry," Paige cut him off before he could voice his thought. Whatever it was, she couldn't bear hearing it right now: not endearment she didn't deserve, nor anger she deserved all too well. "I'm so sorry, Luciferus. I didn't mean to worry you."

Luciferus gave her a long look, brushing a lock of her hair back and squeezing her hand. "You've not been yourself for a long time, Paige. Not since—well, the day I asked you to marry me. Are you sur—"

"Yes! Luciferus, I love you. More than anything, I want to spend my life with you. I'm so sorry I gave you any doubt," Paige said, willing him to believe her.

She saw a spark of relief in his eyes, but the hesitation remained. "But?" Luciferus said, voice resigned. Still, his hand remained on hers.

"But..." Paige's voice cracked, and she squeezed his hand back, not willing to let it go. "But there are things you don't know about me, and I fear once you do, things will change." *You'll hate me. Everyone will.* Paige squeezed his hand tighter.

Luciferus was silent for a long time, and Paige dared not look at his face. Then he began to speak. "When I was seven, I was a bully. I bullied a boy so much once that his family moved away. When I was thirteen, I cheated on all my exams. My math professor found out, but because of my family name, I got away with it. At fourteen, I got in a fight and punched a lad in the face; his tooth cut his lip and he had to get stitches. When I was seventeen, I asked out a girl while I was dating her sister. When I was—"

"Stop!" Paige said, baffled. "What are you doing?"

"Showing you that I'm not perfect either. Nobody is. And I've got a graveyard of skeletons in my closet, same as everyone else. I can keep going," Luciferus said, meeting Paige's gaze.

"Some things are worse than others," Paige maintained mulishly.

"Some are," Luciferus agreed, "but it doesn't take a bad person to do a bad thing, Paige. The intent behind an action is as important as the action itself. And even if the intent is bad—who's to say the person is? People change; people learn. Things are not so black-and-white."

Paige wanted to believe him, but she'd learned by now that wants do not often dictate reality. Believing in wants was a dangerous game. "You'll hate me," Paige whispered.

"Try me," Luciferus returned. She heard a bite in his voice.

"I—I can't." Paige said. "I don't want to lose you." Luciferus' mouth twitched.

"Either you trust me and tell me, or you don't and you move forward with life, Paige. You can't just sit here and wallow," Luciferus said.

"But I—"

"Insufferable woman!" Luciferus groaned, head rolling back. "You think *too much* Paige, and for all of your brains, you cannot see what's before you!" Luciferus got up and began to pace, leaving Paige to miss the warmth of his hand. "Do you trust me when I say I love you?" he asked, turning to her.

"Yes, but—"

Luciferus turned away.

"What do you want from me!" Paige said, scrambling out of bed and turning Luciferus to face her. She was tired of circular conversation and dead ends.

"I want you to *trust* me." Luciferus hissed, eyes narrow on hers.

"I do!"

"Clearly." The sarcasm seeped like molasses from his mouth.

"Fine!" Paige rasped. "Let's go." She shoved her feet into sandals and made for the door, snatching a shawl on the way.

"In the middle of the night? Go where?" Luciferus asked, voice warring between petulance and confusion.

"You want to know me—*really* know me?" Paige hissed, eyes bright and voice low. "Well, here's your chance to see all of me, Luciferus." She opened the door wide and pointed him out. "Hurry up. We've got a human to save."

They marched through the dark alleys toward the Library as if fleeing the hounds of hell. Even Luciferus, with his endless length of legs and robust lungs, seemed to falter for breath.

Luciferus had grown silent since Paige had told him what she'd done, but she had no time to dwell on that. The night was not nearly long enough, and Peter would soon die if she wasn't quick. She'd thought about it long and hard, her mind ruminating on all possibilities, but kept coming back to one simple question: What if Peter simply didn't die? What if he lived past the date and time the Book of Souls had chosen for him? It was clear the Book was done negotiating, so what then? She'd learned much of the inner workings of the Library in the past four years. Now, given all she knew of how Death worked, she had come to one simple conclusion: if she could keep Peter alive past his given death, there would be nothing left to decree that he had to die — at least, not today. He'd be free of a predefined life and death.

They entered the Library and Paige bee-lined toward the Deceased Division, spying a librarian near the front. "You there!" she barked, and the librarian jumped. "The master list of deaths for today. I need it now," she said, putting as much importance in her voice as possible. The librarian shrank, turning around and shuffling through scrolls in an attempt to find the right one. Paige tried to ignore the tick of the clock, each second passing a second closer to Peter's demise.[27] "Quickly, please!" she huffed, and the librarian shuffled faster.

"Here, Miss Vanth," the librarian said finally, turning back around and presenting Paige with a scroll. Paige took it and scanned down the list, finding Peter's name and tracing it to the end. "I need a copy of the Death Agenda for Death #432."

The librarian hesitated, but as Paige opened her mouth to spew forth her argument, Luciferus spoke from behind her. "Miss Bickford, is it? If you could please get the book — I'm afraid it's rather urgent." His soft tone seemed to mollify the librarian into compliance.

Paige looked at Luciferus once the librarian had run away and startled when she met his smoldering, red eyes staring back. She felt her palms get clammy, and she discreetly swiped them on her tunic. She was hesitant to know what he thought of her now.

Before she could speak, the librarian returned, and Paige snatched the Death Agenda out of her hands, flipping through until she found the right page. *Peter Dewett #5271, Date of Death May 15th, 6:32 am. Amsterdam. Run over by a bike.*

Paige looked at the clock; barely an hour left, and she didn't know how long it would take to travel to the human realm. She looked at Luciferus, who was looking at her still. "Come on. We've got to go."

"Hey, wait!" the librarian shouted as Paige rushed past her into the Deceased Division. Beyond the front desk, Paige saw a large stack of Life Tomes, and her

---

[27] It proved quite impossible to ignore.

pace broke as she recognized a familiar spine. She lunged forward, grabbing Peter's Tome without thinking, and then sped up, distantly aware of Luciferus keeping pace behind her.

She'd never been so far into this section of the Library before; the title of "Curator" offered her many privileges, but entrance to the Deceased Division was not one of them. She had no choice now, though; it was simply one more broken rule in a myriad. The Deaths operated from the Deceased Division, so it stood to reason that the entrance to the human realm was somewhere inside.

The temperature plummeted as they went deeper, the Life Tomes here buried deep under layers of darkness and protective dust. Paige's breath rattled harshly in her lungs and exploded out in fog that obscured her sight. Shouts came from behind.

They took a few more steps forward, and then there was no more light. Paige stumbled to a halt. She felt as if her eyes were closed, but they were open as wide as they could be. Luciferus stood just behind her, his heat providing the only solace from the chill that was creeping into her blood.

"I—I think we're lost," Paige whispered, her voice swallowed into the void. She turned her face to and fro as she continued forward, but nothing changed. The shouts came closer.

"This human—Paige, are you sure about this?" Luciferus asked from behind her, voice sounding farther away than she knew he was. "You're risking so much."

"Am I risking you?" Paige asked. She took another step forward into the blackness. She wasn't sure she wanted to know the answer.

"Do you love me?" Luciferus asked, and Paige did not hesitate.

"Absolutely."

"And him?"

Paige sucked in a breath, ignoring the ice in her lungs. "I do, but not in the same way. He's important to me, and his life has shaped mine as much as mine shaped his. I just — I truly don't think his story is over yet, and I need to see it completed in the right way," she said, hoping Luciferus would understand.[28] She wished she could see his eyes, judge his reaction.

She felt Luciferus close in, and his voice came to her ears like a melody in the night. "Just there. Look." Paige felt his fingers on her head, moving her. In the distance was a pinprick of light. "Go. I'll hold them off."

"Luciferus, I—"

"I know. And I don't understand, not fully, but I trust you. And for your passion and idealism, I love you all the more," Luciferus whispered, and Paige felt a flutter of a kiss on her neck. She swallowed the lump in her throat, trying to find her voice, but Luciferus beat her to it. "We'll talk more after — but Satan help you if you're late for our wedding." His voice carried mirth, and Paige's heart swelled.

---

[28] This is a classic example of the lamentable void of empathy between a reader and a non-reader as to how deep feelings for characters that exist mainly on paper can be.

"Go save your human, Paige." Then the warmth disappeared, Luciferus with it.

Paige ran forward, eyes trained on the distant light, ignoring her rasping breath and the freeze of her lungs with each inhale. The light grew nearer, warmer, until suddenly she was there.

She blinked hard, eyes straining even against this dim candlelight, and inspected her surroundings. It was a dark little cave, with tunnel entrances leading every which way. A shadow sat at a desk.

"Destination?" it asked.

"Er, I'm looking for Death 432," Paige said, rather floored.

The shadow looked about as if it were expecting that particular Death to simply appear, but it did not. It turned back to Paige, looking as contrite as a shadow could look.

"Destination?" it asked again, and Paige thought.

"Amsterdam?" she said, hesitantly.

The shadow brightened[29] and got out from behind its desk. "Come, come," it said, shimmering a bit. "This way." It led Paige toward a tunnel near the back. "Through there."

Paige stared into the dark tunnel before her. "Just...through?" She had a feeling she'd failed to conceal the doubt in her voice.

"It helps if you picture where you want to go," the shadow informed her helpfully. It waited.

---

[29] For those who have never seen a shadow brighten, it goes a bit fuzzy around the edges, and sometimes, if it is particularly pleased, iridescent.

"But I've never been there," Paige said. "I don't know how to picture it."

The shadow thought. "Then perhaps you can picture who you want to see?"

An image of Peter formed in her mind, and the tunnel before her suddenly looked more inviting. The shadow glimmered at her side, patient and content. Paige took a step forth, and then another, and was slowly engulfed back into darkness. "How long will it take?" she asked, glancing back, but the entrance was gone now. The picture of Peter still hung in her mind.

Time is running out, Paige. You've made it this far. There's nowhere to go but forward.

And so forward she went.

Paige emerged from a side alley onto a canal. The early morning air was cool on her skin, and the sky shimmered with the earliest rays of dawn light. There was an old church to her left, the clock face on its tower pronouncing 6:24 am.

She looked around, scanning the roads for Peter. Instead, she saw a large, hunched figure shrouded in darkness, scythe glistening above its head. She headed toward it, and as she got near, the world around seemed to quiet.

"Hello," it said, glancing at her as she got close. "Coffee?" The figure shuffled a paperback[30] it had

---

[30] In the darkness, Paige could not make out what it was, but something about it looked oddly familiar.

been reading aside and produced a thermos from the folds of its robes.

"No, thank you," Paige said. "Are you Death 432?"

"Yes," it said, and then took a gulp of coffee. Paige stared at it, suddenly aware that she had no plan for how to proceed. She was not very good without a plan. She felt her hands begin to sweat and her tongue grow clammy. The Life Tome seemed to weigh a thousand pounds, pressed against her chest.

"About Peter Dewett—" she began.

Death 432 seemed to perk up, growing at least a foot taller. "Ah, yes, exciting one, that. Haven't had many deaths by bicycle yet this year, though this is the city for it!" It bent down toward Paige in a conspiratorial stance. "Between you and me, the bicycle is just the catalyst. True cause of death is accidental drowning. Did you know these canals have hundreds of bikes in them? They're a death trap! Peter here is going to fall in, see, and his shoelace is going to get caught on a bike handle. His shoelace!" The Death cackled and seemed to wink at her. "Bloody proud of myself for dreaming up that one. It's the little details, innit?"[31]

"Er, yes, that's rather, uh, imaginative," Paige said, heart pounding. Her mouth was so dry that her tongue was sticking to all sides. Maybe she should have said yes to the coffee. "But the thing is, Peter

---

[31] Death 432 was proud of this death for more than just the little details; it had taken inspiration from the surprisingly unsuspecting deaths that littered Witte's fantasy books. The Death, it seemed, liked irony.

Dewett can't die now."

Death 432 straightened up and took a small book from its pocket. It flipped through the pages for a moment before showing it to Paige. "Begging your pardon, but he's in the book," the Death said. "No mistake. He's dying in" — it glanced up at the clock — "about three minutes."

"Right, yes, except the thing is, it *is* a mistake. He can't die. Not now," Paige said, willing the Death to understand.

The Death had other ideas. It straightened itself out and crossed its arms. "Nah, miss, if it's in the book, it's happening. These names went through about twenty checks on your lot's side. Mistake or no, it's done now. He dies at 6:32 am on the dot, just as it's been written." It took a resolute swig of coffee and then it turned. "Ah, there he is now," it said, and Paige, too, turned and saw Peter Dewett slowly approach them. He was hunched in the morning chill, fruitlessly trying to button his coat without entangling the wire of his overly large headphones. Paige took in the sight of him, heart thumping so loud she could hear nothing else. This was *her Peter*, here, before her very eyes. He was real.

Peter looked up, and Paige's heart nearly stopped, but his eyes looked through hers toward the clock tower.

"He can't see us," Paige said hollowly, and the Death chuckled beside her.

"'Course not. Would give 'em a right fright, wouldn't it?" the Death said. It brought up a hand and swiped at the air, and Paige saw a translucent barrier there. "He'll only see us at the last moment. Well, the scythe at least. I dun' reckon he'll ever see us," the Death said, wrestling its thermos back into its pocket. In the distance, they heard the ring of a bicycle bell, and Paige's stomach sank to the ground.

"What would happen, *hypothetically*, if a human lived past their death time?" Paige attempted to be as nonchalant as she could be.[32]

"*Hypothetically*, that wouldn't happen with me on the job," the Death grumbled.

"But if it did?"

The Death sighed. "A heaping stack of paperwork is what'd happen." The Death looked about as eager at this idea as if it were told to lick a slug. "We'd have to watch that life closely, make sure they don't live for eternity. And, of course, it'd likely cause a domino effect with other Death Dates, so we'd have to fix that. That's what the Book of Souls is *for* — keeping everything tidy. The whole thing'd take ages to muss out." Its voice had a hint of despair at the end.[33]

"So Pe — the human wouldn't die that same day, then." She felt a new surge of confidence.

"Fat chance," the Death snorted. "But this one" — the Death pointed at Peter — "is dying today. In one minute." It nodded resolutely.

Paige watched Peter approach and could bear it no longer. She turned to the Death and prodded it in the

---

[32] Unfortunately, subtlety was not a skill Paige excelled in.

[33] Paige, in contrast, perked up at this. It was better than she'd hoped. Plus, she rather liked paperwork.

chest. "Listen and listen well. I know you've a job to do, but I *will not* let this man die. Not today. You may take him another day. I'll happily do the paperwork," she added helpfully.

The shadows around where the Death's eyes likely were scrunched. "Oh really," it said, elongating the words in one long breath. "Nah, missie, that won't work for me. I've got souls to take, and this here's one of them. I don't mess with divine orders."

"Have you ever thought to try?" Paige said, stalling for time.

"Honestly? No," the Death said, readying its scythe. "I tend to stick within the job parameters." Peter was close now, just a block away.

"Just—look. *Please.*" Paige said, desperation in her voice, and the Death turned toward her. "I'm a Curator at the Library, and, well, I'm no writer[34] like you are, but I read. I read *a lot.*[35] And I know an unfinished story when I see one. Peter Dewett's life is not done. It *can't* be done. Not now. Just give him a bit more time, please," Paige pleaded, and for a moment the Death seemed to wilt and listen. But then the bicycle bell rang out, closer this time, and the Death straightened back into reality.

"Sorry, miss. I sympathize, really, but that decision is above my pay grade," the Death said. Peter was just feet away now, the bicyclist not far behind. "Stand

---

[34] Not a writer, no. Paige was more editor material, it seemed.

[35] The Death, accustomed to the recipients of its written material not being awfully enthused with its work, did not have a particular fondness for readers.

back now. This scythe swings wide."

"And that's all it takes? Just a swipe of the scythe?"

"Yep," the Death said, and brought said scythe up.

"Good. Then without it, Peter can't die," Paige said, and shoved the Death with all her might. Her hands went deep into the folds of the Death's shadow, and for a second Paige despaired they would go all the way through, but then she met resistance.

The Death stumbled off-kilter in surprise, its scythe brandished high.

Peter stepped forward, now within swinging distance.

The bicyclist was close behind, their incessant bell ringing.

Peter, oblivious to all sound but that of his headphones, stepped directly in the bicyclist's way.

And in that moment, Paige placed both hands on the scythe and pulled.

Peter felt the impact of the bike on his right, its handlebars banging into his ribs, and the bicyclist's shoulder cracking against his head. He veered to the left, headphones flying off, tripped over the cord protector[36] of the bridge, and fell toward the water

---

[36] Peter had not-so-secretly harbored a large hatred for these cord protectors and their ineptly minimal height from the ground, which hardly seemed a recipe for protecting anyone from falling into the canals. He'd brought these grumblings before the city council a number of times, but had been largely ignored due to the "historical value" of said cords and canals.

below. Yet, just as he had begun to fall, he felt a force pull him back. His feet, momentarily suspended in air, touched ground once more, and he crumpled backward, clutching his racing heart, and looked up.

Before him stood a tall creature with skin as darkly gray as soot and luminescent amber eyes. Large, leathery wings unfurled to either side, and a long tail slowly unclenched from his midsection. The first brilliant rays of morning light lit her flowing hair and curled horns in blazing brilliance, almost casting the illusion of a halo.

"Are you alright, Peter Dewett?" she asked, and her voice echoed in his mind like a thousand gravelly whispers.

"I—wha—are you my guardian...angel?"

The creature stared at him with a look of deep knowledge, and the corner of her mouth twitched. "No," she said. "Not quite."

"Oh," Peter said. His eyes traveled to the large scythe she held in one hand. "Am I about to die?"

At that, the creature stood straighter and glanced over her shoulder. Peter followed her gaze to nothingness.[37] Beyond, the clock tower showed 6:33 am.

"Not today, Peter. I've made sure of that." She held a long hand down toward him and helped him stand up.

She took a step back, but then paused, giving Peter

---

[37] The nothingness, aka the Death, was in fact muttering about HR violations at that moment while vigorously writing notes in its soggy Death Agenda and shooting eye daggers at Paige.

a long look that left him feeling weak. "Are you feeling alright, Peter?"

Peter realized he was trembling, then, and felt the tickle of sweat on his lip. He touched it, and it came away red. "Oh, yeah, I'll—I'll be alright. It's just a scratch. And shock, I guess, seeing—well, you, and discussing my death, and all." He looked up at the creature. "Was I going to die, just then?" He asked, pointing to the canal. "Was that my death?"

The creature shifted on her feet as one does who wants very badly to lie in that moment. Instead, she shrugged. "Does it matter?" she asked, and Peter wasn't sure how to answer; there were too many things he wanted to say.[38] He settled on shrugging.

"Well, er, thank you, then." Peter dusted himself off. "I do quite like the idea of not dying. I don't suppose I can repay you for, uh, whatever it is you've done to ensure that?" He glanced about. "Fancy a cuppa?"

"You know, I would love to, another day. Right now I've got some long apologies to deliver, and a wedding to attend," the creature said, and her eyes glazed over, a smile widening on her face. Peter got the niggling feeling that her thoughts were now worlds away.

"Right, okay," Peter said, taking a deep breath and wondering what to do with himself now.

The creature glanced at him as if reading his mind,

---

[38] Primary among them being that his death would have been a great deal more undignified than he'd hoped it would be. It certainly wasn't how he'd have written it.

hesitated for a moment, and then reached into her toga, bringing out a slim, leather-clad book. She held it forward, and Peter grasped it, almost dropping it when he saw his name on the front.

"What is this?" he asked in equal parts awe and confusion as he carefully traced the letters.

"It's your life," the creature said. "The important stuff."

A myriad of questions floated in Peter's mind, but only one seemed important enough to ask: "But what do I do with it?"

The creature looked at him and her eyes shone with mirth. "Do with it? Well, Peter, it's a book," she said slowly. "And you're a writer." She chuckled and turned to leave.

She looked back once before she vanished. "The beginning is already there, but the rest? That, Peter, is yours to write."

About the Authors

Kristina Horner is best known as an internet personality and fifteen-time winner of National Novel Writing Month. You'd never know it, though, as she keeps every novel she's ever written hidden deep, deep within the depths of her hard drive. Instead of publishing novels, she runs a podcast about writing and has written for a number of tabletop RPGs, including *Vampire: The Masquerade*. Kristina lives and works out of her home in Seattle, Washington, where she enjoys a quieter life these days alongside her husband and young son. When she's not writing, she can be found playing board games, reading entirely too many books, and working on *Minecraft* at Microsoft. Follow her on Instagram and Twitter at @KristinaHorner.

Stephen Folkins is a friend of a friend; don't worry about it. He works in Legal Billing and uses writing for community and as a creative outlet. He primarily writes humor using fantasy, romance, or horror as a vehicle. He has previously written for the sketch comedy group The Pilot Episode, a cult favorite, he says. Stephen likes urban exploration and watching other people out in the rain. He lives in Seattle, three hours away from his mother's small, toothless dog, Sadie, to whom he is devoted.

Jennifer Lee Swagert is a mapmaker by day and writer by night. She especially enjoys writing fantasy, sci-fi, and speculative fiction that explores power structures and the moments that make us human. She began writing using the library computer after school and still has those stories on an old USB drive somewhere. These days, if she's not creating, she's most likely reading webtoons or congratulating her cats on fitting inside boxes. Her greatest accomplishment to date is having operated one of the foremost British soap opera fandom blogs. She's also a co-founder of 84th Street Press and a Seattle NaNoWriMo municipal liaison. Follow her on Twitter at @jenniferswagert.

Katrina Hamilton spends her time writing, traveling, and outlining the taste profiles of various root beer brands. A constant observer and chronicler of the world around her, Katrina loves finding the interesting within the mundane and turning the ordinary parts of life into engaging and emotional journeys. With experience in playwriting, poetry, short stories, and novels, Katrina chases her ideas into whatever form and genre fit them best. She lives in Seattle with her boyfriend of ten years and several fictional pets.

Shay Lynam is a writer, owner of a fandom-inspired candle business, mom, and wife. Whether writing a young adult thriller/romance or figuring out what scent would be perfect for a K-pop-inspired candle, she's almost always finding ways to be creative. A NaNoWriMo rebel through and through, she usually tries to figure out unconventional ways to get to 50,000 words during the month, whether it be writing fanfiction, short stories, or choose-your-own-adventure novels. Shannon has self-published multiple young adult books as well as contributed to a horror anthology. She lives near Seattle, Washington with her husband, two children, and about 36 houseplants. Follow her on Instagram @shaylynam.

Sunny Everson started creating worlds at age eleven and never slowed down. Their passion for storytelling reaches across numerous genres, but they particularly love writing queer fantasy and science fiction novels dealing with themes of childhood trauma, found family, and environmental stewardship. Although they have always been an eager student, Sunny is a repeat college dropout with a firm belief that a degree should never be a prerequisite for writing your truths. They have participated in NaNoWriMo enough times that they stopped counting and have volunteered with the nonprofit since 2016. They are the owner of a hefty collection of books about writing that they will probably never read and an embarrassing number of blank notebooks. When not writing, Sunny can usually be found wandering through nature with an unreasonable number of dogs. They live with their husband in the Inland Northwest. Follow them on Twitter at @s__everson.

Maria Berejan is an engineer by vocation and writer by passion. She religiously participates in National Novel Writing Month and is a municipal liaison for the Seattle NaNoWriMo region. She writes fantasy and mystery with a good serving of death and is co-founder of 84th Street Press, where she publishes anthologies with her writing group. When she's not writing or actively avoiding writing, she collects hobbies and dreams of inhabiting a rustic cabin in the mountains where she can farm pumpkins and potatoes and think of new ways to idealize writing while not actually writing. She lives with three cats, a bunch of plants, and a husband. Follow her on Twitter @mariaberejan or at mariaberejan.com.

Where to Find Us

Thank you for reading *Boys, Book Clubs, and Other Bad Ideas*. If this prompt inspires you to write your own story, connect with us at
www.84thstreetpress.com.

There you will find more information on our upcoming releases, authors, writing resources, and communities.

To stay up to date on our latest projects, please join our mailing list!

www.bit.ly/84thnewsletter

Next in the Monday Night Anthology series…

The Mistletoe Paradox

Available Dec 2021

Acknowledgements

Thank you to everyone who supported us on this creative journey to publication.

Many thanks to our editor, Morgan Wegner, for her fantastic copyediting and patience as we navigated deadlines for the first time, and to our cover artist, Patrick Knowles, for dressing our book up in the very best way.

Thank you to Taylor Kasony for creating the logo for our company, 84th Street Press, and Zachary Cohn for his counsel on how to best structure our company.

Thank you to everyone that helped us with our Kickstarter, including Gabe Conroy, who created our Kickstarter video; Maria's parents, who let us use their house to film; and Tara Theoharis, who gave us feedback on rewards.

Thank you to Meagan Karimi-Naser, Drew Barth, and Chris Parker for so eagerly working on the audiobook.

Thank you to all the baristas at our favorite writing café for creating a welcoming environment and serving us delicious drinks for six years and counting.

Thank you to all the friends and family who listened to our many ramblings and gave us the space to live in our made-up worlds.

And thank you to *you*, our readers, for supporting this book. We look forward to writing many more!

Thank You, Kickstarter Backers!

Your pledges brought this project to life!

Abbey Conroy, Abbey May Schumacher, Abby Singer, Adam Eaton, Adam Levermore, Addie Mehl, Aimée Heikkila, Alan Lastufka, Alex Carpenter, Alexander JL Theoharis, Alexandra Gray Troha, Alice Suckling, Alison T., Allie Kamel, Allie S., Allison Marshall, Allison Momb, Allyson Laredo, Alyssa Ellyn, Amanda Haynes, Amanda Kyker, Amr Dodin, Amy Cefoldo, Amy Coxe, Amy Piedalue, Anca, Anca & Stefan Colibaba, Anna Diaconu, Anna Todd, Anthony van Winkle, April, Ariana Brinckerhoff, Ash Miller, Ashley Falkenberg, Ashley M. Sousa, Aubrey Smith, Ava Strough, Becca Morgan, Ben Miller, Ben Weitz, BJ Shea's Geek Nation, Brad and Lori Homes, Brad Price, Brandon Lycklama, Brice Goldenberg, Brigitta Spethson, Brittany Buchanan, Bruce Dear, Callahan Noelle Davenport, Callidora L Black, Callier Newton, Carissa F., Caroline Vasquez, Carolyn, Catherine

Dore, Catherine Wresche, Chelsea Holloway, Chiara Buchanan, Chris Parker, Christine Urtz, Chuck & Kathy Hamilton, Colin Barrow, Colin Smith, Cristian Berejan, Cristina Lazar, Dan Anderson, Danielle E., Darinee Louvau, David Edmonds, Denise and David Brumbaugh, Dennis Fang, Diane Lee, Donald Wickman, Ed Bordeaux, Elayna Mae Darcy, Elena Berejan, Emily Burke, Emily Joy Morache, Emily Wilkinson, Emma-Kate Earle, Ericka Mathis, Erin Mills, Evan Lauer, Fiona, Fred W Johnson, Gabe Conroy, Gavin Verhey, Gina Bisceglia, Haley Anne Wink, Haley Conatser, Hana A. Ghani, Hannah Sheridan, Jacob Saueressig, Jamie Linde, Jazmin Merckel, Jenn Godwin, Jennie Drake, Jennifer Padron, Jesse Lee Swagert-Gray, Jessica Rae Sablan, Jessica Skye Merizan, Jessie Aston, Jill Eckhart, Jillian O'Neel, Jimmy Penguin Boy, Joe Farro, Joe Homes, Joe Perella, John Noe, Jorge Antonio Jimenez, Joseph Cardenas, Joshua Howard, Judi Holmes, Julia A, Julie Niblett, Justin Cooke, Justin Hammond, Kaitlin Geddis, Kamil, Karen Botha, Kat Hin, Kate Malloy, Kate Rave, Kathleen Quinlan, Kathy and Chuck Hamilton, Katie & Tim Pedersen, Katie B, Katie Edwards, Katie Moles, Katrina Eames, Kayla Rudolph, Kaylee & Jared, Kelly Dougherty, Kelly Lee, Kendall Bowen, Kevin "Kevimation" McKain, Kristen

Acker-Mohr, Kristen McIntyre, Kyle Reardon, Kyrie Ciricillo, Lainey Martin, Lauren MacAskill, Lauren Pendley, Laurentiu Lazar, Lea Cerron, Leanne, Lily Montgomery, Lindsay Chapin, Liz Leo, Lori Pedersen, Lourdes Orive, LP Kindred, Magda & Radu Jianu, Mallory Shoemaker, Marine Lesne, Mart, Mary Folkins, Mary Kwiatkowski, Matilda Söderlund, Meagan Karimi-Naser, Meg Brown, Megan Glass, Megan McCann, Melanie McClurg, Melissa Anelli, Michaela, Michelle Malew, Mike Zaitchik, MOM, Nash Wiegman, Nick Horner, Nicole Cook, Nicole Hamilton, Nicole Logan, Nicole S, Nitya Tripuraneni, Olive Dunkerton, Patrick Fleming, Pauls Macs, Payton Dixon, R.R.Roseboro, Rachael Bahr, Rachel Cann, Rachel Oblouk, Rebecca Houghton, Richard Patrick, Rob W, Robert Tregillis, Ryan Scarcella, Ryan Williams, Rylee Leingang, Sam Harris, Samantha Cumm, Samantha Thompson, Sarah H, Sarah Jane Spies, Sarah Kerr, Sarah Moustafa, Shannen Angell, Shawn Hostettler, Shay L. Stuart, Shelby Smith, Sherry, Sherry Shi, Stephani Granger-Smith, Stephanie Gildart, Steve Griswold, Steve Macbeth, Sushi, Suzanne Paz-Swagert, Sydney Krause, T. Dowling, Tabitha A. Yamasaki, Tania, Tara Kennedy, Tara Theoharis, Taylor Kasony, Teresa Ward, Tessanie, Theresa Folkins, Tiffany

Musser, Tim Taber, Ty Tew, Tyler-Rose, untappedinkwell, Veda Balliraj, Vicky Ross, Virginia McKee, Weiss, Zachary Cohn, and Zackary Collins

9 781956 273014